"PASSION, TRISH, PASSION."

Jack's gaze searched hers. "Don't you get it? What I'm talking about has nothing to do with sex or lust or anything physical. It's emotion, feelings, plain and simple. The way your heart beats faster when she enters a room. Or the way her smile warms something deep inside you and her laugh makes you melt. It's the way you can't resist making her angry because she argues with her whole heart and soul. It's the reason you've memorized the stubborn tilt of her chin or the wonderful feeling you get when she's wearing your shirt...." Trish's eyes widened—with what? Maybe, just maybe, acknowledgment? He pulled her closer. "Or the way she makes you feel like you were a kid again about to get his first kiss."

"Are you going to kiss me?" She asked, her voice catching.

"Yeah."

"Why?"

"Because I've wanted to for a long time. Because I need to." He stared into her blue eyes and wondered how she, of all people, could have come kicking and screaming into his world to lay claim to his life. "Because you want me to."

"Because I need you to," she whispered.

ParadiseBay

Victoria Alexander

LOVE SPELL BOOKS NEW YORK CITY

LOVE SPELL®

October 1999

Published by

Dorchester Publishing Co., Inc.
276 Fifth Avenue
New York, NY 10001

ISBN 0-505-52350-7

This book is dedicated to
Joanna Cagan,
who has always encouraged me to try my wings
even if it meant occasionally plunging over a cliff.
Thanks for the best birthday present ever.

Paradise Bay

Prologue

The door to the executive suite snapped shut.

"She's not happy about this," Marjorie Caplan said mildly.

"She'll get over it." The head of Evans and Sons, International, grinned at his executive assistant. "Sooner or later."

"And her mother?"

"She'll get over it too." Russell Evans shrugged. "Besides, this is a legitimate assignment. Strictly business. Trish knows that. Evelyn will just have to buck up."

Marjorie raised a brow. "Your wife has never struck me as the buck-up type."

"You don't know her as well as I do."

"Apparently not." Marjorie perched on the

edge of the leather wing chair positioned in front of her boss's desk. "And apparently this was not a good morning for me to be out of the office. Since I walked in on the conclusion of this, let me make sure I have the facts straight. Trish's mother—your wife—is in the middle of planning the wedding of the century for her daughter, your stepdaughter—"

"One of the best and brightest minds in this company," Russ said with pride.

"—coming up in—"

"Five months."

"Four months."

He frowned. "Are you sure?"

"Very." She nodded. "As I was saying, it's four months until her wedding to Elliott Hunt, the son of your second wife, also an up-and-coming employee of the family business—"

"Only because he knows what to kiss and when," Russ muttered.

"That's never seemed to particularly bother you before."

"It has its merits in an employee"—he flashed her a grin—"but not in a son-in-law."

"If he didn't do a good job, you wouldn't keep him around."

"You're right and that wasn't fair of me. Elliot is just ambitious and he's great at what he does. An asset to the company and all that. But what works for the business doesn't work for my family. I'll even admit, on a personal level, he's okay. I've watched him grow up and he's turned out better than I expected. Frankly, I like him—but he's not right for Trish. And she's not right for him."

"Isn't that her decision?"

"She doesn't know what she's doing." His lips pressed together in a stubborn line.

"May I speak freely?"

"You always have."

"That, plus excellent retirement benefits and a good health plan, is the price you pay for nearly forty years of exemplary service," she said primly. "Now then, Trish is almost thirty. She's competent, intelligent and can make her own decisions."

"Not this time." Russ settled back in the chair behind the teak desk, picked up his Mont Blanc pen and tapped it on the polished wood surface. "She's the only daughter I've ever had, and I won't allow her to make the biggest mistake of her life. And the biggest mistake of Elliot's life, too."

"So to save them from themselves you're sending Trish out of town? I believe I heard her mutter something about the ends of the earth?"

"Not quite, but you can see it from there." Russ leaned forward. "Seriously, I think Trish needs time away from the pressure of all this wedding nonsense. She needs to get away from her mother, and away from Elliott. She needs to clear her head and think about what she's doing."

"She's in love."

"I don't think so." Russ shook his head. "I recognize love. Hell, I ought to, I've been married three times myself."

"It's been my observation that that fact hasn't precisely made you an expert," Marjorie said wryly.

"That may be true, but I do know love when I see it. And I don't see it between Trish and Elliot. There's no spark between them. No passion. They're as staid and boring as if they'd already been married for fifty years."

Marjorie studied her boss. She knew that he considered Trish his flesh and blood, even though the girl had been in high school when he'd married her mother. Lord knows, Russ hadn't done particularly well with his own son, although Marjorie had watched that relationship improve in recent years. Maybe he was trying to make up for past mistakes.

In all the years she'd been with him—and Marjorie considered herself as much a guardian of the family as an employee—she'd never seen this protective-parent act before.

"Honestly, Marjorie, I just don't want to see her, them, ruin their lives." Sincerity rang in Russ's voice and shone in his eyes. Still . . . He tapped the pen again.

Marjorie smiled knowingly.

"What?" Russ's eyes widened with feigned innocence.

"You're up to something."

"Me?" Russ shook his head. "Absolutely not."

"I hate to correct you—"

"You love correcting me."

"Be that as it may"—she nodded at his hand—"you only tap your pen when you're concentrating on something, or when you're doing something you don't think I'll approve of."

The pen stopped. "I can't believe you could think such a thing of me. It hurts, it really hurts."

"It only hurts to know I can see right through you." She leaned forward and stared at him over the rim of her glasses. "Now then, Russ, what are you up to?"

"Nothing, Marjorie, nothing at all. And this"—he tapped the pen defiantly—"is just a nervous habit. It doesn't mean a thing."

Marjorie stood slowly and clasped her hands together in her best stereotypical spinster impression. From the moment she'd realized the power "the look" wielded over her boss, she'd cultivated it. It rarely failed to turn this captain of industry into a guilt-ridden schoolboy.

"Apparently I missed a critical detail, since I was not present for the beginning of your discussion with Trish." The pen started again. "Where exactly are you sending her?"

"South Pacific," he said under his breath.

"Of course." Marjorie should have known. It made perfect sense, given a few rather unusual projects she'd dealt with recently. Not that they hadn't been enjoyable, letting her indulge in a secret side of herself and a fondness for the exotic that her boss might well have suspected but never pursued. Add to that Russ's acknowledged love of the place and his firm belief in the magic it could work and . . . well, she was clearly slipping not to have foreseen this. "So the somewhat vague proposal you had me draft last week is something you seriously intend to pursue?"

"Damn straight."

"And if you want to be the first to see the dawn of the year 2000, you'd have to be near the International Date Line. That would put you . . ."

"You've got it." A smug grin, the kind he wore when he had just closed a big deal or beaten a worthy opponent or shaved points off his golf game, creased his ruggedly handsome face. Marjorie never failed to notice that it was the exact same smile on the portrait hanging in the building lobby of the first Russell Jonathan Evans.

"Paradise Bay."

Chapter One

... *although it has long been speculated to have been a significant island nation in the distant past, the true history of Paradise Bay is unknown due to the native islanders' lax, and for the most part nonexistent, record-keeping. While some ancient artifacts have been uncovered, most archeologists of note feel these did not originate on Paradise Bay and may indicate that the island was once an active trade center. For whatever reasons, the original inhabitants and their civilization vanished without a significant trace.*

It was not until the early seventeenth century that Paradise Bay was again inhabited.

17

According to oral tradition, a large group of women from a far distant island were transported to the isolated site as punishment for sins ranging from poor housekeeping to promiscuity. Within several years of their arrival, a British ship, under the command of mutineers, stumbled onto the island to be greeted enthusiastically by the marooned females. Distinctly British surnames and the blue eyes prominent in the current native population give credence to the legend.

It was at that time that the island was first called Paradise Bay.

"Welcome to where the day begins." A garish tropical shirt pulsed in the bright sunlight. The voice attached to the throbbing fluorescent garment yelled in an effort to be heard over the Evans and Sons, International, helicopter. "Come on. Follow me."

Trish Taylor clutched her briefcase, the straps of her laptop carrier and shoulder bag in one hand, the report she'd been reading in the other and hurried out of range of the gale-force winds. The chopper took off immediately.

"Hey." Trish pulled to a stop and stared at the rapidly disappearing aircraft, the ESI blue-and-gold corporate logo glistening in the sunlight. "Where's he going?"

"I don't know." The shirt shrugged. "Back to wherever he came from, I guess."

"Where he came from?" The past day flashed through her mind. It seemed as if she'd been traveling forever: by plane from the U.S. to Australia, then a smaller plane to Fiji and finally the helicopter. It had taken nearly twenty-four hours to get here. Wherever *here* was. Apparently she was somewhere near the 180th parallel and the International Date Line. She'd studied a map on the plane, but it was primarily composed of tiny dots, all purporting to be islands. Now her last tie to life as she knew it was winging its way westward. A wistful note sounded in her voice. "I thought he was staying."

"Not according to the E-mail we received. His job was just to drop you off."

"You have E-mail?" Her spirits perked at his words. How bad could this place be if they had computers?

"Of course," he said in a matter-of-fact way. She stood at least a head taller than the dark-skinned islander and he shielded his face to look up at her. "We're fairly laid back, but we *are* civilized." He stuck out his free hand. "Mo Wellington."

Wellington? Just one of the legacies of the British, probably. Mo's vivid blue eyes were obviously another.

"My dad's the duly elected head honcho of the island, but I kind of manage things," Mo said cheerfully.

Trish shifted the report and shook his hand. "Patricia Taylor. Trish." She glanced around. It didn't look like there was much of anything to manage. "So this is Paradise Bay."

The helicopter had landed on a small dock

that continued as a wooden walkway and turned into a gravel path leading up a slight incline. An emerald green mountain rose in the background, misty clouds teasing its peak. A pristine beach she could have appreciated much more if this was a vacation stretched in an endless curve, bordered by the sparkling sea waters on one side and tropical vegetation on the other. A few rickety boats anchored off shore. It really was a bay, and not a bad one at that. Not bad at all. The island wasn't very big, but it was definitely scenic. Postcard-pretty, in fact. Maybe this idea of her stepfather's wasn't so bizarre after all. "So, where is it? Civilization, I mean."

"The town is just over the rise." Mo raised his eyebrow. "No luggage?"

"I was told the supply boat would bring it."

"The supply boat?" He looked as if he was about to say something else but thought better of it. "Sure. Okay. Let's go."

"Wait." Trish scanned the area again. "Where's the car?"

"There's a jeep, but it's on the other side of the island." He took her briefcase and laptop and started off. "We can walk. It's not far."

"Oh. Good." Swell. She glanced down at her shoes. The ads claimed you could play basketball in these. Fat chance. The manufacturer of her suit had obviously never made similar claims. The designer of the straight-skirted, silk creation had obviously not envisioned its use for anything more exerting than a stroll down a city sidewalk, but Trish had been hustled out of New

York so fast she'd barely had time to pack, let alone change. She groaned to herself and followed Mo up the rise.

"You'll like it here," he called back over his shoulder. "Everybody likes it here. But we don't get many visitors."

"There's a surprise," she muttered. Only the most diehard tourist would attempt the circuitous route to the island.

"So what did you think of the slogan?"

"What slogan?" The hill was a lot steeper than it looked.

He tossed her a grin. "The one I greeted you with. You know: *where the day begins.*"

"Very nice." Maybe it was a mountain disguised as a hill.

"So do you think there's any chance this project will actually happen?"

"I have no idea yet." She trudged along behind him. "Starting a resort from scratch is a massive undertaking. And Russ—Mr. Evans—wants at least part of it ready to go by December 31, 1999. If it can be done at all, that's cutting it close. He's talking about a huge New Year's party for stockholders and other muckety-mucks. Lots of publicity. You know, be one of the first in the world to greet the new century. That sort of thing."

Russ was asking for a miracle and Trish knew it. This whole project was so far removed from her very practical stepfather's usual endeavors, she still found it hard to believe he was serious. But Russ was serious, all right. Otherwise he

21

never would have incurred her mother's wrath by sending her so far away with her wedding looming in the near future. She sighed to herself. She was here to evaluate the project and give her recommendation. She was more than willing to make that recommendation right now. She stopped and pulled off her shoe to pour out what felt like half the beach.

Mo stopped and turned around.

"Those shoes won't be much good here."

Very astute. "They'll have to do until my suitcases arrive."

"Uh-huh." Mo studied her for a minute. "Do you do this kind of thing a lot?"

"Nope." She shrugged. "Usually I hike in really high stilettos."

Mo laughed. "I meant scoping out resort projects. Is that what you do?"

"Not really." In fact, thanks to a corporate takeover several years ago, ESI had an entire separate division that managed and developed resort properties around the world. Trish's specialty was public relations, and she was good at it. Why Russ had decided to send her instead of someone with more expertise didn't make any sense at all, despite his explanation that Paradise Bay was too important to the family history to leave in the hands of strangers. "But that's what makes life interesting, I guess," she said as they continued up the hill.

Mo reached the top of the rise and waited. She stumbled up to him and swiped at her damp forehead with the back of her hand. He waved in an expansive gesture of pride. "Welcome to Paradise."

Trish stared in disbelief. A small town stretched out before them. No, not a town. A village. No, even that was a bit too generous for the sight before her. It was a conglomeration, that's what it was. Or a nightmare. Every conceivable architectural style of the last few centuries was represented, all constructed out of native materials. It was a cartoon interpretation of the sets of every old South Seas island movie ever made, from *South Pacific* to *Hurricane,* created with rapt abandon and a mad disregard for the end result. A tropical Shangri-la theme park run amok. The laughter of children rang out here and there. Laundry in hues that put even Mo's shirt to shame billowed in the breeze. And on every rooftop or next to every dwelling, satellite dishes glistened under the blistering sun like metallic mushrooms.

"Well?" Mo beamed proudly. "What do you think? This will make one hell of a resort. Is this something or what?"

"It's something, all right." Trish smiled weakly and swallowed hard. Mo was right about one thing.

Paradise was already hell.

"So where is she?" Jack Kendall glanced up from the computer screen.

Mo sauntered into the room and plopped

down on the well-cushioned rattan sofa as if he had all the time in the world. The fact was, here on the island, just about everybody did, thanks to the dream—and the farsighted investments—of a nineteenth-century industrialist. "I put her in the guest suite in the west wing."

"What did she think of the house?" The big house was a sprawling Victorian-era tropical fantasy complete with storm shutters and two towering turrets, rendered primarily in an amazing shade of flamingo pink. Its design owed as much to vague ideas of traditional colonial rule as to any legitimate building style. Perched a quarter of the way up the mountain, it was damned impressive, and boasted the only air-conditioned room on the island.

"I think it's the only thing that didn't knock her for a loop. She had a dazed look on her face all the way through town." Mo chuckled. "She's definitely not happy to be here."

"I'm not wild about her being here either." Jack's gaze returned to his screen. Hunched over the keyboard, with his long dark hair and full beard, Jack looked like some kind of computer hermit, which was a fairly accurate assessment. "Did you make her walk?"

"Yep."

"I'll bet she was wearing heels, wasn't she?"

"Yep."

Jack grinned. "She'll be on the next boat back. The one thing this island doesn't need is an Evans flying monkey—"

"Flying monkey?"

"My term for henchman, minion, whatever." A sheepish look crossed his face. "It's from *The Wizard of Oz*. When I was a kid, ambitious corporate types sucking up to the boss reminded me of the Wicked Witch's flying monkeys. I have a stepbrother who's a flying monkey."

"You have a very strange mind."

"Thanks. Anyway, we don't need somebody trying to turn this place into Club Med."

"Yeah. Gorgeous girls in bikinis. Fruit floating in frosted rum drinks. Air conditioning everywhere." Mo sighed. "That would be bad, all right." Mo was an island native, but years spent at a boarding school in the States, followed by UCLA for undergraduate and graduate studies, had left their mark. He still wasn't sure exactly why he'd decided to give up the real world to come back to Paradise Bay. Maybe it was just in his blood. Now this resort proposal offered the opportunity to put his education to better use than the minimal management the island called for. "I don't get it, Jack. Why are you so against this project?"

"This is Paradise, remember? Unspoiled. A heaven on earth." Jack leaned back in his chair and glanced at Mo. "There's no crime. No poverty. No pollution. No—"

"No excitement. No adventure. Nothing to do. Nobody who hasn't lived here all their lives. Dull, boring and predictable." Mo snorted.

"Heaven sucks, Jack. It's a great place to visit, but you wouldn't want to live here."

Jack laughed. "I like living here."

"It's different for you. You're a refugee from the fast lane. You've only been here for four years and you've spent most of your time in front of that keyboard."

"And on the beach," Jack reminded him.

"It would be different if you were a native." Mo blew out a long, frustrated breath. "Except for a few modern conveniences, life here is pretty much the same as it's been for centuries. Half of our young people leave the island—"

"But a lot come back. You did."

"And I'm not sure it wasn't a mistake. I don't want to spend my life lying in the sun." Mo straightened in his seat and leaned forward. "This resort is an opportunity to move Paradise Bay into the modern age. To give the islanders real contact with the rest of the world."

Jack raised his eyebrow. "With all the televisions and satellite setups here, I'd think you'd have all the real world you can handle."

"That's a crock and you know it. Come on, Jack. We're talking the twenty-first century coming up. I want Paradise Bay to be a part of it."

"I think you're wrong, but"—Jack shrugged—"I'll reserve judgment until we know if this proposal is even feasible. How's that?"

"I'll take it for now." Mo narrowed his eyes. "But I want your word that you won't try to screw up her evaluation by making her life miserable."

"Would I do that?" A wicked twinkle lurked in Jack's eye.

"In a minute."

"Okay, okay, I promise." Jack laughed and threw up his hands in surrender. "So tell me about the flying monkey. What's she like? Designer suit for the upwardly mobile executive? Perfect nails for clawing her way to the top? Corporate America is full of that type. She's single, ambitious, her career is her life."

"Not for long. She has a rock the size of a walnut on her hand."

"Okay. I was wrong on that one. But it's probably more of a corporate merger than a marriage. Tough-minded careerwomen don't marry for any other reason. All work, no play. And I'll bet she's a dog, too, right?"

"I've always wanted a puppy," Mo murmured. He should have such a dog. Trish Taylor was Mo's own personal goddess fantasy come to life. Tall and blond and, even in her prim and proper suit, filled out nicely in all the right places. What would Jack think of her? He'd been quite a playboy on the international scene before he'd exiled himself to Paradise Bay. Mo never could figure out exactly why Jack had given all that up for the reclusive life of a computer nerd. Burnout, Jack had said during one of their regular beer binges, usually held the day the supply boat arrived with the island's inventory of goods. "By the way, how is the beer situation?"

"Low." Jack grimaced. "Amos might still have a six-pack at the store and I've got what's left of my last case. But it's rationing time. When's the boat due?"

"A couple of days. Maybe. Who knows." Mo stood to leave. Right now, he wanted to finish the drawings he'd worked on since they'd first learned of the proposed resort. It was a chance to put his architectural skills to good use. His only chance, and a once-in-a-lifetime opportunity. He had no idea if ESI would even consider his ideas, but it was worth a shot. He hadn't planned on returning to Paradise Bay when he'd decided to study architecture, but now he wondered if maybe fate didn't have a hand in his choice. If he could live on the island and do the work he'd always dreamed of, Paradise might just live up to its name.

"See ya." Jack nodded and turned back to the keyboard.

"Later." He'd like to hang around and see Jack's reaction when he met the flying monkey. Hah. With her long legs and blond hair, Trish Taylor was an intriguing combination of Aphrodite and the all-American girl.

Playboy–computer-nerd–recluse meets the flying-monkey–goddess–all-American-girl. Mo smothered a grin.

Maybe Paradise wouldn't be quite so boring after all.

* * *

Jack stared at the screen, but his concentration was shot. Developing a new program to track inventories in a minor ESI division was the last thing on his mind.

Whose stupid idea was this resort scheme anyway? Jack had always thought the island was far too important to the Evans family to be developed in any significant way. The whole of the adult population, just under 300 people was directly or indirectly supported by ESI and had been ever since the first Russell Jonathan Evans had purchased the island toward the end of the last century, when nobody particularly wanted it, only a handful could actually find it and even fewer could afford it. An industrialist with the stature of a Du Pont or a Rockefeller, a hard-headed businessman to the rest of the world, R. J. Evans had the soul of a dreamer. He believed in the popular notion of an ideal society. And his dream was Paradise Bay. He set up a massive community trust fund to provide for every family on the island, with the ultimate goal of turning the place into heaven on earth.

In many ways he'd succeeded. Today, Paradise Bay was a stable, pleasant community with a population of decent, happy people. The trust, managed by ESI experts, had performed far better than even Evans could have imagined. It provided the funding for basics, including an island power plant, sewage and fresh water treatment. Nothing extensive, but adequate to supply the population. The trust paid for health care and education on and off the island. Every family had the opportunity to send their offspring to boarding schools and colleges. About half the islanders, Mo's family included, did just that. Some of the kids returned home; many more did not.

The trust even provided a little extra. Several years ago, in the kind of democratic community decision the first Evans would have appreciated, the residents had voted on whether to bring in air conditioning for every building or televisions for every home. TV was the unanimous choice, and within months Paradise Bay had sprouted satellite dishes like a new crop of wheat.

But even in Paradise there were jobs to be done. Many islanders hand-produced computer components for ESI. There were a few merchants, some agriculture and a small but active fishing fleet. All in all, more than a hundred years after Great-Grandfather Evans bought the island and built his mountain-hugging retreat, Paradise Bay was as close to Nirvana as any community could get.

And it was his sanctuary. Jack blew a long breath and leaned back in his chair. Paradise Bay had held his heart since he first came here as a kid with his folks. He'd loved every inch of it, from the coral sand beaches to the cool green jungle vegetation of the mountain and the bizarre mix of man-made structures. Of course, that was before his mother had died and his dad remarried for the first time. Before he and his father had clashed with all the force of a Greek tragedy and Jack had preferred boarding school and trips abroad and holidays with the families of friends to his own flesh and blood. Before he'd abandoned his father's name and taken his mother's. And when Jack had crashed and burned, physically and emotionally; when his life was a wreck, when he hit absolute bottom, Paradise Bay had still been here for him.

Funny, but in spite of all they'd been through, his dad was too. In his four years on the island they'd had more contact than in the decade before. Mostly E-mails and letters, but his father had found the time to visit a couple of times every year. The island had brought them back together when nothing else could.

Paradise Bay had also given him a purpose in life. He'd always been intrigued by computers, but here, with little else to do, he'd discovered a real talent and a passion for programming. He'd developed dozens of new software programs for the company. That too brought him closer to his dad.

Jack ran a hand through his hair. As much as he hated the idea, maybe it was time for Paradise Bay to join the outside world. In spite of the opportunities available, was it fair to the islanders, Mo and all the others, not to at least look at what the project would mean for today and for the future? Wasn't he just being selfish? Was this resort proposal such a terrible idea? If it could be managed without losing the magic he'd found here, maybe, just maybe, it wouldn't be so bad.

And maybe it was time for him to end his self-imposed exile and rejoin the twentieth, soon the twenty-first, century.

He heaved a heavy sigh, saved what he'd been working on and got to his feet. When this deal was wrapped up, he'd think about going home. Maybe for good. He'd never even met the latest Mrs. Evans, although she'd officially been his stepmother for about thirteen years. It was definitely time. He'd come to the island a spoiled, rich, twenty-six-year-old child. Here, he'd found the man he was meant to be. And his father. And peace.

Later today, he'd E-mail his dad and tell him that he still wasn't convinced, but he'd keep an open mind. Hell, he'd even be nice to the flying monkey. He could probably give her some good ideas. He'd seen more than his share of international playgrounds, resorts catering to the rich and famous. If he worked with her and not against her, he could make sure the end result was something everybody could live with. What was her name again? It had sounded vaguely familiar, but he couldn't quite place it. Oh, yeah, Trish Taylor.

If things worked out, maybe he'd even go back to using his real name.

Russell Jonathan Evans IV.

Chapter Two

. . . volcanic in origin, the island covers a land mass of approximately 100 square miles. Typical of the region, savanna grasslands are prevalent on the west side of the island, dense vegetation dominates on the east with native forest growth covering the mountainous areas. Annual rainfall averages from 70 to 120 inches.

In spite of its proximity to the equator, spells of extreme heat are rare. Steady trade winds preserve a temperate climate, with temperatures ranging from 70 to 80 degrees.

"Temperate, my ass."

Trish lay sprawled face up on the four-poster

bed and stared at the ceiling fan. It revolved too slowly to provide any real relief. Mo had said something about a minor heat wave. The islander apparently had a gift for understatement. Or a weird sense of humor.

Who had put together that damn report anyway? It read like a cross between an encyclopedia entry and a chamber of commerce brochure. No, a travel guide. That's what it was. And an optimistic one to boot. *Spells of extreme heat are rare*. Hah! Tell that to the damp silk blouse clinging to her skin.

"I've got to get out of here," she said to the fan. "Back to civilization. And air conditioning."

The fan whirred on without comment.

"What did I do to deserve this?" Her voice was a pathetic wail, but she was too hot and sticky and unhappy to care. The fan didn't seem to mind either. "I don't know anything about developing resorts." She glared at the fan. "I know public relations. That's it. Period."

The fan wisely refrained from comment.

She still didn't get Russ's reasoning for this assignment. She was in the middle of planning her wedding: the wedding of the year, according to her mother; the wedding of the century, according to Russ, who never failed to speak of the event with heavy sarcasm and an aside on the ever-increasing cost of the celebration. He compared it to the court scene in *Aida*, sans elephants, although her mother had mentioned white doves to be released at the appropriate moment. Trish agreed with her mother, of course. The wedding would be a social affair to remember. Still, the plans were perhaps a shade too spectacular, a tad too overdone and a lot more virginal than she would have liked. Her stepfather had never particularly minded spending huge amounts of money, and Trish suspected his sudden concern for cost meant he wasn't quite as pleased about her impending marriage to Elliott as her mother was. Otherwise, why would he feel compelled to point out that the wedding hoopla was eerily similar to the preparations of South Seas islanders for throwing virgins into volcanoes? Or mention that if native fathers had to pay what he had to pay, they'd jump in the molten lava themselves. He mentioned over and over again that sacrificial virgins were, in some island societies, actually marrying the god of the volcano.

"If they threw them in during one of these *rare* hot spells, they'd probably be just as happy," she muttered.

It might have been all those cracks about islands and sacrifice that prompted Russ to send her here. She was pretty sure he wanted to give her a chance to think about her future with Elliott. Russ was the only real father she'd ever known, and she adored him. But he'd always thought he knew what was best, and she wouldn't put it past him to pull a stunt like this.

She definitely felt like a virgin sacrifice. Okay, strictly for the sake of accuracy, make that a human sacrifice. Oh, sure, there was a mountain here instead of a volcano. And the islanders—

the only one she had met anyway, in his flowered shirt and khaki shorts—seemed friendly enough. Probably not the type to throw anyone, virgin or not, into a volcano, unless it was a dire emergency. From the looks of things, Paradise Bay residents would be more likely to try a sacrifice to the gods of satellite dishes in hopes of better reception.

Why wouldn't Russ want her to marry Elliott? Technically, he was more or less a part of the family, even though Elliott's mother had been married to Russ for less than two years. And Elliott was an asset to the company. His rise owed nothing to nepotism. On the contrary, Russ expected Elliott—and Trish, for that matter—to work harder than anyone else. Elliott was smart and conscientious and ambitious. If he sometimes verged on sucking up, Trish shrugged, so what? Everybody did at some point. What she felt for Elliott wasn't a grand passion, but it was comfortable and secure and solid. Just like Elliott himself. He would make any girl a wonderful husband. They were a perfectly matched pair with both feet firmly on the ground. Once again, she ignored the vague thought in the back of her mind that had plagued her more and more with every day closer to the wedding: Maybe, just maybe, that wasn't enough.

She groaned aloud. Whatever her stepfather's true purpose might be for her exile, she was stuck with it. Allegedly, she had to evaluate the potential for a resort and the feasibility of opening in time for a private gala for New Years Eve 1999. She'd love to turn in that report now:

It is my considered opinion that Paradise Bay is inappropriately named. While the island is scenic, aside from a preponderance of satellite receivers, its development is primitive, its terrain rugged and its climate too damn hot.

Yeah, right. That would go over well. Especially since she'd been on the island less than twenty-four hours and hadn't seen anything beyond the walk—no, the hike—no, the endurance test—to the house. She'd stripped off her clothes and collapsed, sleeping fitfully through the rest of the afternoon, all night and, apparently, most of the morning. Her bags were nowhere to be seen, and she'd been forced to put on the skirt and blouse she'd worn yesterday. Just that effort in the unbearable heat was enough to do her in.

No, she had a job to do here and in spite of her concerns about her qualifications to do it, she was determined to give it her best shot. Her best *objective* shot. And fast. The sooner she got to work, the sooner she could go home.

She propped herself up on her elbows and glanced around the large bedroom. Grudgingly, she had to admit that it was very nice, furnished with Victorian antiques probably brought here when the house was built by the first R. J. Evans, the lunatic ancestor who'd bought the island.

Trish slid off the bed and pushed her feet into her ruined shoes. As soon as the supply boat arrived with her bags, she'd change to athletic shoes and shorts. There was no need for formality here.

If there was electricity to run ceiling fans, there had to be a refrigerator and, hopefully, ice. A cool drink would definitely improve her mood. Food wouldn't hurt either. She stepped out of her room and wandered down a long hall to the wide main stairway, wondering how anyone had managed to create this Victorian masterpiece set in the middle of nowhere. Even in the 1890s, it must have cost a fortune. Carved wood glowed with warmth from years of careful polishing. The furniture was antique and in pristine condition.

She descended the stairs to a huge receiving hall and looked around. Mo said there was a housekeeper here somewhere. On one side of the foyer, open pocket doors led into a parlor. Trish peeked in. Furnished in the same period as her room upstairs but empty of people, it had a pleasant air of welcome about it. A second set of pocket doors on the other side of the foyer mirrored those leading to the parlor, but these were closed. For privacy? Yeah, right. From whom? She vaguely recalled someone at the office saying that the house was maintained strictly for members of the family and the occasional family friend who might want to vacation in the middle of nowhere. Trish stepped to the doors, grasped the brass handles, slid the doors open and gasped.

Cool air poured over her. Sweet, delicious, cool air.

"Thank God." She closed her eyes, raised her chin, lifted her hair off the back of her neck and sighed in pure, hedonistic delight. "Oh, yeah. Air conditioning. I love air conditioning."

"It's for the computer."

"It's wonderful. I never knew just how wonderful a simple thing like—" Trish snapped her eyes open.

She stood at the top of three steps that descended into a huge sunken room. Dark wood paneling gleamed in the sunlight streaming in through windows that reached nearly to the high, coffered ceiling; cases crammed with books lined the walls. Assorted knickknacks, obviously valuable antique collections and a wide variety of unidentified items littered empty spaces on the tables and shelves.

A man dressed in standard island-issue khaki shorts and a gaudy flowered shirt sat in front of a state-of-the-art computer setup. At least, she thought it was a man. With long, dark shaggy hair and a full beard, who could tell if this hulking beast was human or not?

"Who in the hell are you?" she asked incredulously.

"I might ask you the same thing." The hulking beast's tone was surprisingly mild, in direct contrast with his rather frightening appearance.

"This house—"

"Before you say another word, shut the door," he said firmly. "The air conditioning in this room isn't enough to cool the whole house."

Trish turned, pulled the doors closed and swiveled back to her previous position, placing her hands imperiously on her hips. "Now," she said in her best representative-of-the-family voice, "this house is the property of the Evans family."

He leaned back in his chair and studied her. "What's your point?"

"My point is: I seriously doubt that you're supposed to be here." She glared at him. "Whoever you are."

"How do you know I'm not supposed to be here if you don't know who I am?" The beast smirked at her.

"I don't have to know who you are in order to know that." She started down the steps. He looked disreputable, but she doubted he was dangerous. There wasn't a dangerous person on all of Paradise Bay. At least, that's what the travel guide, or rather the report, said. Of course, it wasn't entirely accurate about the heat.

He certainly did seem right at home, though. The relaxed way he sat before the computer, his authoritative tone when he told her to shut the door and his casual attitude were not indicative of a trespasser. But surely someone back at the office would have told her about this beach-bum creature apparently working here at the mansion. On the other hand, she'd been so furious and was rushed out of town so quickly, she couldn't be completely certain that he hadn't been mentioned. Still . . .

"I know who I am, and that's enough."

"Not for me." He grinned. "But I'll bite: Who are you?"

She grit her teeth. No, he wasn't dangerous. Just annoying. "I'm Trish Taylor. And I'm supposed to be here."

"I heard you were coming. Some off-the-wall idea about turning the island into a resort." He stared thoughtfully. "Taylor. That sounds so familiar. Why can't I place . . ." His eyes widened. "Patricia Taylor?"

"Yes?" Caution edged her voice.

"Patti?"

"I haven't been called Patti since I was in high school." How did the beach bum know her name? Or anything else, for that matter?

"Patti Taylor—"

"Trish," she said sharply. "It's Trish Taylor."

"Okay, *Trish*." He chuckled. "I should have expected this. I knew he had you working for the company. You're the princess."

"Excuse me?"

"The princess. The stepdaughter." He shook his head and laughed. "You're my—er—the boss's kid, by marriage anyway."

"Russ Evans is my stepfather," she said slowly. "How did you know that? Who are you?"

"I'm—" He paused for a moment. What was

41

he doing? Making up a name? "I'm Jack. Jack Kendall."

He stared at her as if he expected some kind of reaction. "Is that supposed to mean something?"

"I guess not. I thought maybe you might have heard of me."

"Nope. Not a word. Hard to believe, I know." He looked thoughtful, or was it disappointed? Add arrogant to the list of his sterling qualities. "You must be some kind of state secret."

"I wouldn't be at all surprised."

"So now that we've been properly introduced: Who are you and what are you doing here?"

Jack Kendall, beach bum, hulking beast, nodded at the computer. "I develop software. Programming. That sort of thing."

"Here?" Shock sounded in her voice.

He grinned again. It was a surprisingly nice grin, what she could see of it through the beard anyway. The kind of smile that made you feel as though it came from his soul, honest, with no pretensions. The kind that made you believe that this was a man you could trust.

"This is a great place to work. No distractions. No problems. No hassles. Terrific beaches, great areas for hiking or climbing. It's got everything a man could ask for." His gaze flicked over her. "Almost."

She grimaced to herself. On second thought, trust was out of the question. The beach bum, hulking beast, computer nerd was obviously interested in the same thing every other man was. Not that she hadn't checked him out too. She was engaged, not dead. There was a possibility, under all that hair, that he was fairly good-looking. Not that she cared. He was obviously not her type of man. Not like Elliott. With luck, she could just get rid of him for now. "Are you telling me you work for ESI? Here?"

"That's pretty much it."

"I don't understand." She studied him carefully. "I thought this house was only for the family. And maybe friends of the family."

"Hey, Princess, what makes you think I couldn't be a friend of the family?"

Long hair, full beard, sandals—nope. "You don't look the type."

"I'll have you know I clean up pretty well."

"You'd have to." A horrible thought dawned on her. "So . . . where do you live?"

"On the island."

"No, I mean where exactly?"

His grin widened.

"Oh, great." She stalked to an overstuffed chair, collapsed into it and stared at the ceiling. "The beach bum is my roommate."

"Beach bum?"

"Sorry." Now that she knew he was legitimately supposed to be here . . . "Hey." She sat up and glared at him. "How do I know you're telling me the truth?"

"I guess you don't." He shrugged, as if he could care less if she believed him or not. "You could ask Mo, I suppose, or send an E-mail." Her spirits rose. "Of course, I have the only working modem on the island."

"What about a phone?"

"Only on the island. Off island we use radios or E-mail."

"How—"

"I have a satellite link."

"I should have known." She stared for a moment. "In that case, how about an ID? Driver's license, credit card, employee ID?"

He unfolded long legs and slowly rose to his feet. She was five-foot-eight, but he was taller by a good half-foot. And very tan. In fact, with his dark skin, he would have resembled an islander if he hadn't been so tall—and if his eyes were blue. Instead, they were a deep, dark, smoldering brown. Kind of nice, actually. Just how well did he clean up?

He patted the pockets of his khaki shorts. "Sorry. Must have left my wallet in my other pants."

"Figures." She sank back into the chair, leaned her head back and closed her eyes. As much as she hated to admit it, his story made a certain amount of sense. He obviously belonged here. And it was just as obvious that she did not.

"What about you, princess?" the beach bum asked.

"What about me?"

"How do I know you're who you say you are? I think I should see some ID myself."

44

"Sorry." She let the sarcasm drip from her words. "Left it in my other pants."

This was just great. No phones. She hadn't any idea how to work a radio. And the Robinson Crusoe clone controlled her only access to E-mail. Basically, she was incommunicado, held hostage from the rest of the world. Trapped in a Victorian mansion with a hulking beast on an island in the middle of nowhere.

Paradise just got better and better.

Man's best friend. With great-looking legs. They stretched out in front of her forever. Maybe he'd been on the island too damn long. He'd seen great-looking legs before. But the rest of her was just as good. Blond hair hitting just above her shoulder, pert little nose, snapping blue eyes, a body filled out nicely in all his favorite places, and she was tall. He liked tall women.

After all, there was no blood or emotional bond between them; although, in the bizarre American family structure of multiple marriages and divorces, in a convoluted way she was his sister. Even if he'd never met her. Or ever lived in the same house with her. He smiled to himself. Until now.

He wasn't exactly sure why he hadn't told her of their family connection, but somehow it seemed like a good idea to keep it to himself. Until he got to know her, anyway.

"I don't get it, Ms. Taylor—"

"Trish." Her voice was resigned. "Call me

Trish. Apparently, we're roommates."

"Okay, Trish. You're obviously not real happy to be here."

"You could tell that, could you?"

"It's pretty hard to miss," he said wryly. "It oozes from you along with the sarcasm. So what's the problem?"

"Problems, plural." She raised her head and looked at him. "The problems, Mr. Kendall—"

"Jack."

"Jack, start with the fact that I'm really not qualified to determine whether this island is suitable for what Russ wants to do. I'm out of my league and that bothers me. A lot. Resort development is not my field of expertise. I have no training for it. I'm in public relations."

"I should have figured."

"What do you mean by that?" Her eyes narrowed.

"Nothing really." Had he struck a nerve? "Only that every little rich girl who wants to go to work for Daddy's company seems to end up in PR. It's a good place to put a relative with few skills other than looks."

"Mr. Kendall. Jack." Her voice was cold. "Not that I care what you think, but I majored in public relations in college, minoring in journalism and business. I worked for three years on my own, freelancing and consulting, until I had enough experience to land a job with Evans. My stepfather does not believe in handing out jobs to people who don't deserve them."

He smothered a laugh. Some things never changed. From the first R. J. Evans on down, no offspring who couldn't handle the job had been taken into the company. If memory served, aside from his aunt, Trish was the first female to be involved in the business. He was curious about whether his father had bent the long-standing family tradition for her. Apparently not. His estimation of her notched upward. "Sorry."

"I get that kind of crap all the time." She shook her head. "It's not easy to convince the world that qualified and rich are not mutually exclusive. It's like being—"

"Smart and pretty?"

"That's about it."

"So you have two stereotypes to overcome."

"Don't forget blond," she muttered.

"Oh, yeah." He laughed. "The dumb blonde syndrome. Must be tough."

"I can handle it," she said.

He'd just bet she could.

"For what it's worth, I think this resort idea is crazy too. It's totally impractical. The costs will be astronomical. And there's no way it can be pulled together in the time frame Russ wants."

"In time to greet the year 2000," Jack murmured.

"Right." She scoffed. "Frankly, I think it's bogus. I think my stepfather just wanted to get me out of the country and away from everything going on in my life."

"This is a great place to get your act together."

"My act is just fine, thank you," she said in a haughty tone. "Bogus or not, I've got a job to do. I just wish to hell I knew where to start."

"Well, we start at the beginning. A visual survey of the island. A laundry list of what is already here and what needs to be built. A general idea of—"

"We?" She raised a brow.

"Sure. I'm an ESI employee too." *And a member of the family.* "Didn't anybody tell you I was supposed to work with you on this? That's what my E-mail said." The lie rolled off his lips without hesitation. "I've lived here for four years. I know this place inside and out."

"Really?" Her expression brightened. "Nobody said a word about you. At least not that I can remember—but everything happened so fast. . . . This is great. Maybe we can wrap this up quickly and I can go home. Thanks." She smiled for the first time, and it did something odd to the pit of his stomach. "That will help with another of my problems. I'm in the throes of planning my wedding."

"Oh?" His gaze dropped to her hand. Mo was right: The diamond on her finger was obscene.

"That's really why I think Russ sent me away. I don't think he's all that wild about my marriage."

"He doesn't like your fiancé?" What was his father up to?

"Oh, he likes him all right." She pulled her brows together in a thoughtful frown. "At least

I always assumed he liked him. But I'm beginning to wonder if Russ thinks Elliott is the right man for me."

"Elliott?" No, it couldn't be. "Elliott Hunt?"

"Yeah."

Elliott? "He's a wimp."

"He is not!" Suspicion narrowed her eyes. "How do you know anything about him, anyway?"

"I haven't always lived in Paradise Bay. I'm familiar with the real world. And Elliott Hunt." He pulled himself to his feet and strode across the room to a small refrigerator concealed in the woodwork. Beer ration or no beer ration, this news called for a drink. He opened the door, grabbed a can, popped the top and pulled a long swallow. "Your stepfather is right: Elliott's not for you."

"How would you know?" She stood up and crossed her arms over her chest. "You don't even know me."

"Yeah, but I know Elliott. He's a wuss." He shook his head in disgust. He'd lived in the same house with Elliott for two long, horrible years. Even as a kid, Elliott was a suck-up and a tattler. Jack hadn't run into him in years—in fact, he hadn't seen him since their parents' divorce— but he couldn't imagine he'd changed much. "I can't believe it. Elliott."

"Elliott is a wonderful man," she said staunchly.

"Elliott is a jerk, and that's the nicest thing I

can say about him." He took another pull from the can.

"He's intelligent and ambitious and steady and we're perfect together."

Fire sparked in her blue eyes. Elliott would take that spark right out of her or, at a minimum, dim it, which was just as bad. They'd have their perfect life with two-point-seven perfect children, or whatever the average was these days, and live in a perfect house, in a perfect, exclusive area of the city. Secure and stable and boring with a capital *B*. Everything a woman could ask for. Only he knew as sure as he'd ever known anything in his life that Elliott was not the man for Trish. He'd bet big bucks his father knew it too. She was probably right. The whole resort idea was a scam to get her away from Elliott and everything else in her life and give her the opportunity to come to her senses. The least Jack could do was help out his old man. It wouldn't be easy. She looked like the stubborn type. But time was the key. The longer he kept her here, the better the chances of success.

"Besides, it's none of your business," she added.

Of course, he wouldn't get very far if she hated him. "You're right." He ran his hand through his hair. "It's none of my business. As you pointed out, I don't even know you. Sorry."

"Apology accepted," she said grudgingly. "You're going to have to tell me how you know Elliott. And how you got here in the first place."

"Sure." He shrugged. "Later."

Her gaze dropped to the can in his hand. "Is that cold?"

"Yep." He raised the can. "I'd give you one, but we're on tight rations until the supply boat comes."

The tip of her tongue flicked across her lips. "Oh, I see. In that case . . ."

"I'd offer you a sip but, as you said, I don't even know you."

"Right. I'm not generally a beer drinker anyway. It just looked good. And cold . . ." She sighed. "At least the boat will be here this afternoon. It's bringing my luggage."

"You were told the supply boat was coming today?" he said slowly.

"Yes. Well . . ." She looked longingly at the beer. "I imagine there's a kitchen here? With a refrigerator? And food? And ice?"

"We have all the comforts of home."

"Not my home."

"Head down the hall past the stairs; you can't miss the kitchen."

"Thanks." She turned to leave.

"You know," he said slowly, "if you're really serious about getting this job done, why don't we start with a tour of the island? Today. This afternoon."

"I'd love to, but I don't have anything to wear." She gestured at her expensive, wrinkled skirt and blouse. "I've already learned business clothes aren't exactly Paradise Bay–friendly."

"Maybe Maude can lend you something."

"Maude?"

"Maude Wellington, Mo's sister. She takes care of the house."

"Oh, the mythical housekeeper." Trish shrugged. "Sure. That would be great." She smiled again, pulled open the door and closed it behind her.

Jack stared at the door. How would Trish react to Maude? He'd bet the princess had never met a housekeeper like Maude Wellington before.

He turned back to the computer and settled into the chair before the keyboard. He needed to make sure his hunch about his father's plan was right. He pulled up an E-mail form, typed in the ESI address and stopped, his fingers poised above the keys.

What if he was wrong? What if his father's purpose in sending Trish here had nothing to do with her marriage to Elliott? Abruptly, he realized that regardless of his father's intention, Jack couldn't let her marry Elliott. He couldn't let anybody he liked marry Elliott. And he definitely liked Trish. She might be a little too uptight and serious, and he suspected she was a bit of a snob, but he'd work on that. He used to be quite charming and a lot of fun, even if he was a little out of practice. He grinned and typed a quick note.

The flying monkey didn't stand a chance.

Chapter Three

"Why didn't you tell her you're her brother?" Maude lounged against the kitchen counter, a cup of her killer coffee in her hand.

"I'm not her brother," Jack said, his tone a bit sharper than he'd expected. He stirred the coffee sitting on the table in front of him, surprised as always that the spoon didn't dissolve. "Our parents are married, but there's no real connection between us. We're related only through a quirk of fate."

" 'The unpredictability inherent in human affairs is due largely to the fact that the by-products of a human process are more fateful than the product,' " Maude said.

Jack looked at her curiously. "And which one of your philosophers said that?"

"Eric Hoffer." Maude sipped her coffee. "I have to keep in practice. Who knows when a real job in a real university will come up? I have to be prepared."

"Beats taking care of me, right?"

"You're not so bad." Maude grinned and slid her glasses higher on her nose. "Most of the time."

Jack laughed. Maude was a fascinating contradiction. From the dark tone of her skin to her black hair, she looked like Hollywood's version of a Polynesian princess. Except for her amazing blue eyes. And the tortoiseshell glasses. And the air of intelligence that surrounded her like a rare perfume. She barely came up to the middle of his chest and he probably would have fallen hard for her if they hadn't become such good friends first. She'd returned to the island about the same time he'd arrived. They'd had a brief fling, but back then he'd needed a friend much more than he'd needed a lover.

"How goes the job hunt anyway?"

Maude shrugged. "Same old stuff. There's not much out there for doctors of philosophy except the occasional off-the-wall think tank and academia. And tenured philosophy professors are notoriously long-lived."

Jack braced himself, took another sip of coffee and tried not to wince. Maude was a genius when it came to knowledge of the world's philosophers, and an expert gourmet cook, but her coffee-making skills left a lot to be desired. She had a passion for coffee so strong, the spoon could almost stand up by itself, and it took several spoonfuls of sugar to be palatable enough for Jack to bravely force it down.

"It's been almost four years." He paused, already knowing her reaction. "Why don't you let me talk to my fa—"

"We've been through all this before." Maude shook her head. "The trust fund gave me the best education money could buy, from high school through my doctorate program. I don't want ESI taking care of me for the rest of my life. Period. End of discussion."

"You are one stubborn philosopher." He had to admire her, though. She'd had a few offers here and there, but she was looking for just the right opportunity. ESI could easily set up a think tank through one of its nonprofit operations, but Maude refused to even consider that route. Instead, she kept up a long-distance job search, wrote articles for various journals and worked on her own philosophical treatise, parts of which he'd read but didn't really understand. Once a week, she took over his computer and held long, rambling discussions with like minds around the world.

"Speaking of stubborn, you changed the subject." Maude poked him with her finger and looked thoughtfully at him. "Why don't you want her to know who you are?"

"It just seemed like a good idea at the time, I guess." He still hadn't quite figured that one out himself. "Besides, if she's right about why my father sent her here, I don't want her to think the whole family's ganging up on her."

"Maybe you just don't want her to think of you as a brother."

"Oh, and why wouldn't I want that?"

Maude took a thoughtful sip. "You tell me."

"Come on. I just met her," he said irritably.

"Mo said she's gorgeous. A goddess, I believe is the way he put it."

Jack laughed. "Mo thinks any blonde who towers above him is a goddess."

"And what do you think?"

"She's pretty." Very pretty. With incredibly long legs. Jack pulled himself to his feet. "Hopefully, she'll be down any minute and you can see for yourself. What's she doing, anyway?"

"She was in the shower when I went up. I put the clothes you asked for on her bed, plus a pair of old tennis shoes of Mo's. But I don't know if any of my things will fit. From Mo's description, I got an image of a fair-haired giant. A very well-built fair-haired giant."

Jack grinned wickedly.

Maude narrowed her eyes. "It's been a long time since you've been in a relationship with a woman—"

"Other than you."

"Scarcely counts. I'd hate to see this Amazonian creature break your little heart."

"That's not even a possibility. I'm going to work with her on this resort scheme, and in the process convince her that Elliott is not the right man for her."

"And how do you know that?"

"I know Elliott." Jack heaved a deep sigh. "He's not an evil stepbrother or anything like that. He's just a follow-the-rules, don't-make-waves, straight-and-narrow, suck-up-to-authority jerk. A genuine pain in the ass."

"Maybe he's changed."

"If he'd changed, my father wouldn't be against this wedding."

Maude's brow quirked upward.

"Don't give me that look. Yeah, okay, I admit it." He stepped to her side and set his cup down in the sink. "My old man isn't the idiot I once thought he was."

Maude laughed. "I never imagined I'd hear you say that."

"You and me both."

"Just be careful, okay?" Maude took his hand. "I have weird vibes about this whole thing."

"Then everything's fine. Because, my dear, sweet friend"— he pulled her into his arms and grinned down at her—"while you have the philosophies of the world at your fingertips, your vibes are never right."

Trish placed her hand against the swinging kitchen door and paused. Low voices and laughter sounded on the other side. The hulking beast must have company. Female company, from the sound of it. Maybe it was the alleged house-keeper? Or maybe it was the midget who'd left clean clothes on her bed. Trish glanced down ruefully. The T-shirt, emblazoned with the words PHILOSOPHY: UNINTELLIGIBLE ANSWERS TO INSOLUBLE PROBLEMS, stretched across her chest and barely came to her waist. The shorts fit, more or less, although generally she preferred shorts that didn't hit a mere inch below her butt. There was scarcely enough room in the pocket to slip in a couple of index cards and a pen. But she couldn't stand to put back on her dusty, ru-ined suit. Besides, her clothes would arrive soon. At least the shoes, grubby as they were, fit. And the bite she'd grabbed earlier, coupled with the shower, made her feel almost human again.

She drew in a deep breath and plastered what she hoped was a pleasant smile on her face. No need to alienate the natives, after all. She pushed open the door and stepped into the kitchen.

Jack and a woman stood near the sink wrapped in each other's arms. Tiny and perfect, with black hair swept up in a ponytail, she looked like a doll. South Seas Barbie. Her stom-ach lurched.

This is all I need. Maybe, if they hadn't seen her, she could just back quietly out the door and—

"About time you made an appearance, Prin-cess," Jack said. He and the doll casually re-leased each other and stepped apart.

"I'm sorry if I . . . I mean, I hope I didn't . . ." Damn. She hadn't the vaguest idea how to get out of this extremely awkward situation.

Jack grinned, obviously enjoying her discomfort. Right then and there she wanted to kill him. Or somebody.

"There's nothing to be sorry about, and you didn't." Barbie gave Jack the same kind of look a mother gives a naughty child. She stepped toward Trish and stretched out her hand. "I'm Maude Wellington."

"You're the housekeeper?" *Some housekeeper!* Trish took her hand numbly. "For him?"

Maude laughed. "It's more a favor than an actual job. Jack needs someone to take care of him."

"I'll bet." *And exactly how much care does he require?*

Maude dropped her hand, her eyes, a remarkable shade of blue, narrowing slightly. "I really don't do all that much."

"She feeds me," Jack said cheerfully.

"How nice," Trish murmured. *What else does she do?*

"Jack, weren't you going to show Ms. Taylor—"

"Call her Trish."

"Of course." Trish forced a polite smile. Why did this woman rub her the wrong way? She couldn't remember ever taking an instant dislike to anyone before. Although she'd never met a "housekeeper" who obviously wasn't one before either. "I've always enjoyed friendly relationships with, um, the staff."

Jack sucked in a loud breath. "Whoa, hold on, Trish. You don't under—"

"Jack." Maude's gaze locked with Trish's. "Didn't you say you were going to show Trish around? Why don't you go outside and wait for her."

Jack shook his shaggy head. "I don't think—"

"We'll have some coffee and she'll join you in a minute."

"Coffee sounds good." She'd love a few moments alone with Island Barbie. They needed to get a few things straight. It wasn't as if she cared anything at all about Jack. She didn't even know him. He could do whatever he liked with whomever he liked. But not here. Not with her in the same house. Her family's house. And not under the guise of housekeeping.

"I really think I should stay here." Jack glanced from Maude to Trish and back again. "On second thought, I'll be right outside." He turned on his heel, yanked open a screen door and stepped through, the wooden door banging shut behind him. Hah! And he called Elliott a wimp.

Maude poured a cup and handed it to her. "So what's your problem, Princess?"

"Problem?" Trish accepted the coffee and pulled a long sip. It was black and strong. Extremely strong. Just the way she liked it. "To start with, I don't like to be called 'Princess.'"

"Okay. I'll make you a deal." Maude refilled her own cup. "I won't call you 'Princess' if you don't look at me like I'm Jezebel seducing an innocent."

"Although I doubt Jack Kendall is innocent in any way, shape or form, it certainly looked like I walked in on something that falls outside of the strict definition of housekeeping."

"Don't believe everything you see. Jack and I are friends. Good friends. Nothing more." Maude studied her for a minute. "Most of the young people on the island who go away to school don't come back. My brother and I are two of the exceptions, but there aren't many of us. This place is very much like any small town anywhere. There's not a lot of opportunity to use a college education. And not a lot of people you can relate to.

"I came home shortly after Jack arrived. At the time he really needed a friend." She shrugged. "And that's pretty much all there is to it."

"So why are you working as a housekeeper?"

"It gives me something to do, but it's not much of a job." Maude smiled. "I took it off my mom's hands, but all I really do is a little vacuuming and dusting once a week."

"And cook," Trish said pointedly.

"That's the best part. I am one hell of a cook. Gourmet. It's kind of a hobby."

Great. Make that Gourmet Barbie.

Maude crossed her arms and leaned her back against the counter. "My turn for questions."

"Shoot." Trish kept her tone cool.

"Why do you care?"

"Why do I care about what?" she said uneasily.

"About Jack and me and what we may or may not be doing together."

"Well, I have to share this house with him and you're working here and . . ." You'd obviously jumped to conclusions, reacting to Barbie in a totally irrational way. She'd think she was jealous or something. "Beats me. There's no reason why I should care about him and you one way or the other." What was wrong with her, anyway? She pushed her hair away from her face. "Three days ago, I couldn't even remember ever hearing of Paradise Bay. Now I'm on the other side of the world from where I should be and where I want to be. I'm hot and tired and I have no idea how I'm going to pull off the impossible."

Maude stared at her silently.

"I apologize. I don't know what's the matter with me. I'm not usually such a—"

"Snob?"

Trish wrinkled her nose. "I was going to say bitch, but I guess snob covers it too." She pulled a deep breath. "I'm willing to start over if you are. Beginning with thanking you for the clothes." She glanced from Maude to her outfit and back. "I assume these are yours."

"They're mine all right." Maude's gaze swept over her. "Not exactly your size, are they?"

Trish smiled wryly. "You noticed that too?"

Maude's eyes twinkled behind her glasses. "It's pretty hard to miss. Although my brother would love you in those."

"Mo?"

"He has a thing for tall leggy blondes. You're his dream girl."

"Swell."

"Don't worry." Maude laughed. "He's my brother—my twin actually, even though most of the time we don't agree on anything. I'm older by a couple of minutes and lord it over him every chance I get, but he's a good guy and relatively harmless."

"Great." That was a relief. One complication she didn't need to deal with was a lovesick islander. She already had Jack to contend with, and who knew what was on his mind. She took another sip of her coffee. "What about Jack? Is he harmless too?"

"Jack is an interesting guy." Maude thought for a minute. "That computer literally saved his life. His fa—ESI set it all up for him, and once he got into programming and whatever else it is he does, his whole world changed. He was lost when he got here."

"What do you mean?"

"It's his story. He'll tell you if he wants. In the meantime"—Maude gestured at Trish's clothes—"I'll try and see what else I can come up with for you to wear. But I warn you, most native islanders are much shorter and smaller than you are. We might have to resort to borrowing some of

Jack's shirts. Of course, he's much bigger—"

"I'd rather go with too big than too small," she said quickly. "Besides, my things will be here when the supply boat comes today."

"Today?" Maude pulled her brows together, then shrugged. "Whatever. You'd better get going."

"Thanks again." Was it her imagination, or did everyone on the island act a little strange whenever she mentioned the supply boat. She turned to leave, then turned back. "I really am sorry."

"Forget it." Maude smiled. "Go on. Jack's waiting."

Trish returned the smile. Maybe she and Maude could even be friends. Or at least civil. She pushed open the back door and stepped onto the veranda that wrapped around the house like a life preserver. There wasn't a lawn. Instead, a stone pathway wound through free-form beds of what were probably native flowering plants. The garden filled a space of less than thirty feet before the mountain foliage took over and the terrain rose sharply. A small gingerbread Victorian gazebo stood off to one side, matched on the opposite end of the grounds by an oversized gardener's shed. It was obviously well kept and looked like a scene from a gardening book, taken straight from a chapter entitled "Island Fantasy." If Maude was the housekeeper, Trish wondered what the gardener looked like.

Kendall was nowhere in sight. Trish walked down the three steps from the porch and headed around the house. Maybe he was out front. She still couldn't figure out why she'd had such a strong reaction to the sight of Jack and Maude together. It couldn't possibly have been jealousy, although it had felt suspiciously like that. She was being ridiculous, of course. She didn't know Jack well enough to be jealous. She didn't know him at all, although she had to admit that there was something about the man that she automatically liked. Something familiar and comforting. Something that warmed her deep inside.

Abruptly, she stopped up short. Of course, that was it. It was his smile. There was something about the guy's smile that grabbed at her. Maybe they'd met somewhere before? No. She would have remembered that smile and those eyes. This was very weird. She shook her head and continued walking around the house. Smile or no smile, she wasn't interested in anything from Jack Kendall, other than his help.

Even if she didn't have Elliott, she could never be interested in someone like Jack. They had nothing in common; they were complete opposites. You could tell just from looking at him that he wasn't at all stable. He probably didn't have a serious bone in his body. And he sure didn't look like any computer nerd she'd ever met. No, he looked like the kind of guy who'd actively seek out adventure. And Trish had no desire for adventure.

On the other hand, Jack was apparently dedicated to his work. No one had really explained exactly why he was here in the first place, but she didn't doubt he was legitimate. Still, there were facets to this man that hadn't been revealed. Something didn't quite mesh. The hulking beast was definitely a mystery. In Trish's book, mystery ranked right up there with adventure on her list of dislikes. She'd much rather know all the answers up front. No unknowns, no shocks, and no surprises.

She'd bet Jack Kendall was just full of surprises.

She rounded the corner of the house and spotted Jack lounging lazily on the front steps of the porch.

His gaze flicked over her. "Nice outfit."

She snorted. "Hardly. I feel like a waitress at Hooters."

"Yeah." He grinned. "That's what I meant."

She ignored his leer and looked around. "I'm ready to go. Where's the car?"

He unfolded his long legs and got to his feet. "There's only one car. A jeep. And it's—"

"I know." She grimaced. "It's on the other side of the island." She heaved a resigned sigh. "So what do we do? Walk?"

"Nope." He strode off down the stone walkway that led to the road and stopped beside a large palm. A small motorcycle, or maybe it was a scooter, leaned against the tree. Either way, it certainly didn't look very substantial.

"What is that?" She pointed to the childlike vehicle

"It's a bike. A scooter, really. Italian." He threw one leg over the seat and settled down. "Standard mode of transportation on Paradise Bay."

"I should have known." Motorbikes were not her idea of a good time. Too open, too fast and too damn terrifying. Deathtraps.

He nodded behind him. "Hop on."

She eyed the bike skeptically. And a tiny deathtrap at that. "Where?"

"Right behind me. There's plenty of room." Jack patted the seat.

Plenty of room? Hardly. She'd be plastered up so close against him, it would be quite an intimate encounter.

He raised a brow. "Come on, Princess."

"Don't call me 'Princess,'" she muttered. "Look, I hate to admit it, but these things really scare me."

"Would you rather walk?"

She could wimp out, but for some obscure reason she didn't want him to think she was a coward. She was, but that was beside the point. Trish sighed and climbed on behind him. There was no other place to put her hands, and reluctantly she wrapped her arms around him, holding herself as stiff as possible.

"That's better." He turned the key and the engine sputtered to life. It didn't sound too bad, actually. In fact, it sounded a lot like the

Tinkertoy it resembled. She released the breath she didn't know she held.

Jack maneuvered the scooter in a long, slow curve and headed downhill on the mansion's gravel drive. He was surprisingly cautious and handled the bike with an easy confidence at a reasonable speed. Maybe this wouldn't be so bad after all. She relaxed her grip. Maybe it would even be the tiniest bit enjoyable.

The drive ended at the road that Mo had said circled the island. Midway up the slope of the mountain, halfway between the community and the Evans' family private property, the road marked an unofficial boundary. Straight ahead would lead down into the village. Instead, Jack turned onto the main road and headed east.

"Where are we going?" she called over the noise of the engine.

"I thought we'd start on the other side of the island. That's probably the best place for the resort." He glanced over his shoulder. "Are you okay back there?"

"Fine." It was true, she was fine. The wind blowing through her hair, the easy pace of the bike, even the solid warmth of the man in front of her, all combined to ease her fear. And the scenery was magnificent. The mountain rose solidly on their left. On the opposite side, the road was high enough to look out over the junglelike vegetation and beyond to the beaches and shocking blue water, but not high enough to be scary. Not bad. Not bad at all. Maybe she'd even try to drive one of these herself. Maybe she'd ask Jack, or Mo, if she could rent or borrow—

"Great. Then hold on."

Without warning, Jack gunned the engine and the bike leapt forward like the proverbial bat out of hell. Trish's heart lodged firmly in her throat and she clung tighter to Jack for dear life. She yelled into his ear, "Slow down!"

"I can't hear you," he yelled back.

Of course he could hear her! She could hear him, couldn't she? The man was just being annoying. He probably drove this way all the time. It was a wonder he was still alive.

The bike hit a bump in the road and at once they were airborne. She screamed, squeezed her eyes closed tight and waited for the inevitable pain that dying in a motorcycle crash was bound to bring. *Please let it be fast!* DOA or something. She didn't want to suffer.

The bike slammed back to earth. The man really did know what he was doing. Incredibly they were still upright, still moving at the speed of light and still alive. Good. She'd rather kill him herself. She tightened her grip.

"Still okay?" She could hear the laughter in his voice.

"No!"

His laughter floated back to her. The scenery whizzed by in a nauseating blur. She gritted her teeth and buried her head in his back. She couldn't bear to watch. Oh, Jack Kendall was a dead man, all right. But it wouldn't be fast. No way. He didn't deserve fast. It would be slow and painful and last forever. Just like this ride from hell. Each and every time she thought there was a chance for survival, they'd hit another bump and leave the road again. She had no idea if they'd been on the damn bike for a lifetime or only a few minutes; terror vanquished all sense of time. Abruptly she realized thinking about slow, torturous ways to kill him took her mind off her own impending death. . . .

Maybe there was some special tropical-island torture specifically for those virgins who refused to jump into the volcano. Or better yet, the young men who made sure the victims no longer qualified for sacrifice. What would be more perfect? Jack was probably a virgin despoiler from way back.

The bike shuddered to a stop.

"You can let go of me now," he said.

"Are we alive?" She was afraid to look.

"More or less."

She raised her head, released her grip and practically fell off the bike in her eagerness to get her feet back on solid ground. He stretched, winced, then rubbed his stomach. "Boy, Princess, you sure do have a death grip."

"It goes along with the death ride!" She glared at him. "What in the hell were you doing, anyway? I told you I don't like those things. You scared the crap out of me!"

He got off the bike, kicked a stand into place

and settled the bike. "I always drive like that."

"Even with a passenger?" How could he be so laid-back? He'd taken her life in his hands and it didn't even seem to bother him.

Jack's brown eyes twinkled with amusement. On second thought, death, even slow and torturous, was probably too good for him. "I never have passengers. Just about everybody I know here has their own bike."

"You had a passenger today, and you nearly killed me." No, there had to be something he deserved more than death.

The corners of his mouth quivered, as if he was trying not to laugh. "You were perfectly safe."

"Safe? Hah!" She planted her hands on her hips. "I nearly fell off the damn thing every time you decided to leave the ground. We could have slid sideways on the gravel. We could have plunged off the cliffs. We could—"

"Taylor." He put his hands on her shoulders. "Have you looked around at all?"

"—have crashed into a tree. I could easily have had a heart attack—"

"Trish." Gently, he turned her around. "Look."

"I don't want to look," she snapped and glanced around in spite of herself. Her breath caught in her throat. The land gently sloped away from the road down to the beach below. The mountain rose sharply behind them. Sapphire water lapped at a dark, sandy beach, glistening in the sunshine. Slightly behind her to her right, a waterfall crashed down the side of the mountain in a ribbon of white and green, scattering droplets of water that sparkled like the finest diamonds.

"This is where you should put your resort. This is Paradise."

Chapter Four

"So what do you think?" Jack struggled to hide the pride in his voice. "It's something, isn't it?"

"It's something all right." Trish stared at the scene laid out before her like a kid at the gates of Disney World.

"Isn't it?" He smiled to himself. Of course she loved it. Who in their right mind wouldn't? This was without question the most beautiful place he'd ever seen, and he'd seen most of the acknowledged scenic wonders of the world.

"I can see why you brought me here." She breathed an appreciative sigh. "It does take your breath away."

"Happens to the best of us." He'd had the same reaction the first time he stood here as a kid with his parents. Even as a moderately smart-mouthed ten-year-old he was struck silent by the magical vista, the same now as it was then. The deep blue of the sea stretched out forever to meet and meld with the endless sky, in startling contrast to the dark, nearly black, volcanic sand found only on this side of the island. The mountain loomed at his back, lending an air of strength and majesty to the setting. The crystal purity of the falling water tied it all together like an iridescent ribbon on an unexpected gift.

"In your opinion, as someone familiar with the island, is this the absolute best place for the resort?"

"I wouldn't put it anywhere else," Jack said absently. His father had said his reaction to the setting was probably genetic: Each and every member of the Evans family had fallen victim to the spell cast by this spot since the first R. J. Evans had set foot on the island. His grandson and great-grandson had shared a special closeness on that visit long before Jack's mother had died and teenage resentment had driven the generations apart. Time and the island had healed those wounds, and to this day the mystical serenity he found here never failed to—

"Damn." Trish glared at the fountain pen in her hand, shook it vigorously, then scribbled on a file card. "There. That's better."

He glanced over at her. "I'm glad to see the scenery hasn't overwhelmed you completely."

She raised her gaze, considered the shoreline

with a speculative look, then glanced down and continued writing. "I said it was pretty."

"You said it took your breath away."

"Yeah, okay." She stepped away from him and turned to study the mountain, tapping the end of the pen against her bottom lip. "Its breathtaking."

Trish's eyes narrowed, as if she was considering some significant point. She flipped over the card in her hand and again scrawled a few words. Even in the intriguing too-tight, too-short outfit Maude had lent her, she appeared the model of corporate-trained efficiency.

"Are you sure you don't know what you're doing?"

"I'm sure," she said without looking at him.

"Then what are you—"

"I already told you I'm out of my league here." She pushed back strands of blond hair that stubbornly refused to stay tucked behind her ears. "But I also told you I'm not stupid. Neither is my stepfather. No matter what his ulterior motives, he still expects me to do the best I can. And I'm going to." She waved the file card at him. "See. I'm taking notes."

"Uh-huh." He craned his neck and tried to make out the unintelligible scratches on the small rectangular card.

"Oh, no, you don't." She jerked the card out of his line of sight. "The last thing I need is you watching over my shoulder." She turned her back to him.

Nice shoulder, though, a lecherous voice noted in his head. He bit back a grin. It was good to know that in spite of his years on the island he could still appreciate a nice shoulder and all that went with it when he saw one. Not that he'd been completely without female companionship.

"Okay." She glanced back at him over that intriguing shoulder. "I'm done."

"What do you mean, *you're done?*"

"I've seen all I need to see. I can write my report now."

He stared in disbelief. "That's it? That's the sum total of your study? A quick once-over and you've reached a decision? What happened to *do the best I can?*"

"Hey." She swiveled toward him and waved the alleged notes under his nose. "I took notes. Look, Kendall. Jack."

Trish drew a deep breath and gazed at him the way a kindhearted adult might look at a child. A young child. A very young child who didn't speak English. She gestured in a wide, expansive wave that took in the beach, the sea and probably the rest of the world. "It doesn't take a genius to figure out a few basics about this project. Even I can see that the problems are insurmountable. There is no way this can be pulled off. Definitely not in time for New Year's Eve 1999, and probably not at all."

"You're kidding."

"I've never been more serious. This is all I need to know." Again she fluttered the card at him. "I wasn't just screwing around here. I've written down everything I've seen. I've made notes of all the other things I've noticed that would effect this project. Bottom line: No way, no how, can this be accomplished."

"And that's what you're going to say?"

"Yep." She flashed him a brilliant smile and slipped the condemning index card into her back pocket. "My work here is done." She turned and headed toward the bike. In spite of his annoyance, he couldn't help but notice the interesting way her hips moved in the tight shorts and wondered idly how she managed to wedge even a mere card into that pocket. "You can take me home now."

"I don't think so," Jack said under his breath, filing away his appreciation of her backside for further consideration at a later moment.

Nice butt aside, there was no way he would let her shortchange this spot—his spot. Oh, sure, he still had doubts about the whole resort idea, but somehow Trish's quick dismissal of the proposal irritated him. Besides, until his dad responded to his E-mail and told him otherwise, Jack was operating on the belief that keeping Trish on the island was his father's real purpose. She might think her work was through, but his was just beginning.

"Well?" She climbed on the back of the scooter. "I'm ready."

"Don't bet on it." He strode toward the bike, settled in front of her and cranked the key sharply. The engine roared to life, and he felt her tense behind him.

"Take it easy on the way back, would you, Jack?" She sounded way too casual, as if she didn't have a worry in the world, but her arms tightened around him.

"Sure." *On the way back.* He turned the bike in a long, easy circle, passed the direction they'd come from and aimed straight for the beach.

"Kendall?" Caution edged her words. "What are you doing? Where are we going?"

"Just trying to help you do your job," he called over his shoulder. "Hold on."

"What do you mean, hold on?" Her voice rose. He glanced back. Her eyes were wide with terror. "Jack?"

He grinned and turned toward the water. He probably should tell her that he'd ridden down to the beach this way a hundred, even a thousand times, usually at much higher speeds, without incident. Maybe he should mention that the slope from the road to the beach looked far steeper than it was. At the very least he could warn her exactly what he planned.

Naaaah.

The bike hit an outcropping and flew through the air for an exhilarating, and sorrowfully brief, moment before dropping back onto the rough earth. She screamed and once again buried her face in his back. He could get to like having her so close if he wasn't fairly certain her nails were leaving permanent marks on his skin. In another minute or two, firm ground gave way to sand. Their speed slowed, he jerked the handlebars to one side and the bike skidded to a stop.

Trish gripped him as if he was the only life preserver left on the *Titanic*. Her face was still hidden in his shirt.

"Taylor?" He tried not to laugh. "Trish?"

Her voice was muffled. "Do you know how many ways I can come up with to kill a man when my life is flashing before my eyes?"

"No," he said innocently. "How many?"

She muttered something he didn't quite catch and figured he was better off not knowing.

"Come on." He slipped off the scooter and grabbed her hand.

She snatched it away and crossed her arms over her chest. "I'm not going anywhere."

"You haven't seen anything—"

"I've seen enough, thank—"

"Damn," he shook his head, "you are one stubborn princess."

Her eyes narrowed. "And you are one irritating computer nerd hulking beast."

"It's part of my charm." He stepped forward, pulled her off the scooter and in one quick move threw her over his shoulder.

"What do you think you're doing? Put me down!"

"In a minute." He started toward the water, one arm hooked around her legs, his other hand resting on her nice firm rear end.

"Watch where you put that hand, pal," she growled and tried to squirm free.

I am watching. He shifted her on his shoulder and grunted. "You know, you're heavier than I thought."

"Good! I hope you get a hernia or a bad back or something."

"That would put me in my place, all right. Lucky for me we're not going far." He stopped a few feet from the water's edge and deposited her flat on her backside in the sand.

She glared up at him. "Happy now?"

"Ecstatic." He squatted beside her. "If you'd stop being so put out for a moment and just listen to me—"

"I can't imagine anything you might say—"

"Shut up, Taylor, and look." He gestured at the sea. "What do you see?"

She surveyed the vista and clenched her teeth. "Nothing."

"Come on—"

"No, really." She scrambled to her feet and whipped the note card out of her pocket. "I even wrote it down. There's nothing here. Absolutely nothing. No dock—"

"There's only one dock on the island."

"Exactly. So we either build another dock or drive from the other side of the island. But for that we'd need a road. A highway. Even a street." She swiveled toward the road. "And that's it, right?"

"Well—"

"And it's not even a real, legitimate, paved road."

"Real roads are in short supply on Paradise Bay."

"Besides"—she was on a roll now and he almost regretted not letting her go back to the house—"there's no airstrip—"

"Not now but—"

"Nope." She shook her head. "The infrastructure alone needed for a luxury resort will make the cost astronomical. Then there's equipment, materials, construction workers—everything and everyone will have to be transported by boat or plane, probably from Australia or New Zealand." She shoved the note card back in her pocket. "It's just not feasible."

"You haven't given it much of a chance." He crossed his arms over his chest. "You've hardly seen any of the island—"

"You said this was the only place for the resort."

"Well, yes, but—"

"Then I consulted an expert." She smiled smugly, and for a second Jack wondered if maybe she didn't deserve Elliott after all.

"But—"

"But nothing. I was sent to evaluate the possibilities of putting a resort here and I have. It's not my fault it turned out to be so easy. I mean, aside from a location that I admit is nice—"

"Breathtaking."

"Okay, okay—breathtaking. Regardless, this

81

whole idea is impracticable, unrealistic, etc." She planted her hands on her hips. "I've seen all I need to see. All there is to see. Now, will you take me home?"

He shook his head. "Where is your imagination, Taylor? Your sense of adventure?"

"Don't have one, don't want one. Take me home."

"Not yet. I listened to what you didn't see, now you can listen to what I *do* see." He grabbed her shoulders and turned her toward the falls, sharp against the lush foliage of the mountainside. "What do you see there?"

She sighed in resignation. "A pretty—no—a breathtaking waterfall."

"Good. That's just for starters." He pulled his brows together and thought for a moment. "You see the natural terrace to the side of the waterfall? I see that expanded, but in a way that fits into the scenery, so it looks like it's part of the mountain. I see a pathway that splits and leads in that direction"—he nodded away from the beach—"to a golf course and tennis courts. All designed with nature in mind so that it seems like it's always been there and you'll miss it if you aren't looking for it. And over here"—he turned her a half-step— "across the road—"

"A real road, or will that be *au natural* too?"

He ignored the sarcasm. An odd sense of excitement built within him. He could picture it clearly in his mind. Maybe his father's idea wasn't so farfetched after all. "Across the *real road* is the center of the resort. Come on, use your imagination."

"I don't have one," she said sharply.

"Sure you do, you just don't know it. Look, right there." He pointed to an area slightly off the road. "That's the spot for the main lodge or clubhouse or some kind of central building connected to smaller units designed to house guest rooms. I don't know exactly. I'm not an architect, but I can see everything perched along the slopes of the mountain and the beach."

"Maybe, I guess—"

"And here." He turned her to face east and the blue waters reaching to infinity. Jack stepped behind her, bending a little to speak softly into her ear. "What do you think I see here, Trish?"

"A dock?" Her voice seemed strangely weak, and without thinking he pulled her a bit closer to him.

"The dock will be off to the side." He stared into the distance. "Here, Trish, right here, I see the night chased off by the first rays of day but reluctantly, in no real hurry to leave. I see long purple fingers stretching out and changing so slowly that at first you barely notice it."

She leaned back against him, and it seemed only natural to wrap his arms around her. "And all of a sudden you realize the purple is now a deep, rich pink, and then orange, and before you know it, the sun is peeking over the rim of the world so bright it hurts to look at it. You know you have to pull your eyes away before it blinds you, but you stare anyway because you've never seen a sun so huge or a sunrise so magnificent as it is right here."

"Wow." The word was no more than a breath. He stared at the invisible sunrise until abruptly, the scene vanished from his mind, and he was all too aware of just how nicely Trish Taylor fit against him. "Trish?"

"Hmmm?" She twisted in his arms and gazed up at him, and for a split second he thought she too noticed how well their bodies might just be made for one another. Her eyes widened and she stepped back, crossing her arms over her chest, as if she was suddenly cold. Her gaze met his. "Very nice, Kendall. I'm impressed, I really am. And I admit, when it comes to the dreaming department, you've got me beat. But"—her chin rose a notch—"as lovely a dream as it is, that's all it's ever going to be. I've made my decision."

"You're crazy if you think Evans is going to drop this project just on your say-so."

"What's crazy is this whole, stupid idea. And frankly, I'm more convinced than ever that my being sent here was a scam to get me out of town. My stepfather may be a world-class meddler, but he's not an idiot. He's one hell of a businessman—"

"And a dreamer in his own way."

"A dreamer? Russell Jonathan Evans the Third?" she scoffed. "Get real. What he is is practical and solid and stable. And I'd bet he already knows the cost of this project is prohibitive. My recommendation is to dump it. Period."

" 'The cost is prohibitive'?" His tone dripped with sarcasm. "Whoa. Big words from the flying monkey."

"Flying monkey?" Her brows pulled together in confusion. "What's a flying monkey?"

"Forget it." He shook his head in disgust and headed up the slope toward the road. Trish only saw what she wanted to see, and she didn't want to see the possibilities here. She didn't want to even consider the excitement and adventure of creating something fantastic out of nothing.

"Oh, I'll forget it, all right." She struggled to keep up with him, muttering at a level just loud enough for him to hear. "Anthills. That's it. Staked out to anthills. Naked. Covered with honey. In the desert . . ."

She wanted him dead. Again. Man, despite what she claimed, she had an imagination. A wicked imagination.

". . . the blistering sun beating down . . ."

Why couldn't she see what he could see so clearly? Oh, sure, it was a wild, impractical idea, but with enough creativity and enough money, both of which ESI had in abundance, the resort could be built. Why not?

Of course, this really could be just a plot on his father's part to separate Trish and Elliott. Jack wouldn't put it past his dad to concoct a mythical project.

But what if he could change his father's mind? The more he'd tried to get Trish to see the po-

Victoria Alexander

tential here, the more he'd seen it himself. God knows it wouldn't be the first time an Evans had taken the impossible and made it a reality. And what if . . .

He stopped in his tracks.

What if Russell Jonathan Evans the third had always had every intention of building a resort on Paradise Bay? And what if this project could serve a few other purposes as well, like separating his stepdaughter from her fiancé and luring someone on the fringes of the company completely into the fold? Someone who loved the island and would guarantee progress didn't destroy but enhanced it? Someone like, say, a black sheep—

"You're grinning like an idiot, Kendall." Trish marched past him to the bike. "What's so funny?"

Or a prodigal son?

"Nothing." He shook his head, but he couldn't wipe the smile off his face.

Or Russell Jonathan Evans the fourth?

He had to hand it to his old man. His dad had never once suggested he take a bigger role in a business that would fall to him to run one day. Instead, Jack had been painlessly integrated into the company through his programming. Now that he thought about it, he was familiar in one way or another with every division and most departments in the megaconglomerate that was ESI. The past few years had simply prepared him like nothing else could to run the company his family had built through the last hundred-plus years.

"So how do you drive this thing?" Trish circled the bike.

"You don't. I do."

"I watched you do it." She threw a leg over the seat, settled herself and bounced experimentally. "It doesn't seem too tough."

He cocked a brow. "Have you ever ridden a bike like this?"

"Nope. But it looks about as complicated as a kid's toy. How hard could it be?"

"Harder than it looks. I'd be happy to show you the basics later. Right now—"

"Right now, if you're driving, I'm walking." She scrambled off the bike. "There's no way I'll get back on that deathtrap with you."

"You don't trust me?" He gasped in mock distress. "I'm crushed."

"I'm sure."

"I haven't lost a passenger yet."

"There's always a first time. Thanks, but no thanks." She started off down the road. He opened his mouth to call after her, then snapped it shut. Let her walk. He could use the time it would take to get back to the house to fire off another E-mail to his dad. For the first time he regretted the reluctance of each new generation to upgrade the communication facilities on the island. Right now he could sure use a basic long-distance phone service.

She stopped and turned back to him. "I hate

to admit this"—she drew in a deep breath and squared her shoulders—"but I haven't the vaguest idea where I am. I have no sense of direction without street signs and traffic lights. And everything here looks the same to me. This is the way back, right?"

That way would bring her back to the house the way they'd come and take her maybe twenty minutes to half an hour. The other direction would also ultimately get her back to the house, but she'd end up circling the rest of the island and it would take her a good three hours.

"This way is probably better." *For me, anyway.* He nodded in the opposite direction and pushed away a twinge of guilt. He really did need the extra time to contact his dad and find out if any or all of his speculation was accurate. Besides, she'd said she wanted to do the best she could, and it was part of her job to get a good feel for Paradise Bay. All of it. He was simply helping her do her job.

He climbed on the bike, started the engine and sidled up next to her. "See ya."

She stared at him suspiciously. "Aren't you going in the wrong direction?"

"I know a shortcut. There's a ravine that runs along the side of the mountain and if you hit it at just the right spot you can—"

"Never mind." She shuddered. "I'm safer walking."

He laughed. "I was right: you have no spirit of adventure."

"Oh, yeah? Well, you . . . you . . ." Her eyes narrowed. "You have too much damn hair."

"Good comeback. That put me in my place. Later." He gunned the motor and headed down the road.

And wondered just what method of murder she was planning for him now.

". . . baked on a spit turning over an open fire . . ."

Scenes from old black-and-white movies featuring cannibals dancing around a big pot played in her mind.

". . . no—boiled. Much better. Much slower . . ."

How could he have left her to walk back by herself? The least he could have done when she'd said she wanted to walk was talk her out of it. She had admitted she had no sense of direction. Jack Kendall was without a doubt one of the most irritating men she'd ever met.

In some rational, sane corner of her mind she knew her reaction to him wasn't completely justified, but she didn't care. She was going on gut instinct, not logic. Besides, so far he'd implied she owed her job to nepotism, called her fiancé a wuss, terrorized her on a Tinkertoy and practically said she was fat. Who wouldn't be pissed?

The old movie in her head shifted to show Jack popping up from the center of the pot with all the fanfare of a stripper springing from a cake at a bachelor party. A wide grin stretched across his face and a wicked twinkle shone in his eye.

She trudged onward, barely noting the sparkling sea on her right, the verdant ferns and heavy undergrowth creeping up the mountain to her left. It was probably the combination of that damn twinkle and his infectious smile that set off her warning signals. In spite of his too-long hair and his too-full beard, those eyes and that grin were deadly. Plus, he was smart, and his expert handling of the bike confirmed her initial impression of his adventure-loving personality. If she'd had any doubts whatsoever about his athleticism, they vanished the moment she'd put her arms around him. Only a dead woman would fail to notice the hard muscles of his chest beneath his shirt.

She wiped her forehead with the back of her hand. Where were those island breezes the report—no, travel guide—talked about? The sun seemed much hotter now than when she'd started out. Why hadn't she brought a hat? Surely Maude had a hat that she could have borrowed Even a baseball cap would be better than nothing. Kendall should have offered her something. She'd be burned to a crisp by the time she reached the house, and it would be his fault. Add inconsiderate to his list of attributes—good and bad.

The list was growing by the minute. She checked the items off in her head. Inconsiderate. Check. Smart. Obviously. Handsome? Who could really tell with all that hair? Okay. She sighed. She could tell. Check. Flirtatious? No doubt about that. Adventurous? Definitely. Any way you looked at it, the sum total added up to dangerous. Jack Kendall was dangerous. Thank God she was already in a relationship. A man like Kendall would want to be in charge. He'd expect to be in control.

And hadn't he been in control ever since she walked into his air conditioning?

Of course, it had been partly her fault: She never should have admitted that she didn't know what she was doing. It was obviously some sort of tropical dementia on her part. And he took full advantage of her weakness, damn him. She hated not being in control. She'd hated it for as long as she could remember.

"And wouldn't a shrink have a good time with that little confession," she said aloud glaring at a bird that swooped and squawked overhead. Trish had never given into the temptation to go to a psychiatrist, although most of her friends had. What was the point? She knew what even the most incompetent analyst would say. A freshman psychology student could figure it out.

"Blame it on my father. Blame it on my mother," she muttered to herself. She could practically hear the headshrinker now. . . .

"My dear, your need for control stems from your childhood. The fact that you were the center of a nasty custody battle with your future and your life totally out of your hands—"

"But, Doctor, I was only seven at the time. A mere child. Children don't get to decide their own fate."

"Nonetheless, Patricia, your sense of helplessness burned into your subconscious, leaving you with the need to control life around you."

"Well, I suppose . . ."

"Now"—he leaned closer—*"shall we talk about the subconscious motives behind your marriage to Elliot?"*

She blinked hard and shook her head. Where on earth had that come from? This was ridiculous. If she wanted someone throwing totally insane ideas at her, she could go to a real shrink, not the Dr. Freud look-alike two semesters of college psychology courses had firmly planted in her mind.

"Hah. Who has an imagination now, Kendall?" She kicked at the ground and a sparse spray of gravel flew out in front of her. A few feet ahead, some sort of lizard scurried across the road. She stifled a scream. Wild lizards. Swell. The closest she'd ever come to a lizard was a pet chameleon owned by the brother of a friend. What other kind of awful creature might be lurking just out of sight, waiting to pounce on her? The urge to scream rose again, this time out of frustration. Not that it would do any good. She was definitely alone, at least when it came to two-legged company.

Shouldn't she be able to see the house by now? Maybe not. After all, she had no idea how long the ride out had taken. An eternity would have been her best guess. She'd kept her face buried in Kendall's shirt, so nothing she passed now looked familiar. Or actually, everything looked familiar: one beach, one palm, one wild lizard looked pretty much like the next, although she had the weirdest feeling she was missing something.

She slowed down and studied her surroundings. While the site Kendall had shown her was right up there on the top ten list of the most beautiful places she'd ever seen pictured, it's beauty wasn't out of the ordinary here. Every place she walked by was lovely—amazing, as a matter of fact. The beaches were gorgeous, the plants and trees as perfect as if master gardeners tended them. Grudgingly she admitted Paradise Bay lived up to its name at least in the scenery department. There wasn't a single spot that wasn't nice—all right—breathtaking.

How long had she been walking anyway? A good twenty minutes at least. Maybe longer. Trish glanced at her watch and grimaced. The delicate little gold trinket was as out of place here as she was.

Kendall fits in like a native.

Why was he here, anyway? For that matter, who was he really? Oh, sure, his name probably *was* Jack Kendall, and she didn't doubt that he worked for ESI: In a community the size of Paradise Bay, someone who didn't belong would never be able to hide his presence. But beyond that, nothing about him made sense. South Seas Barbie—or rather, Maude—had said he was lost when he'd arrived. Yeah, right. Kendall didn't strike her as the kind of guy who could lose his way. Nope, he was the kind who was always in control of everything up to and including his emotions. You could tell by the air of confidence that hung around him like a force field.

It was irritating not to know his story. It gave him the upper hand. He certainly did seem to know a lot about her. But if he called her "princess" one more time, she was going to have to punch his lights out. Not that she had ever punched anyone's lights out, but sheer enthusiasm would probably make up for her lack of practical experience.

Maude had also said that the company had arranged for his computer system. Maybe he was a refugee scientist from an Iron Curtain country seeking asylum with corporate America, but had been forced to hide out in the South Pacific first, until things cooled down. She laughed out loud. For one thing, he had no accent; for another, there wasn't any Iron Curtain anymore. Maybe he was simply an international criminal hiding from the authorities? See, she had loads of imagination; she just didn't flaunt it—that's all.

More than likely, Kendall was a very distant Evans relative. That would explain why she had never heard of him before, and why he was living in the mansion. Chances were he just needed a secluded place to recover from some horrible trauma and developed software in his spare time. Still pretty strange, but it made much more sense than the mad-scientist or evil-genius-on-the-lam theories.

Too bad she wouldn't be here long enough to find out the truth. If she remembered, she'd ask her stepfather when she got back to civilization—but probably not. Once she got out of here she'd put Paradise Bay and its resident hulking beast out of her thoughts forever.

At the moment, Kendall's past wasn't the only vague and elusive thing hovering at the back of her mind. She glanced toward the water and shook her head. What was wrong with this picture? This scene was just as postcard pretty as every other setting she'd admired today. The mountain foliage to her left just as lush and green. The sea on her right just as blue and inviting.

The mountain to her left and the sea to her right?

She smacked her hand against her forehead and bit back a curse. He'd sent her the wrong way! She have been too stupid not to notice until now. She wanted to throw something. Or kick something. Or someone. Trish clenched her fists and picked up her pace. Eventually she'd get back to the house, and Jack Kendall had better watch out.

She'd make boiling by cannibals look like a day in the park.

*   *   *

Russ leaned back in the custom-made leather chair in his library and studied the monitor. He narrowed his eyes and tapped the end of his pen thoughtfully on the antique desk in front of him. It had been a long time since anything had taken him by surprise. But he had to admit he was surprised now, and more than a little pleased.

He reread the E-mail for the third time. He knew Jack was smart when it came to the complexities of programming, and he figured the kid had a fair amount of common sense, but he'd never realized just how intuitive his son was. Jack's E-mail mentioned Trish's theory as to why she was sent to Paradise Bay and Jack's own suspicions that she was right. It was an easy call, really. Russ would have been disappointed if Jack hadn't caught that one.

Jack's decision not to tell Trish about their family connection had caught him off-guard initially. Russ never considered the idea that Trish wouldn't recognize his son's name. But on second thought, Jack's reasoning about not wanting it to seem like the entire family, or at least the male half, was against her made a great deal of sense. Russ had no problem playing along, for a while.

But as for the rest of it . . . Russ chuckled. He thought he'd been too subtle for Jack to figure out that the Paradise Bay project had originated out of Russ's desire to bring Jack fully into the company where he belonged. And when it was wrapped up—to bring him home. It had been far too long since his son had been under his roof.

On the other hand, Trish's reaction to Paradise Bay came as no surprise at all. He'd known she'd hate it. Way too much fresh air and sunshine for a city dweller. Russ knew Trish didn't appreciate anything she couldn't control, and her life was far too organized for him. She had her future carefully laid out with the precision of a corporate day planner. Even when she was out of her element she refused to relinquish the upper hand. Over the years he'd watched her successfully bluff her way out of any number of business and personal situations.

Well, she was definitely out of her element now, and with Jack's help, she'd stay there long enough to realize her marriage to Elliot would be an unmitigated disaster. Russ knew better than most that there was nothing worse than a boring marriage; his brief stint with Elliott's mother had proved that.

He rested his fingers on the keyboard and considered the tone of his note. It was nearly midnight here, but it was midafternoon tomorrow on Paradise Bay. Jack probably wouldn't get back to him with Trish's response until later tonight. Later tomorrow? Those damn time zones always threw him, although he and Jack had worked out a schedule for E-mails and online talks: midday for Jack, late night for Russ, when he was at home and could relax.

Russ thought for a moment. Trish wasn't

going to be at all happy about this. But he was certain that if anyone could handle her, Jack could. Family working with family had always been one of the strengths of ESI. Once Trish learned the fine art of give and take, they'd make one hell of a great team. He grinned again and started to type.

If they didn't kill each other first.

Chapter Five

Paradise Bay is roughly circular in shape. A bay located in the southeast quadrant is the predominant coastal feature. The single main road circling the island, and the relatively small total land area, makes it virtually impossible to get lost. Anyone walking continuously in the same direction will eventually return to the point from which he started.

Trish jerked open the pocket doors to the library with a vengeance. They slid on their runners, shot into their slots in the wall and bounced back at her in a blatant attempt to get even. She thrust her hands out, and the doors smacked into them with surprising and painful force. She winced. One more complaint to add to her list.

"Kendall, are you in here?" It took a moment for her eyes to adjust to the dim light.

"Yeah, Taylor. What's up?" Jack sat in front of the computer, his brow wrinkled in concentration, obviously working on something absorbing. Maybe something important. Even crucial.

Tough.

She clenched her jaw. "Look at me."

He glanced at her, then turned his gaze back to the screen. "You look hot."

"I am hot," she said, spitting the words out one at a time.

"The temperature usually doesn't get very high here." He tapped a few keys. "We're having some kind of weird heat wave, I guess."

"I'm also sunburned." Anyone in his right mind would realize from the tone of her voice alone that she wasn't happy and pay her the common courtesy of at least looking at her.

He hit ENTER and studied the monitor. "I thought you looked kind of red. You probably should have put on sunscreen, or at least worn a hat."

"A hat? You think I should have worn a hat?" Her voice rose. The man probably couldn't even spell courtesy. "I don't *have* a hat. Where would I get a hat? My stuff isn't here yet, remember?"

"Oh, yeah," Jack tapped out a few more words. "It's coming on the supply boat."

"Is it here yet? It's supposed to be here. Today. Any minute now."

"Yeah, right," he said absently, scribbling on a notebook beside the mouse pad.

She huffed a short, angry breath. "The least you can do is offer me one of your beers."

"Nope. Strict rationing." He shook his head. "Sorry. What took you so long, anyway?"

"What took me—" The words caught in her throat and all she could do was sputter.

"I figured you'd be back at least an hour ago." He talked as though she'd just enjoyed a relaxing stroll in a garden.

"Well, it takes a while when you're tricked into walking around a whole frigging island!" She glared at him with all the enmity she could muster. "As you well know!"

He glanced across the room at her. About time that she managed to get his attention. A tiny bubble of satisfaction rose within her.

He raised a brow. "Isn't that part of your job? To see everything here?"

The bubble hovered uncertainly. "Yes, but—"

"Is there any better way to do that than on foot?"

The bubble dropped like a rock. "I suppose not but—"

"Then I was simply helping you do what you came here to do in the first place." A pleasant smile lifted the corners of his mouth. The kind of professional smile one co-worker gives another.

She wanted to belt him.

"By the way, you have an E-mail." He rolled his chair from the computer to a state-of-the-art laser printer and picked up a sheet of paper lying in a wicker IN basket. "From the head honcho himself."

"Well, it's about time." She sounded much bitchier than she'd intended, but she didn't care. This was obviously her ticket out of here. She stepped toward him and reached for the E-mail. "Russ has probably come to his senses. I'll bet the minute I walked out of his office he realized what a stupid idea this resort business is." Trish snatched the paper from his hand. "He probably wants me to come home right now."

"Oh, yeah, I'm sure that's it," Jack said under his breath and rolled back to the computer.

She resisted the childish but tempting urge to stick out her tongue and turned her gaze to the message.

Subj: Paradise Bay Project
To: PB1@evansandsonsintl.com
File: C/PARADISE.DOC (67503 BYTES)
DL Time (TCP/IP): < 1 minute
Good Morning Trish,

I trust you are enjoying Paradise Bay. It's always been one of my favorite places.

I'm sorry I haven't been in touch, but more pressing problems demanded my immediate attention. It now strikes me that I may not have made myself clear when I sent you to the island.

Your purpose is not simply to evaluate the

feasibility of the project. I am well aware of the problems facing us.

"That's something anyway," she muttered.

Your job is to determine how to overcome those obstacles.

"What?" A heavy knot settled in her stomach. "He can't be serious."

Jack Kendall knows the island intimately and will be of invaluable assistance. I expect you to draw on his expertise and work closely with him.

Jack Kendall? She glanced from the E-mail to Jack. *Work closely with Jack Kendall? Not in this lifetime!* He ignored her, intent on whatever he had on the screen. It was probably a video game. He'd tied his hair back at the nape of his neck and looked almost human. Still, the man was irritating and dangerous and had made her walk around the whole damn island. The last thing she wanted to do was work with him, closely or any other way.

Trish scanned the rest of the page. Disappointment battled with dismay and deepened at every word. Her stepfather had obviously thought this out. He instructed her to involve Mo Wellington, and his knowledge of architecture, in the plans. He wanted the project to be a family affair, and as a native islander, Mo was considered family.

While I understand the nature of the costs involved in a project of this type, I am confident that the attention to detail and its exclusive nature will ensure its financial success.

She couldn't believe it. Kendall was right all along. Her staid, stable stepfather was a major-league dreamer and now had trapped her firmly in a tropical nightmare.

However, while the development of the Inn on Paradise Bay is first and foremost a business venture, it means a great deal to me on a personal level, and I want members of my family intimately involved.

I expect you to pull this off, Trish. I further expect you to stay as long as it takes to do the job. Everything here is in your mother's capable hands, and Elliott will certainly understand.

Russ

Trish's spirits crashed. *Stay as long as it takes?* She stared at the E-mail, wondering if there was any chance at all that this was some horrible cyberspace mistake, and Russ's real note telling her to come home would appear any minute. And knowing full well it wouldn't. She was stuck here, with that insufferable hulking beast.

Elliott will certainly understand? Swell. Elliott could understand all he wanted. *She* didn't understand. Not one tiny bit. She wanted to bury her head in her arms and cry. To weep and wail and make as much noise as possible. This was a horrible end to a perfectly rotten day, and nobody deserved a good weeping and wailing more than she did. She wouldn't, of course. Not now, anyway. Not in front of anyone, and especially not in front of the hulking beast.

"So, do I take it your work here isn't done after all?" Jack asked innocently.

She pulled her gaze from the page and stared at him, her frustration swept aside by resentment. "As if you didn't know."

"Come on, Taylor, don't shoot the messenger. I just received the E-mail. I didn't write it." He shrugged. "I was only doing my job."

"And what's in that job description, anyway? Stool pigeon? Tattletale? Spy? You told him, didn't you?"

"Told him what?" His eyes widened.

"Don't give me that little-boy-falsely-accused look. You told him that I had already decided to veto this project. That I was getting off this island as soon as possible." She clenched her fists. "That I want to go home!"

He leaned back in his chair. "Now why would I do that?"

"I don't know." She threw up her hands. "And frankly it doesn't make sense to me." She folded her arms over her chest and paced the width of the room. "I would have expected you to throw every kind of obstacle in my path and do practically anything to make me decide against this project."

"Why would you expect that?"

"For God sakes, Kendall, do you ever look in a mirror?" She stopped and wrinkled her nose. "You look like something time forgot. Like you were shipwrecked on a deserted island surviving on roots and berries instead of living in a Victorian mansion with high-tech toys at your fingertips. In short, pal, you look like a stereotypical, crazy, retro-Sixties tree hugger."

He jutted out his chin and fluffed his dark beard. "You don't like the beard?"

"Are you kidding? It looks like some kind of mange-ridden animal curled up on your face and died. It would be different if it was trimmed and shaped and not quite as—well—overwhelming." She shook her head. "Obviously you've been here way too long. Beards like yours are for . . . I don't know, cave-dwelling hermits. Or Santa Claus wannabes. Or goats."

He frowned. "Goats?"

"Goats."

"You think I look like a goat?"

"No, I don't think you look like a goat!" She bit her lip to keep from screaming and mentally counted to ten. "And I don't want to talk about goats anyway. Goats have nothing to do with anything. The point I was trying to make is that I don't understand why you would want this resort. I would think anyone who's lived on this island the way you have would be violently opposed to any kind of development."

"I admit the idea didn't appeal to me at first, but then I realized, with a little help from a friend, that if it's done right, it will be great for the island and the people who live here." He glanced at the monitor. "By the way, there's a file that goes with the E-mail."

"A file? Great. That's just what I wanted to hear." In the world of ESI, a file only emerged when a project was more than just a gleam in someone's eye. A file spelled *official*. Russ's edict gave her no choice. Her only options were to concede gracefully or continue a futile battle with the hulking beast. And the beast didn't play fair. Why, a minute ago she'd been practically screaming and he hadn't so much as raised his voice. She heaved a resigned sigh, walked over to stand behind him and bent to view the screen.

"So." Defeat washed through her and she sighed again. "Can you print it for me, or do you want to hand over the computer and I'll read it off the monitor?"

He turned his head and looked up at her, his face only a few inches from hers. Their gazes locked. His eyes were much darker than she'd realized. They were brown: a deep, rich, chocolaty velvet brown sparkling with gold flecks. The annoying, amused twinkle she'd noticed before had vanished. Replaced by something else. Something smoldering. Something smoky and hot . . . very hot. When had the room gotten so warm, and why was it so hard to breathe?

"Is, um, the air conditioning working?"

"Uh-huh." His gaze never left hers.

Abruptly her mouth was dry, and without thinking she licked her lips. His gaze flicked to her mouth, then back to her eyes. Beard or no beard, this guy was something else. Something dangerous. Something threatening. Or something wonderful? Those lips. Those eyes.

I want members of my family intimately involved.

She sucked in a short, hard breath and jerked upright.

"What?" Confusion colored Jack's face. "What happened? What did I do?"

"You!" She aimed a shaky finger at him. "You're related to Russ, aren't you?" She asked accusingly.

"What do you mean *related?*" he asked slowly.

"You know. A relative, a cousin, a nephew. Something like that." She took a step back. "You are, aren't you? Admit it."

He lifted a casual shoulder. "Okay, I confess. I'm a relative."

"That's what I thought. I knew you had to be some kind of member of the family to be staying here—and Maude told me the company set up this computer stuff, so nothing else makes sense." She nodded with satisfaction, pleased with her deduction and eager to continue this nice, safe, neutral subject. "So what's the connection? I've never heard of any Kendalls in Russ's family. You must be pretty distant—a third cousin a couple of times removed or something."

He smiled, and she noticed how his grin was reflected in his eyes. "Distant and removed about covers it."

"No, seriously—"

"Okay, seriously." He paused for a moment. "Kendall was Evans's first wife's name. And I'm—"

"You're related to her." Triumph rang in her voice.

He grinned.

"I knew it." She smiled back. It certainly did feel good to be right and finally have the upper hand on something. Even a tiny victory over Jack made her feel more comfortable again. "It was obvious. Same last names."

"You catch on fast."

"Thanks."

"So . . ." His tone was light, as if he really didn't care one way or the other, but there was a cautious look in his eyes. "What else did Maude say about me?"

"Nothing, really. She said you'd tell me your story if you wanted to. So what is the story?" She studied him for a moment. "I know; you're hunted by the police for some terrible crime. Or you left some poor woman standing at the altar and she's out to get you. Or maybe you're a movie star who was horribly scarred in an accident and the beard is part of your disguise. Or you—"

"Whoa. Hold it right there, Taylor." He shook his head and got to his feet. "Nothing nearly as interesting as any of your scenarios. But I have to hand it to you. You had me fooled."

"Did I?" She grinned up at him, oddly pleased with herself. "About what?"

"I thought you had no imagination." He stepped closer. "But right now, I think the only thing you really need to know is that you and I aren't related."

"Sure we are. By marriage." Her voice sounded weak.

"Doesn't count." He moved nearer.

"Okay, well . . ." Why was he so damn close? Didn't he know he was invading her space? This close, she could touch him if she wanted to. Worse, he could touch her. "Um . . . we're both employees. And employees really shouldn't . . . um . . ." Warmth spread into her face.

"Shouldn't what?"

"Shouldn't fraternize," she whispered. God help her, his eyes were doing that smoldering thing again.

"I kind of like the sound of that." He bent his head toward hers. Was he going to kiss her? Was she going to let him? Worse. Was she going to kiss him back? A tremor of excitement rushed through her.

Oh, yeah.

She held her breath and closed her eyes. She could feel his breath on her lips, sensed his mouth closing in on hers. A feather-like touch tickled her chin and she jumped.

"What now?" He ground out the question.

"Your beard." She rubbed her chin with a vigor that she hoped would cover a trembling in her hand and various other parts of her body. "It tickled."

He groaned and rolled his eyes toward the ceiling. "I don't think—"

"No, Kendall, I'm the one not thinking." She edged around him and sprinted for the door. "Chalk it up to tropical dementia."

"What?"

"Never mind. I have a lot of work to do and I need to get going." She reached the doorway and didn't trust herself to look back. She didn't think she could take any more of his smoldering. "Now. I'll get that file from you later."

"It's the goat business, isn't it?" he called after her. "You can't get it out of your head, can you? Wasn't there a Greek god—a heavy-duty partier—who was half-goat? Can't you think of it that way?"

"No! And I take it back about the goats, anyway." She yanked the doors open but couldn't resist a parting shot. She drew a shaky breath. "Actually, a goat's beard is really a hell of a lot nicer than yours." She stepped over the threshold and pulled the doors closed behind her. His laughter trailed after her.

She leaned back against the library doors and tried to catch her breath. The man had completely disarmed her. Once again, he was in complete control. At what point had her passionate anger turned to just plain passion? It was lust, plain and simple. Good Lord, she groaned, she had the hots for the hulking beast. This could lead to all kinds of disaster. It was just a good thing his beard had tickled when he tried to kiss her.

She pushed away from the doors and headed toward the stairs on wobbly knees. Obviously, the only way she was going to survive Paradise Bay was to focus on work. That's exactly what she'd do. Work and nothing but work. Starting this minute.

And she absolutely refused to listen to a nagging voice in the back of her mind that wondered why the one excuse she didn't think of when Jack was about to kiss her, the one perfect excuse, the one excuse no could possibly argue with . . . was Elliott.

The deep-set eyes stared back at him with unflinching candor.

Jack braced his hands on the edge of the old-fashioned bathroom sink and leaned closer to the mirror. It had been a long time since he'd taken a good, hard look at himself. He'd never been especially vain, even though he'd always considered himself to be fairly good-looking. Women seemed to think so, anyway. Still, when a man didn't face a mirror every day to shave, he might not have a realistic picture of himself.

He inspected the face staring back at him with an assessing, critical eye. His brow was broad, but not Neanderthal broad. His eyes were an interesting shade of brown with specks of a lighter color scattered here and there. He waggled his brows in his best lecherous Groucho Marx imitation and grinned. Okay, so it was egotistical of him, but he'd always counted his eyes as one of his greatest charms.

He turned his head first one way and then the other and examined his profile. The broken nose he'd gotten in a game of rugby as a teenager had turned a classic Roman feature into a nose with character. A nose a man could be proud of, with just enough imperfection to tell the world that this was a man who would face life head-on. A take-no-prisoners kind of nose. All in all, he looked pretty damn good.

Except, and he had to admit it was a big exception, for the hair.

Jack blew out a long, resigned breath. There was no getting around it. Trish was right: There was way too much hair. It fell past his shoulders in dark waves that would have looked great on an air-brushed romance cover model but on him looked just plain stupid. His beard filled the space between his lips and his chest with a cloud of—what? Brown cotton? He really hadn't noticed how disreputable his appearance had become. And really hadn't cared. Until now.

He straightened and picked up the scissors lying on the edge of the sink. First, the beard. He should have done this long before now. When it came right down to it; he wasn't all that fond of the beard. It had been itchy when he'd first started growing it—how long ago? But then he'd simply ignored it, too mired in his own sorry emotional state to pay attention to physical appearance or discomfort.

"It's a far, far better thing that I do, than I have ever done," the hairy creature in the mirror announced in an accent that would make Charles Dickens proud. "Damn straight, pal."

He snipped carefully until the shape of his chin could finally be seen, then stepped back and studied his image. There was no need to get rid of it all. In fact, now that it was trimmed closely it gave him a distinguished look—like a professor or an artist. A successful artist. Not bad. Not bad at all.

Now for the hair.

"I wonder if Samson felt this way?" his image muttered.

He pulled in a deep breath, then attacked the task with cautious resolve. Inch by inch the scissors took their toll, until his hair waved softly around his neck halfway between his shoulders and his ears. He'd never especially appreciated the slight curl nature had bestowed on him, but now it helped give the illusion of an even cut. He

114

ran his fingers up his neck, under and through the dark stands. Nope, definitely not straight. He'd never be able to get a paying job in a hair salon, but it would do.

Once again he stepped back to get a better view of his handiwork.

"Goat, my ass."

The hairy hermit in the mirror had vanished, replaced by a relatively sophisticated image that would fit in as well on the Champs-Elysees or the Via Veneto or Wall Street as on Paradise Bay.

He nodded with satisfaction. Trish Taylor would have nothing to complain about now. The next time he tried to kiss her—

The thought stopped him cold. Would there be a next time? Hadn't that one attempt—okay, those two attempts—just been some kind of momentary flash of insanity on his part? After all, she was engaged. Not that he particularly cared about her engagement. He was only committed to breaking up that little arrangement, strictly as a favor to his dad. Nothing else.

Absently, he picked up a wicker wastebasket, grabbed a fistful of hair from the sink and tossed it into the basket. There was no way Maude would clean up in here. The woman did not have what it took to be a really great maid. If she saw this mess she'd kill him.

That seemed to be a continuing theme around here these days. Trish already wanted to kill him—so many times he'd lost count. After she'd returned from her hike—he grinned at the memory—and their encounter in the library, she'd hidden in her room for the rest of the day and the evening. He'd brought the resort file to her, but she hadn't even opened the door, claiming she wasn't decent. He'd assured her that he didn't mind, but she insisted on his leaving the file on the floor in the front of the door anyway. He'd brushed off his disappointment and gone on about his business.

Why was he disappointed, anyway? Sure she was pretty, just his type, actually. And yeah, it had been a long time since he'd been around an All-American princess like Trish. But she was also stubborn, with a tendency to bitch. A lot. Granted, some of her complaints were justified. He ignored a tiny twinge of guilt. He really hadn't gone out of his way to make her first day easier. Poor kid. She was even stuck wearing someone else's clothes. Not that she didn't look damn good poured into clothes that were at least two sizes too small. But for someone like Trish, someone used to wearing designer everything, it was probably a hardship on a par with flying coach. In her own reluctant way she was being a good sport.

Which still didn't explain why he wanted to kiss her. He threw another handful of hair into the basket. It wasn't because she was pretty, although that certainly didn't hurt. Or the fact that technically her engagement to Elliott made her off-limits, and anything you couldn't have always seemed a little more attractive. Or even the flash he'd had of what he suspected to be a wicked sense of humor and humor was right up there with long legs on Jack's top-ten list of what he liked in a woman.

He flicked on the faucet and watched the hypnotic swirl of the water swishing around the sides of the sink. No, it was far more intangible than a nice body or a quick comeback. It was vague and elusive and hard to put his finger on. But there was definitely something there. Something he'd glimpsed during that long moment when she'd leaned over his shoulder and her gaze had locked with his. Something intriguing and exciting and . . . right.

Right?

He scoffed. Hardly. He'd just met her. *Right* would put this in the category of love at first sight, and that was the craziest thing he'd ever heard. Lust at first sight maybe. But even that wasn't completely accurate. He hadn't been interested in her at all until that one moment. That one insignificant moment when he'd looked into her eyes and seen whatever it was that grabbed him and made him wonder what it would be like to kiss her. No, made him *want* to kiss her. Just once. Or maybe twice. Or maybe over and over again until she melted in his arms and his insides turned to mush and all he could think about was the heat of her skin next to his and the fire of her lips on his and—

Whoa. Hold it right there, Kendall.

Jack stared at the tiny whirlpool in the center

of the sink. Where had all that come from? Sure, he'd wanted a kiss. One lousy kiss. Big deal. But the rest of it? He turned off the faucet and watched the water disappear down the drain, carrying with it the last bits of his beard and leftover debris from his haircut.

And his old life as well?

Maybe. His reflection in the mirror shrugged. Why not? He knew he was ready to go home. Ready to face the world again. But what else was he ready for? Somewhere deep inside he knew that any involvement with Trish wouldn't be just another enjoyable fling. Not for him, and definitely not for her. Anything with Trish would be serious. Possibly even permanent. Funny, that idea wasn't quite as terrifying as it once had been. He really had grown up on this island. Still, maturity didn't necessarily mean it was time to settle down. Even if he had no intention of returning to his old way of life when he left Paradise Bay, he also didn't plan on his new lifestyle including a committed relationship. Not yet, anyway.

Still, there was something about that woman. Something . . . dangerous. He'd have to watch his step. Take it slow. See where things led.

If he was Samson, then she was definitely Delilah. His new, sophisticated, professorial, artistic reflection smiled wryly back at him.

And everyone knew how that story had turned out.

Chapter Six

It is not uncommon for visitors to Paradise Bay to confuse today's residents with the stereotypical representations of tropical natives depicted in the popular films of a half-century ago. However, its islanders are neither as isolated nor as quaint as a newcomer might initially assume.

While upon first glance the inhabitants of the island appear to view life with a casual, relaxed attitude, the majority of the population is hard-working, industrious and creative. Evidence of this is borne out by the impressive percentage of offspring who, over the years, have excelled off-island in pursuits as varied as music theory and physics.

The people of Paradise Bay take their individual and collective responsibilities seriously, particularly as they pertain to anything that directly impacts their home and its future.

The oversized floral dress billowed around her as if it had a life of its own. Trish struggled to control, or at least contain, the vast yards of material and at the same time make her way down the front stairs without tripping. If she could just cinch the waist a bit tighter . . .

"That's not working any better than the shorts, is it?"

She glanced toward the foot of the stairs. Maude stared up at her, her lips pressed tightly together, obviously holding back a smile.

"Go ahead and laugh. Even I can see the humor in this."

"I am sorry." Maude chuckled. "But you said after the shorts, you'd prefer big to small."

"It's okay." Trish swatted impatiently at the fabric. "I do feel like I'm wearing a tent, though." She sighed and walked down the last few steps to the main floor.

"Actually, this particular tent is my mom's. She's a couple of sizes larger than I am."

Trish raised an eyebrow.

Maude laughed. "Okay. More than a couple." Her gaze flicked over Trish. "Maybe if you pulled it up and kind of bloused it over the belt?"

"It is bloused," Trish said wryly and looked

down at the dress. Maude's mother might be wider than her offspring, but she obviously wasn't any taller. Any more blousing and the tent would barely cover her butt. The hem already hit somewhere between the tops of her knees and her thighs. Self-consciously, she tugged it down.

"I'll see what else I can come up with for you. This was the best I could do yesterday."

"Thanks. I appreciate it," Trish murmured, and tried to readjust the belt and the reams of material gathered at her waist.

Maude leaned against the ornately carved newel post. "As much as I hate to say this, you look—"

"Horrible? Like something the cat dragged in? Or just awful, like one of those people caught on the fashion dos and don'ts pages? I'm a cover model for the *don'ts*."

"Oh, it's not all that bad." Maude's voice lacked even the mildest conviction.

"No?" Trish laughed and caught the hem of the dress in each hand and stretched it wide on either side of her. "I suppose if you ignore the fact that there's enough material here for an entire wardrobe and try not to notice the predominance of neon yellow in the pattern, which is not one of my personal favorites even at the best of times"—Trish twirled around—"then I think you're right. It's not bad at all. In fact, it's definitely me."

Maude shook her head and grinned. "I'm not sure it's anybody." Her expression grew thoughtful. "Actually, the outfit wasn't what I meant. You look . . . well, tired. And red."

"Too much sun yesterday and too little sleep last night." Trish shrugged.

"Funny," Maude's tone was casual, "visitors usually sleep quite well here. Something about the trade winds, the fresh smell of the sea, the scent of native blossoms—"

"I know, I know, it's wonderful, really it is," Trish said quickly. "But between the sunburn and everything I've got on my mind, I wouldn't have been able to sleep anywhere. First and foremost, I have to figure out how to get this massive project off the ground." *And Jack Kendall out of my head.*

"It's a big deal, all right."

"Very big." Big enough to occupy her every waking moment, if her every waking moment wasn't already occupied with thoughts of a hairy, annoying computer expert. "It's no wonder all I did last night was toss and turn."

"Uh-huh." Maude looked like she didn't believe her for a second. She studied her for a long moment. "Did Jack tell you I get vibes about things?"

"Vibes? You mean you're psychic?" *Swell. South Seas Barbie reads minds.*

"Not exactly." Maude paused. "It's more like I have a very highly developed sense of intuition."

"Oh, yeah? So what's it telling you now?" The moment the words shot out of her mouth, Trish wanted to take them back. The muscles in her shoulders tightened. Did she really need to know what Maude's intuition had to say?

Maude straightened, pulled off her glasses and polished them on the bottom of a T-shirt that proclaimed THINKING: THE TALKING OF THE SOUL WITH ITSELF—PLATO. Regardless of any psychic abilities, the woman apparently had a thing for obscure quotes. "Jack says my vibes are always wrong."

"Is he right?"

"I let him think he is. It works better that way." Maude held her glasses up, tilting them until they caught the light for a thorough inspection. "Nobody likes a prophet. It's like being the bearer of bad tidings."

"Tell me about it," Trish said under her breath remembering her reaction to Jack's delivery of her stepfather's E-mail.

"Right or wrong, I get the very distinct feeling your lack of sleep has nothing to do with the resort."

"Well, as hard as it is to admit it, for once Jack was right." The lie came without hesitation. "Your vibes are wrong."

"Hard to believe, but okay. It doesn't really matter, I guess." Maude put her glasses back on her nose. "If you do decide you want to talk . . ."

"I appreciate the offer, but aside from my job, there's nothing to talk about." Would Maude's *vibes* tell her this too was a lie?

"Whatever." The single word spoke volumes. Trish would bet Maude's intuition was right-on when it came to recognizing the truth.

The islander nodded toward the closed pocket doors across the hall. "Apparently the library has been designated the center of operations. It looks like some kind of war room in there. I just dropped off coffee and fresh croissants."

"Fresh croissants? Homemade?"

"With my own special fruit chutney and caramel butter." The smile of someone who's an expert and knows it crossed her face. "I told you I was a good cook."

"It sounds wonderful," Trish said with relief. Food was one subject she could be completely truthful about.

"You'll have to let me know what you think." Maude started down the hall toward the kitchen, then stopped and pinned Trish with a steady, no-nonsense stare. "By the way, I consider Jack a really close friend. If you hurt him, even a tiny bit, I'll have to rip your heart out." Maude smiled pleasantly.

Trish stared down at the determined, diminutive creature and realized she probably would do just that. "No problem. The only relationship I want with Jack Kendall is a business one."

Maude's eyes widened skeptically. "Business?"

"Absolutely." Trish kept her voice firm. "Nothing more."

"Yeah, that's what I thought." Maude turned and walked briskly toward the kitchen, throwing a final comment over her shoulder. "This afternoon I'll see what else I can dig up for you to wear."

"Thanks, but I'm sure the supply boat will be here today."

Maude said something Trish didn't quite catch, but the laughter trailing behind her, even after she disappeared into the kitchen, was unmistakable. There *was* a supply boat, wasn't there?

Trish blew out a long sigh and sank down onto the bottom step. Obviously, Maude's vibes didn't believe her declaration about a strictly business relationship with Jack. Maybe if she'd had a little more sleep, and a lot more practice, she'd be a better liar. She'd have to work on that. Right now, Maude's coffee would do wonders.

Sleep would make a big difference too. She propped her elbow on her knee and rested her chin in her hand. Her mind was a mess of conflicting emotions all centering on what hadn't happened between her and Jack. And whether or not she was glad or merely relieved or even . . . disappointed?

She hadn't especially wanted to examine those emotions last night. Not about Jack, and definitely not about Elliott. For the life of her, she couldn't quite figure out exactly where Elliott fit into the equation. And he should fit. Perfectly. After all, he was her fiancé. The man she fully intended to marry. Of course, Elliott was Elliott and could be counted on to be there for her when she needed him. That was one of the nice things about going into marriage with your head on straight. About marrying a man who was more or less your best friend. You knew exactly what to expect, with none of that throw-me-on-the-floor-and-screw-my-eyes-out passion messing everything up. Still, her stomach clenched when she realized she actually felt guilty lying to Maude, but betraying Elliot by kissing another man didn't bother her at all.

Damn. That was exactly the kind of idea Russ had sent her here to consider in the first place. Well, she'd show him. She simply wouldn't think about Elliott right now, and any disturbing questions could be nicely avoided.

Not that it had worked with Jack. Yesterday, she'd decided that locking herself in her room and avoiding Jack was the best way to avoid thinking about him. She hadn't counted on her subconscious dwelling on the man and fueling her body with a restlessness that defied sleep.

Trish stared across the wide foyer at the library doors. The hum of the air conditioner droned on faintly behind the walnut panels. He was probably in there right now. Waiting for her. For what? Business? The doors seemed to swell and throb like a cartoon. Or pleasure?

She jerked up straight and shook her head. She had to knock it off, and right now. Thinking like this could only lead to trouble. She had a job to do and she had neither the time nor the inclination for silly distractions.

When it came right down to it, Jack's attempt

to kiss her was just another way he had of taking control. She nodded sharply and ignored the thought that she really hadn't done much to stop him and it was only the brush of the primeval growth on his chin that brought her to her senses. Thank God for facial hair, although she'd never particularly liked or appreciated beards before now.

Still, he does have those dark, smoldering eyes . . .

"Stop it!" Trish sprang to her feet. This was ridiculous. She hadn't let Kendall get away with anything yesterday and she certainly wasn't going to let him get away with anything now. Plus: this was her project. The E-mail from Russ and the file in her room spelled that out in no uncertain terms.

She marched to the library and gripped the door handles with a determined grasp. If this was a war room, she was ready to do battle—with him and with herself if necessary. It was time to stop behaving like a teenager with a crush. She was in charge. She was in control. She was the boss. And it was about time she proved it. She would be businesslike but not tyrannical. Masterful but not overbearing. Authoritative but approachable.

And absolutely, under no circumstances, would she let herself even think the word *smoldering.*

She drew a deep breath, planted her best professional smile on her face, imagined she wore a designer suit instead of a flowered tent and slid the doors open with a firm yet gentle hand.

No one seemed to notice.

Her smile slipped just a bit. She didn't spot Jack, but Mo was bent over a table on the far side of the room, drawing with one hand and gesturing with the other. A tall man stood next to him. Both were too involved in their discussion about whatever Mo was sketching to notice her presence.

Who in the hell was this? She pulled her brows together in annoyance. And where had he come from? He obviously wasn't an islander: For one thing he was way too tall, and he was wearing a pale gray golf shirt and dark shorts. Positively sedate compared to the flowered fabrics islanders seemed to go for. His hair was dark and casually curly in a rumpled, movie-star kind of way. Very nice. Of course, this guy too had a beard. She groaned to herself. Why was it that every interesting man—make that every interesting, *tall* man—she'd met lately had an aversion to shaving? Not that she cared. It was merely a point worth noting. Still, the newcomer's beard was closely trimmed and neat and really rather distinguished. From this side of the spacious room he looked fairly attractive. No. Very attractive. And sexy. Not that it mattered. Again, it was simply another fact worth noting.

Was he an architect or engineer sent by Russ to work with Mo? But how had he gotten here? Even though she'd finally fallen asleep around dawn, and ultimately slept much later than she'd planned, surely she would have heard a helicopter. Unless . . .

Unless he'd come on the supply boat!

At once her sagging spirits lifted. With her own clothes and makeup and all the other necessities of life her luggage held, she could handle Kendall and everything else.

Trish stepped toward the men, and this time, her smile was genuine. She extended her hand. "Good morning. I'm Trish Taylor. I don't think we've—" The stranger raised his head. Her heart skipped a beat. "—met?"

Amusement danced in dark brown, smold— no, anything but smoldering—eyes. "No? I could have sworn—"

"What have you done to yourself?" She could barely croak out the words. In spite of the too-long hair and overgrown beard, Jack Kendall had been attractive. Now he was deadly.

"I figured it was time for a new look." He rubbed what was left of his beard self-consciously, as if her answer was important to him. "Does it work?"

She swallowed hard and nodded.

"I'll take that for a yes." His gaze shifted to her hand, then back to her eyes. He raised a dark brow. "Did you still want to shake?"

"No, of course not." She dropped her hand and forced a cool note into her voice. "I just didn't recognize you for a minute, that's all."

"Jack looks practically human again. I barely

recognized him myself." Mo chuckled. "It's a pretty radical change."

"Don't let it fool you." Jack's comment was directed toward Mo, but his gaze lingered on Trish. "Inside, I'm still the same old Jack I was yesterday."

A shiver coursed through her and she wrenched her gaze from his. Apparently, he wouldn't make it any easier to focus on the job at hand and nothing else.

For the first time she noticed the library. Jack wasn't the only change this morning. Maude had called it, all right: this room did look like a campaign headquarters. The long computer table was barely visible under assorted debris: papers, cups and who knew what else. The floor wasn't much better, littered with balls of crumpled-up paper. Two large library tables she vaguely remembered being along a wall had been moved into the center of the room. Most of one was covered with sheets of oversized drafting paper that flowed off the surface and piled in drifts on the floor. The other had an assortment of odd little white boxes scattered here in precise patterns and there heaped with rapt abandon.

"Now that we all know who we are"—Mo tapped his pencil on the table impatiently—"what do you think, Trish?"

"I think it's a pit," she muttered, stepping carefully around a pile of drawings.

"Not the room." Mo gestured toward the boxes on the other table. "What do you think of this.

It's all tentative right now, just ideas I've been playing around with."

"Take a look." Jack moved to the table and brushed aside paper and other litter until the rectangular shapes sat alone. "Mo's been working on this since we first heard about the resort. When I came down this morning he had already set everything up."

Trish stepped closer and examined the display. She could see now that what had appeared to be white cardboard boxes were actually building models.

"Interesting," she murmured and bent down until her eye was level with the tabletop. There were two distinct arrangements: one precise and geometric, the other random clusters with no two groups alike. "Why different layouts?"

"I wasn't sure what we were going for." Mo stepped to her side. "I've got it all on computer, too, but I think it's easier to get a real feel for a design when it's three-dimensional. But like I said, I was just playing. When I started I didn't know if I'd get to work on this or if ESI would bring in outsiders."

"My—Evans wants this to be a family project. That includes you." Jack moved to her other side. "Mo couldn't do much until we got the file with the specifics, but he has come up with these options to help us decide exactly what kind of feel we want for the place. Or rather for The Inn on Paradise Bay."

"The Inn on Paradise Bay." Trish rolled the

phrase over in her head. "That's what Russ called it in his E-mail. It has a nice ring to it. Understated and classic. I like it."

"Works for me," Jack said.

"Yeah, I like it too. Now"— Mo circled the table—"Over here, I've arranged the buildings in a formal, elegant style. The grouping closest to you is more laid-back. Not haphazard exactly, but—"

"Casual. Relaxed." Jack crouched down next to her and tapped the top of a cardboard building. "This layout says this is a spot to kick back and forget about the rest of the world and just enjoy life."

"While the other setting proclaims the kind of pampered exclusivity the clientele we want to appeal to expects," Mo pointed out.

"I see." Trish stood up slowly. "I'm impressed, Mo. You've done a hell of a lot of work in a very short time."

Mo rested his hands on the table and leaned forward. "Frankly, Trish, this is the chance of a lifetime for me professionally. I also think it's an opportunity for Paradise Bay to take its place in the world without losing any of what makes it unique in the process."

Jack nodded in agreement.

"Plus there's the added benefit of piña coladas and a jumping nightlife with great-looking women in skimpy bathing suits." Mo grinned.

"Spells Paradise to me." Jack's face was a picture of innocent enthusiasm.

"I get the idea," Trish said dryly.

"So," Mo drew the word out slowly, "which plan do you like better?"

"I'm not sure." Trish turned her full attention to the presentations. She was right: This was interesting. And intriguing. Her gaze slid from one model to the other, then back again.

"Well?" Polite impatience sounded in Mo's voice.

"I'm thinking." Trish considered the options. For the first time the project seemed not only possible but real, and exciting. Maybe even fun.

Across the table, Mo shifted nervously from foot to foot. Trish spoke without looking at him. "Would you do me a favor, Mo? Sit down, and try to relax. You're involved one way or the other, so chill."

"But my favorite—"

"Don't tell me," she said sharply. "I want to make up my own mind."

Mo heaved a long-suffering sigh.

"By the way, Maude said there was coffee." Trish walked around the table, her gaze never leaving the miniature resorts. "Could one of you bring me a cup?"

A minute later Jack placed a hefty mug in her hand. His fingers brushed hers, and for a second her growing enthusiasm for the project was eclipsed by excitement of a completely different kind.

She took a long swallow of the heavy brew and focused on the work at hand, bending down again to study the models from a different perspective. Mo was right about the effect of a formal arrangement. It announced to the world that this was a place where one's every need would be taken care of without hesitation, regardless of cost or difficulty.

Trish straightened and considered her choices. She doubted either man would be terribly disappointed one way or the other, although it was obvious each had his favorite. But the ultimate success of the inn might well hinge on this decision, and each and every decision to come. This was the price one paid for power, the cost of being in control.

She glanced at Mo. "This would be easier if we had some representation of the layout of the site itself. You know, the beach, road, mountain, that sort of thing."

"That will come," Mo said quickly. "Keep in mind, this is basically a three-dimensional rough draft."

"Again, the idea here is to decide what kind of overall atmosphere we're after. What'll it be, Trish?" Jack waved at the formal setting, "Plan A," then at the relaxed version—"or Plan B?"

"I don't have anything to base this on. No research, no stats, nothing like that. I'm relying on gut instinct alone, but here goes." She gestured at the more precise grouping. "This arrangement practically screams perfect, exactly what the very rich expect in an exclusive and expensive resort."

Mo beamed.

"On the other hand"—she circled the table to the second set of models—"those same people who demand luxury are always searching for something new. Something unexpected and unique. Obviously, Paradise Bay in and of itself provides that but"—she drew a deep breath—"I think the ambience we're striving for needs to reflect that one-of-a-kind atmosphere.

"I'm sorry, Mo." She shrugged in apology. "It just seems to me Plan A is too perfect and too typical. It doesn't take advantage of the natural assets we already have.

"But with Plan B, the facility itself can conform to the layout of the land." She narrowed her eyes and stared at the jumble of box-shaped forms. "The buildings need to fit into the scenery, to be harmonious with nature, not oppose it. You know, a terrace to the side of the waterfall. Golf courses and tennis courts that look like nature designed them instead of man."

"And the guest rooms?" Jack said. "The inn itself?"

"The same thing." It was laid out in her mind as clearly and distinctly as a photograph. "The buildings should be nestled beneath the mountain, perched along the sides, trailing down to the beach as if they had grown like vines instead of been built. The main focus of the complex, clubhouse or whatever, should be oriented toward the east to take advantage of the magnificent sunrise."

"The sunrise?" Jack's voice was soft.

"Yeah." She nodded. "I can see it in my head. The sky changing from blue-black to purple, then pink, and the sun peeks over the horizon so bright . . . *you know you have to pull your eyes away before it blinds you but you stare anyway because you've never seen a sun so huge or a sunrise so magnificent as it is right here . . ."*

Trish snapped her head around to meet Jack's gaze.

"That's pretty much how I saw it." He smiled, but there was an odd look in his eyes. Her breath caught. Time slowed. Her gaze meshed with his. His eyes dark and intense and smol—

"Okay. I know when I'm outnumbered." Mo's voice shattered the tension he hadn't seemed to notice. "Plan B it is, then. Now I've got some ideas for the buildings themselves. . . ." Mo moved to the other table and shuffled through piles of printouts.

Jack ran his fingers through his hair. Was she mistaken, or did his hand seem to shake? Quickly, she downed the rest of her now luke-warm coffee and chalked up her own trembling to the sudden rush of caffeine.

"Good coffee," she mumbled. Jack and Mo traded skeptical glances. "Seriously, I like it."

"Good," Jack said, his tone abruptly brusque and businesslike. "You're going to need a lot of it if we're going to pull this project together in the time frame Evans has laid out."

"No problem." If he could be all business, so

136

could she. "We need to start with a preliminary list. What we have and what we need. The style of the inn, even the design, is the fun stuff. Everything else is going to be a grind." She nodded at the computer. "Jack, do you want to take this down or should I?"

"Your wish is my command, Princess." He swept an exaggerated bow.

"Just sit down and don't call me Princess." She couldn't resist a quick laugh.

"What about boss?" He dropped into the chair in front of the monitor. "Chief? Head honcho? Lord and master?"

"I like that one." She pretended to consider it for a minute. "Oh, yeah, let's go for lord and master." She gave him her best royalty-gazing-at-the-peasants look. "And you can be the loyal minion."

"Could be fun." His tone was mild, but his gaze bored into hers with a wicked challenge. "The lord and master and her loyal minion."

"You two sound like you're playing weird games over there," Mo said absently, selecting a printout and studying it. "Although technically it should probably be lady and mistress. Either way, I warn you, if I hear anything that sounds like a suggestion to play pizza delivery boy and bored housewife, I'm out of here."

Trish choked back a strangled laugh. Jack snorted. They both grinned. Jack's gaze flicked over her lecherously. "Which one do you want to be?"

Mo glanced in their direction. "Upgraded communication facilities."

"What?" they said in unison.

"The list," he said pointedly. "That's the first thing we need to look at. After that—"

"Heliport," Trish said. "It's mentioned in the file. Russ doesn't want anything as invasive as an airstrip. If you can't afford to get here by helicopter or boat, you can't afford to come. Period."

"Got it." Jack's fingers flashed across the keyboard. "Transportation. Communications—"

"A reliable source of supplies," Trish said dryly.

Jack nodded. "Plus we need an assessment of the island's waste disposal capacity, power capabilities—"

"Guest occupancy," Mo said. "What are we talking about in terms of complex size?"

"That's in the file too. I left it on my bed. I'll run up to my room and get it." Trish turned to go.

"Don't bother," Jack said. "It's in the computer."

"I know, but I want to get my laptop too. We'll need two computers just to keep track of what we're doing." She started toward the door.

"What about water?" Mo said to Jack. "Will we need to upgrade . . ."

Trish reached the doors and slid them open. Excitement surged through her. Who would have believed it? Maybe they could pull this thing off. It would take a lot of effort. A lot of long hours. They'd have to work very closely together. Of course, Mo would be there most of the time as an unknowing chaperone. Or, given his comments, possibly a very astute chaperone. Did he get the same vibes his twin did?

"Before you go, Taylor, there's something I've been meaning to say to you."

"And what would that be, Kendall?" she said lightly, but her heart raced. Surely he wouldn't refer to yesterday's almost kiss in front of Mo.

A grin stretched across his devastating face. "Nice dress."

"Bite me." She smiled and closed the doors, then muffled her face in her hands and laughed. The man was incorrigible.

Maybe they didn't need a chaperone after all.

Maybe they needed a referee.

Chapter Seven

While ideally suited to recreational pursuits, there has been little development of such facilities on Paradise Bay. Residents have traditionally enjoyed water-based sports, including swimming, diving and surfing, but the absence of boats capable of achieving the high speeds necessary for activities such as waterskiing and parasailing has prevented their introduction.

Trish stared dubiously at the water lapping around her legs. How in the hell had she gotten here anyway? One minute she'd been setting up her laptop, talking with Jack and Mo about myriad details and wearing that goofy tent dress. The next Jack had been muttering about recreational opportunities and seeing the island from all angles, Mo had been nodding in agreement and Maude was hustling her back into her abandoned T-shirt and shorts for use as a bathing suit. All three of them had ignored her protests, as if she were speaking in a foreign and completely unknown language.

Something swam by her feet and she bit back a scream. Before she'd realized what the hulking beast and his cohorts were up to, she was on the back of Jack's motorbike, holding on for dear life, zipping to the bay.

Jack had leapt into the water as if he were some sort of dolphin. Or some sort of seal. Or some wildly attractive, more-than-a-little-primitive bad boy you knew would break your heart and make you hate yourself for being a fool later, but, oh hell, at the moment, you just didn't care. And now that he'd cut his hair and trimmed his beard and was half-naked in frayed, bleached cutoffs that clung to him, well . . .

She shivered with the unmistakable feel of aching desire. Jeez, it had been a long time since any man, let alone a man she scarcely knew, had triggered a feeling that strong within her.

"Now then, Patricia, do you think your reaction to this stranger bears closer scrutiny?"

"Not really." She shrugged. *"I'm a normal, healthy female and he is one great-looking guy. It's*

*only natural to feel a certain amount of attraction
toward him."*

"Is it?"

*"Of course," she said defensively. "It doesn't
mean a thing."*

*"Perhaps we should explore why he triggers
these sensations yet your fiancé does not."*

*"Perhaps we should talk about something else,
doctor," she snapped.*

*"As you wish," he said in the noncommittal
way he had perfected to a fine art.*

*"Besides, it's not as if I was going to act on my
feelings."*

"Aren't you?"

"Absolutely not!"

"Are you quite certain?"

"Absolutely." She sighed. "Not."

"Are you coming?" Jack waved and bobbed from
a distance she wouldn't have attempted to reach
with a rowboat.

"It's great. Really great." She smiled and nodded and waved back in hopes he'd leave her
alone and go do that recreational nonsense by
himself. She was perfectly willing to accept a
written, or even an oral, report in the place of
seeing anything for herself.

"Come on in," he called.

"No thanks. I can see just fine from here. You
go ahead and have a good time without me." The
water was a fairly pleasant temperature, not too
cold, not too warm, but there were all those unidentified *things* swimming in it.

He walked toward her, his stride swift and determined, without that odd, slow-motion look most people had when they walked through water. Damn. Were even the forces of nature against her today?

At least he was far enough away to give her a few moments to get adjusted to the idea of being alone with him. Alone and wet. With every step, more of his bronzed chest was exposed to view. The man certainly did keep himself in shape.

"Don't tell me you can't swim?" he asked incredulously.

"Of course I can swim." *I just prefer to swim in a nice clean, chlorinated pool.* "But overall, I'm not the athletic type. I'd rather drive than walk, I prefer elevators to stairs and I don't think half-naked people should be running through the streets on their lunch hour unless they're being chased by muggers. However," she added, "I'm not a total couch potato. I see the health benefits of staying in shape. I do belong to a health club."

"Oh, yeah?" He laughed. "And do you ever go?"

"All the time," she lied. If pressed, she could probably find her membership card, and she was certain she'd at least driven by the club.

Jack waded closer, the water now barely covering his shorts, hanging low on his hips. He was a god of the sea in denim. And she'd thought he was hot when he was *dry*.

"Then what are you waiting for?"

"Nothing," she said, without so much as a touch of conviction, and jerked her gaze away from him to stare at the water surging gently below her knees. It was better to wonder what else might swim by than to concentrate too long on Kendall's far too obvious appeal.

"So?" His legs splashed into view and she jerked her chin up to meet his gaze and his grin. "What's the problem, Princess?"

She sighed and gave up. "Princesses are not especially fond of being extremely close to, well, nature."

"Oh, yeah," he said, as if he had just realized it himself. "No concrete. No chlorine." He waggled his brows wickedly and leered at her. "No towel boys."

She resisted the urge to tell him what a great towel boy he'd make but couldn't hold back a quick laugh. "No beach chairs. No bar, either."

He shook his head mournfully. "No beer."

"*You* have beer." She raised an eyebrow and smiled. "Some people just never learned to share."

"I'll make you a deal." He stepped backward and held out his hands. "If you come in the water, I'll give you a beer when we get home."

She crossed her arms and shook her head. "I don't really like beer."

"It'll be cold," he cajoled, as if he were the devil offering temptation for her soul.

"Doesn't matter." She shrugged. "I don't want it."

"Sure you do. You want anything you can't have."

"Oh, I do, do I?"

"Hey, you're a princess. It's a princess rule."

She started to protest, then grinned instead. "You're right. It's in the handbook. But as a *corporate* princess, I am open to negotiation. So here are my terms: I'll come all the way into the water. I'll even swim—"

He gasped in exaggerated shock. "You can swim?"

She ignored him. "—for oh, say, a case of beer."

"A case? An entire case?" He shook his head in fake regret. "I don't think so. Best I can offer is two beers."

"Two? No way. Half a case, then."

He snorted. "Don't forget, we're rationing. A six-pack and that's the absolute best I can do."

"Well, I don't know . . ." She narrowed her eyes and stared into the water for a long, thoughtful moment.

"Come on, Taylor, I could easily pick you up and dump you in the water right now."

"It's a deal," she said quickly.

"Great." He thrust out his hand. "Shake on it."

"I don't need to shake, but . . ." She grasped his hand and nearly jumped at the electricity that sparked between them. Her gaze shot to his and he looked as startled as she felt. She snatched her hand away and started wading toward the open sea, two steps ahead of him. "Now what?" She struggled to keep her voice light.

"A few more steps and we can swim. See where the bay curves?" He waved to the right, and she hadn't realized he was quite as close as he was. "See the boat moored out there? That's where we're headed."

She studied the shoreline. "Wouldn't it be much easier to walk along the beach and then swim?"

"This is much faster."

"I have all the time in the world, thank you." There was no way she was swimming with Charlie the Tuna and who knew what else if she didn't have to. She pivoted and smacked right into Jack's hard, solid chest. He grabbed her to keep her from falling. Or at least that's what she told herself.

She stared into his eyes. Heat simmered, smoldered, calling to a similar fire that flared deep in her midsection. His gaze slipped to her mouth, and she didn't want to lick her lips, but they were incredibly dry. The muscles of his arms tensed slightly, and she wondered,or maybe hoped, if he was as affected by their closeness as she.

"I'm going to walk." Her voice was breathless and she couldn't seem to pull her gaze from his.

"Okay." He made no move to release her. The heat of his bare chest warmed her breasts through her shirt. Good God, was the man feverish? Was she?

"Well, um . . ." He let her go and she headed back toward the water's edge. "I'll meet you over there."

"Sure. Just be careful."

"Careful?" She stopped and turned. "Careful about what?"

"Oh, you know." He shrugged. "Wild lizards, tarantulas, snakes—"

"Snakes?" Was he telling the truth? Probably not. Even if he was, it was a definite toss-up between which was more dangerous: big hairy spiders and tropical snakes or Jack Kendall.

"I'll watch it." She started off. At least, once the swimming was over, she'd get to ride above the sea instead of in it.

"Whatever. See you at the boat." He paused, then called after her. "By the way, don't let anything you might see in the water spook you. Potato cod are kind of scary looking, but they won't hurt you. Try not to step on a manta ray though; they get really testy about that. Oh, and we rarely get sharks longer than four feet in the bay."

Her heart stopped and she swiveled to face him. "Sharks?"

"No big deal." He raised his broad shoulders in a casual shrug, then turned and dove into the water.

"Sharks." She groaned. She really didn't think there was any serious danger; at least that was what she told herself on a rational level. Emotionally, the idea of sharks of any length made her want to run screaming from the water. Straight into the waiting grip of giant spiders or killer snakes.

If there was even the remotest chance of being

eaten by sharks, she'd just as soon be by Jack's side when it happened. She waded after him. At least this way she had a fifty-fifty chance. With any luck, sharks would prefer tanned, well-muscled meat to a pale blond offering and eat Jack first.

At least that way she'd die a happy woman.

"Whoa. You really can swim. I'm impressed." Jack grinned and treaded water by the side of the boat. "I guess the health club did its job after all."

"Yeah, I'm a regular mermaid." She grabbed the rung of a ladder dangling over the side of the modest but well-equipped cabin cruiser. "Are we going onboard?"

"Not today."

"Not today?" Her brows pulled together and her voice rose. "What do you mean, 'not today'? I just swam across half the Pacific Ocean to get here with God knows what lurking in the water. You said you were going to show me the island from a new angle."

"And you thought that meant a boat?"

"Yeah." She drew the word out slowly.

He shook his head in mock sympathy. "Sorry."

"Then . . ." She narrowed her eyes. "Oh, no you don't. I'm not swimming around this whole island. I walked it yesterday and that was bad enough, but there's no way—"

"Now why would you do that? That would be silly." Why did he suspect that she wasn't going to like this? "What we want is on the other side of the boat." He started off with long, easy strokes. Behind him, she sighed in resignation, then splashed after him.

He had to admit she was a decent swimmer, really not half-bad. He figured it must come naturally to her. Short of a dynamite body, showcased nicely in her wet T-shirt and shorts, there was no indication Trish Taylor had any kind of athletic ability at all.

He circled the boat and spotted his objective, looking like a baby whale nudged up against its mother. "This is it."

"This is what?" she said suspiciously

"It's a jet ski." He pulled himself onto the water vehicle. "There's another in a shed on the island, but I keep this one out here." He flashed her his best wicked grin. "You'll have to ride with me."

"You're kidding. That thing is nothing more than one of those annoying little motorbikes on water." She looked longingly at the cabin cruiser. "Couldn't we just take the boat?"

"It wouldn't be much of an adventure that way."

"I could live with that."

"I'll bet. Now, give me your hand." He reached down and she reluctantly grabbed his hand. He pulled her up and swung her onto the seat behind him, only catching a tantalizing glimpse of transparent T-shirt plastered to luscious breasts.

He himself might need a quick, cooling dip in a moment.

"At least it gets me out of the water." She wrapped her arms around him. "Do you drive this thing like a bat out of hell too?"

"Usually."

"The things I do for my job. Okay." She tightened her grip and rested her forehead on his back. "I'm ready."

He had planned to drive at his usual high speed, but something about Trish's reluctant good sportsmanship held him back. Her aversion to adventure wasn't hard to miss, and obviously being in the water was too close to nature for her. She was definitely out of her element.

He gunned the motor. Full out, this model probably wouldn't do more than forty miles per hour at best. Still, for anyone not used to it, that was a fairly death-defying speed. He held it to a moderate pace and aimed toward the opening of the bay to the sea. He wanted to show her the possibilities here, but he also hoped, at some point during the day, that he could clear up that little misunderstanding about who he really was. He didn't know her well yet, but he was pretty sure she wouldn't like being deceived. Even when the deception was as insignificant as his parentage.

"Can this thing go any faster?" Apprehension sounded in her voice.

"Sure."

"Are you planning to go any faster?"

"Nope."

She was silent for a moment then he felt her sigh. "Thanks."

He grinned and drove through the entrance of the bay to the left, heading in a clockwise circle around the island. Jack pointed out various places he thought would be ideal for basing some of the recreational facilities he and Mo had discussed.

He spotted the first location he wanted to show her, about halfway between the bay and the site for the resort, and aimed the jet ski toward the beach, cutting the engine when the vehicle was about ten feet from the shore. He hopped off into knee-high water.

"I'd suggest putting another dock here, a serious working dock. We talked about one at the site, but I think that should be more for aesthetics, while this one would serve a practical purpose."

She slid into the water and looked around. "It's very pretty."

"Breathtaking?"

"Isn't everything here? This whole place looks like a movie set," she said wryly and helped him pull the jet ski onto the beach.

"We're about five minutes by land from where the resort will be. Access would be easy, but the dock and everything that goes along with it won't be intrusive."

"Keeping the views from the hotel pristine and postcard perfect." Her voice was thoughtful. "Guests who want water activities will have them close at hand, and those who don't won't be bothered. Great idea."

"Thanks." He plopped down on the beach and patted the sand beside him.

She looked warily at him. "Any nasty beach creatures I should be aware of?"

"Nah. Anything really dangerous doesn't come out until after dark."

"Swell." She settled down next to him. "Does that include you?"

"Oh, I'm always more dangerous after dark. Just wait till sunset."

"Thanks for the warning." She laughed and changed the subject. Apparently the thought of him after dark made her nervous. He smiled to himself. "So what exactly are we talking about here? What do you see us providing for guests?"

"Well, first of all, we'll want to have scuba gear and equipment available for diving and snorkeling." He leaned back on his elbows. "There are more than three hundred different species of reef coral, and you can find most of them in this area. Plus the variety of fish is practically endless. There's as much to see under the water as above it. We'll definitely have to offer big-game fishing—"

She slanted him a suspicious glance. "How big?"

"Big. Tuna, marlin, sailfish. I'll take you out

on the boat and let you try it for yourself."

"I'll pass. I prefer my fish already sautéed when I first meet it."

"There's a surprise." He chuckled. "I think we need to bring in a few decent-sized boats for leisurely cruises around Paradise Bay and some of the other islands. Maybe set up day cruises—"

"Complete with gourmet picnics on the beach."

"Now you're getting into the spirit. Plus, we'll offer sailing, jet skis of course—"

"Of course," she murmured.

"—windsurfing, parasailing—"

"Parasailing? Isn't that where normally intelligent people strap themselves onto flimsy little kites and are pulled along by boats until they're airborne?"

"That's it, all right. Ever tried it?"

"No, thank you." She shook her head. "I make it a rule not to fly on anything that doesn't have a bathroom and meal service."

He raised a brow. "I gather that means you'll pass on the hang gliding too?"

"You figured that out all by yourself?" She laughed. "You're the one who pointed out my big character flaw. You know, no spirit of adventure." She stretched out in the sand, rolled on her side, leaned on one elbow and propped her head in her hand. "Have you done all that stuff?"

"Pretty much." He stared out at the crystal-blue waters, seeing beyond the tropical serenity to a lifetime filled with seeking ever greater thrills and challenges and excitement.

"Why?"

"Because it's there?"

"Isn't that the answer for climbing Everest?"

"Been there." He shrugged nonchalantly. "It's overrated."

"Yeah, right." She looked at him as if he was a new form of life. "Seriously, Jack, I don't get it. I guess I can see the appeal—dimly, but I can see it—of high speeds and roller-coaster type fun, but I don't understand the thrill being worth the risk."

"It's the challenge, I suppose." He thought for a moment. "The idea of pushing yourself as far as you can, in some cases farther. Discovering your limits and surpassing them. Facing your fears and overcoming them."

"Why did you quit?"

"Who says I did?"

"Well, you're here, in the middle of nowhere, working with computers. Correct me if I'm wrong, but there's not a lot of danger involved in that."

"Maybe not. But it's a different kind of challenge. Intellectual instead of physical. Someday everybody grows up. I just reached a point where I realized risking my neck wasn't as satisfying as it used to be. I finally figured out my life was going nowhere and I needed to find a real focus. Something to challenge my mind the same way I'd challenge my body." He shrugged. "Now I'm a computer nerd in Paradise."

"Do you regret it?" she asked softly.

"Not at all." His gaze caught hers. "It's not easy to face your own demons, but now I'm actually fairly content. I've found my niche in the world and I like it."

"I'm impressed." She smiled. "It's a shame more members of this family can't do the same."

"What do you mean?" he said cautiously.

"Well, Russ's son is still roaming around the world, risking his neck. Spending his father's money." She snorted with disdain. "Russell Jonathan Evans the fourth—what a jerk."

A sinking feeling settled in his gut. "He's not so bad."

"Oh, please. He's a grown man. He's got responsibilities to his family that he's completely ignored. He's going to own the whole company someday. And what does he do? Nothing. *Nada*. Not one little thing." Disgust underlaid her words. "You can call me a princess all you want, but the prince in this fairy tale definitely needs work. RJ the fourth is a playboy in the worst sense of the word. He hasn't done anything but wander the globe with the jet set for years."

"I gather you don't think much of him," he said slowly.

"Honestly, I've never met him." She blew out an exasperated breath. "Can you believe that? His father married my mother more than a decade ago and in all that time he's never once come to visit. As far as I know, Russ hasn't even seen him in years. He's never met his stepmother. His father doesn't deserve this kind of treatment."

"You blame his son for all that?"

"Completely. Look." She sat up and crossed her legs Indian style. "Like most really successful men, Russ thinks he's never wrong. He wants everything under his control. That attitude is a pain in the butt to deal with—"

"—and it put you here—"

"—Exactly. But Russ only does what he does because he cares about me. He can't accept that I'm an adult and can make my own decisions." She grinned ruefully. "That's my problem and I'll deal with it as soon as I get home. Russ has been more of a father to me than my biological father ever was. He's a good guy and he deserves better than a son who treats him like he's the scum of the earth."

"I think you're being a little hard on"—he tried not to choke on the words—"RJ the fourth."

She scoffed. "I'm not being hard enough." She paused and stared for a moment. "You know him, don't you?"

"Well, I—"

"Of course you do." She clapped her palm to her forehead. "I should have realized it. From what you've said, it sounds like your life and his were pretty similar until you came here. He's what? Your cousin?"

"Something like that," he muttered.

"So am I being too hard on him? Do I have the wrong impression of the crown prince?"

Jack considered his words carefully. This was definitely not the moment for any revelations of his own. But if he was going to avoid her hatred when he did spill it all, now was the time to set a little groundwork.

"M—RJ the fourth's mother died when he was just a kid. He took it really bad. And right or wrong, he blamed his father."

"I can't imagine ever blaming Russ for that."

"You have to realize, in those days Russ was a typical workaholic. I think a man who inherits a family fortune, and business and all the tradition that goes along with it, can go one of three ways. He can squander everything having a good time—"

"Like the prince."

"—or he can run in place, maintain the status quo; or he can build what he's got to even greater levels. That's the path men like Russ take." For a moment, childhood memories rushed through him. "Don't get me wrong: Russ was a good father and husband and, from what I saw, it seemed like a decent family relationship all the way around. The three of them were close. But Russ was gone a lot and work kept him busy, even when he was home.

"When his wife got sick, there was nothing he could do. It was too late to go back and rewrite the past, and I'm sure he went through a hell of his own. When she died, I think his son was too caught up in his own grief to notice Russ's pain. Plus Russ married again, disastrously, fairly soon after his wife's death. His son had a real hard time with what he saw as a betrayal of his mother's memory."

"I don't care, it still stinks," she said grimly. "He was all Russ had left and he dumped him."

"I know." Guilt surged through him. It had taken Jack and Russ the last four years to work through all this and come to grips with the past. Even though they now had the kind of relationship they always should have had, he couldn't help regretting the time they'd wasted and the pain they'd inflicted on each other. "But I think you can understand it."

"Not me. I can't." Her voice was cold. "I've never been able to understand it. Or forgive it. And I never will."

He picked up a handful of sand and let it drift through his fingers. This was going to be a lot harder than he thought. She really hated him.

"What about Russ? Has he forgiven him?"

"I have no idea." She shrugged. "I haven't lived with him and my mother for years. I don't know what the latest is on his relationship with the prodigal son."

"If Russ has forgiven him, could you?"

"I don't know that either." She rested her elbows on her knees, clasped her hands in her lap and gazed out at the water. "You may have noticed, I'm rather protective of Russ. He's my dad," she said simply, as if that explained everything.

For a moment, envy, hard and fierce, gripped

him. His father had filled a void in this woman's life and had earned her undying loyalty and love. For so long, Jack had been too stupid and resentful and just plain stubborn to see what he had and what he was missing. He could only thank God that they'd reconciled before age and the passage of years had made it impossible.

He and his father were close again, but Trish couldn't stand him. And he'd bet it would take more than a recommendation from Russ to change her mind. He had his work cut out for him. Talk about a challenge. . . .

"You know, for years I swore that if I ever did meet RJ the fourth, I'd knock his block off." She tilted her head towards him and grinned.

"Oh?" He drew his brows together. "Somehow I can't quite picture that. Have you ever knocked somebody's block off before?"

"Nope. But there's always a first time." Her blue eyes twinkled. "I figure desire will more than make up for my lack of experience."

"Desire usually does," he drawled. Without warning, he was aware of the double meaning of his words and could see that she caught it too.

"When it comes to knocking his block off, I mean," she said quickly.

"Yeah." He gazed into her eyes. "That's what I thought you meant. What else?"

"Nothing." She scrambled to her feet. "Well, if there's more to your tour, we'd better get going." She headed for the jet ski. "We have a lot of work to do."

He leaned back in the sand, enjoying the sight of her retreat for just a moment before heaving himself up and starting after her.

"Oh, yeah, Princess. A lot of work. And you don't know the half of it," he said softly to himself.

Chapter Eight

No discussion of Paradise Bay would be complete without mentioning the scenic vistas presented to the visitor from virtually every point on the island. Whether one stands on a beach at sea level or observes the surrounding area from the highest peak, it is impossible not to find a location with panoramic views that delight the senses with the majesty of nature's tropical splendor.

The spectacular sunrises on Paradise Bay are equaled in beauty only by the sunsets.

"Is there any spot here that isn't breathtaking?" Trish sat on the steps of the porch and gazed out over the island.

"Not really." Jack lounged beside her, precious beer in hand. "I've always thought there was magic on Paradise Bay."

"It does seem enchanted." She held up her beer can. "And this isn't bad either. Thanks."

"Hey, you won it fair and square." His words teased, but his tone was remote, as if he was thinking of something he didn't want to talk about. He stared straight ahead, over the rooftops of the village and into the setting sun.

He'd been somewhat pensive ever since they'd returned to the house. They'd checked in with Mo and agreed to jump into the project first thing in the morning. She wondered how long it would be before they'd have another peaceful day like this.

She hated to admit it, but she'd had a great time with Jack. Aside from those unexpected moments that kept cropping up. Like when her gaze had drifted to his lips and she'd wondered what would have happened if he had kissed her yesterday. If his kisses were subtle and sensually persuasive or hard, demanding and not to be refused. Or when she'd been forced to wrap her arms around him on the jet ski and she'd wondered if his body temperature was higher than normal or if his heat was in response to her own. Or when his gaze had caught hers and it seemed as if they were saying all kinds of things without words. Moments that triggered crazy thoughts she'd tried to ignore but that hung on in the back of her mind, nagging questions she didn't know how to answer.

She glanced over at him again. His brow was furrowed and he appeared lost in his own thoughts. Initially, she'd thought he was simply tired. God knows she'd been exhausted. She'd gone straight to her room and collapsed on the bed for a quick nap, waking just in time for the sunset. She'd wandered downstairs to find Jack alone on the porch and had demanded her first beer.

She didn't know what was bothering him and it was probably none of her business anyway. She didn't really know him well enough to pry. Technically, he wasn't even family. But it was weird just how natural it felt to be with him. It was as if they'd known each other forever. Not quite like an old friend, but more like . . . what? She didn't know and wasn't particularly eager to find out. Of course, the ease she felt in his presence vanished the instant he looked at her with that smoldering gaze of his, or she was forced to hold on to him for dear life or any one of a dozen different innocent actions that with him became anything but innocent.

Still, if she had to be exiled in paradise, he wasn't a bad choice to be exiled with. As long as she could keep things on a friendly—but not too friendly—basis. And they did have a job to do.

That was pretty strange too. She'd been convinced that this whole resort deal was a scam to get her out of civilization and away from Elliott and the wedding plans. She still wasn't completely certain that wasn't part of Russ's true purpose. But The Inn on Paradise Bay was apparently something her stepfather really wanted to pull off, and she was the one he'd charged with doing just that. "I suppose if he's going to try to control my life, he sure couldn't have picked a more magnificent place to do it in."

"What?" Jack looked over at her.

"Sorry." She took a sip of beer. "I was just thinking. I didn't realize I said it out loud."

He studied her thoughtfully. "You have a real problem with control, don't you?"

"Probably. Stems back to my childhood, according to Psychology 101." She grinned. "But seriously, I don't know anyone who wants to let other people run their lives and make their decisions for them. Especially about things like career choices and where to live and—"

"Whom to marry?"

"That too." She raised her beer in a toast. "I just want to make my own choices, and if that means making my own mistakes, so be it. You of all people should be able to understand that."

"Me?" he asked with surprise, clinking her can with his own. "Why me?"

"It sounds like you've done exactly what you've wanted, made your own decisions, run your own life."

"And made more than my share of mistakes," he pointed out.

"That's the price you pay for freedom, and it doesn't seem at all high to me." She squinted into the sunset and sighed. "I know Russ is only thinking of my best interests, but I really hate being lied to."

"Who's lied to you?"

"*Lied* might be too strong a word. Let's say deceived. Or misled."

"Okay, so who's misled you?"

"Russ, of course. He told me he wanted to build . . ." She realized the truth the moment she said the words and laughed. "He told me he wanted to build a luxury resort on Paradise Bay and apparently, he really does. I guess he didn't mislead me after all. But that doesn't mean he's not still trying to run my life. He just found a legitimate way to do it."

"So." Jack let the word hang in the air for a moment. "What are you going to do about it?"

"Do? Not much I can do, really. I'm a little too old for youthful rebellion. Besides, he's not just my stepfather, he's my boss." She took a long swallow of beer and considered her options. "About the only thing I can do is show him that, regardless of any ulterior motives he might have had in sending me here, he made the right choice. I can work my butt off, Kendall, and, with your help, pull together the best damn resort Russ or anybody else has ever seen."

"I'll drink to that." Jack clinked his can against hers again.

They lapsed into an easy silence. Relaxed. Natural? She shook her head to clear away the idea. She didn't even know Jack Kendall and had no business being natural, or anything else, with him. His personal life was his own.

On the other hand, even though they'd never met before, his personal life did overlap with hers in an odd way. And Trish would be an idiot if she didn't take advantage of the opportunity he presented.

"Tell me about him," she said casually.

"Who?" Jack's brow furrowed.

"The crown prince. Russ's son."

"Why do you ask? I thought you hated him."

"I do. I'm curious, that's all. It's not a big deal." She shrugged. "It's just that you're the first person I've met, other than Russ, who knows him. And I'd never talk to Russ about him."

"Aren't you forgetting about Elliott?"

"I would never forget about Elliott," she said a shade too quickly. "He's always on my mind. He's my fiancé. I'm going to . . ."

Jack's dark brow arched upward.

". . . marry him." She groaned to herself. She was babbling like an idiot. It was an unavoidable by-product of her effort to smother the persistent voice of her mythical psychiatrist, reminding her that she hadn't thought of Elliott much at all today. In fact, as the annoying voice had pointed out, Elliott was the farthest thing from her mind when Jack had come so close to kissing her.

"That's very nice, but"—the corners of his mouth quirked upward—"what I meant was:

why don't you ask Elliott about him? He knows him."

"Oh." A wave of heat washed up her face. She didn't just sound like an idiot, obviously she was one. She drew a deep breath. "Elliott really isn't the one to ask. He hasn't seen RJ the fourth since his mother and Russ divorced. I only know they hated each other when they were kids."

"With good reason," he murmured.

"That's right, I almost forgot. You don't like Elliott either."

"Not particularly."

"You guys are just one big happy family, aren't you?" Until now, she'd never realized how fraught with conflict Russ's family was. Oh, sure, she knew about his split with his son. And Elliott had always made his feelings about Russ's offspring clear. Now, there was cousin Jack who didn't like Elliott.

He blew out a resigned breath. "What do you want to know?"

"You said I was too hard on him. What's he like?"

"He's okay." Jack shrugged. "He always struck me as being kind of lost. I think his careening around the world at a breakneck pace was—is—his way of avoiding life. It's easy to do in the international set he ran—runs in. I don't think he could face those responsibilities you talked about. And I think it took him a long time to come to grips with his feelings about his parents."

"You actually sound like you feel sorry for him." A note of amazement sounded in her voice.

"I guess I do in a way. It's not easy being a crown prince," he said dryly.

"You think I've misjudged him, don't you?"

"Not entirely. I can see why you don't like him. But people do change. Everybody grows up sooner or later."

She snorted. "Not him."

"You never know." He hesitated. "What would you think if he did change? If, say, he worked out his problems with Russ? If he came home and took a position in ESI?"

"I think that will be a cold day in hell. I suppose I could give him the benefit of the doubt, but it wouldn't be easy. I don't know if I'd believe him anyway. It could be that coming home is just something else for him to play around with. He'd have to prove he'd changed." Her tone hardened. "And he'd have to make up with his father. If Russ was willing to forgive him, maybe I could too. But I'm not making any promises."

"You're tough, lady."

"I have my moments. I care a lot for Russ and I think his son really hurt him."

"Do you think RJ knows that?"

"Yes." She kept her voice light, as if it didn't matter, but it did. A lot. "I've never told anyone this before, but I wrote to him once."

"You did?" A startled expression crossed his face.

"Don't look so surprised. It was right after I graduated from high school, when I was not above a little meddling. I wrote this long, passionate letter. I poured out my heart to him. I told him what I thought of his treatment of Russ and how lucky he was to have a father like that.

"I blasted him for his total disregard for his father's feelings and urged him to see Russ and straighten out all the trouble between them. And I finished it up with my own rather scathing opinion of him and the life he led."

"And did you hear back from him?" he asked slowly.

"Nope. Not a single word."

"He was probably terrified."

"I'll bet."

"Realistically, there's a good chance he never got your letter. People who don't have a permanent mailing address tend to miss a lot of correspondence."

"Oh, yeah, I'm sure that's it." She couldn't help the sarcasm in her voice. "It's not that he didn't care. He just didn't get the letter."

"You never know."

"And probably never will. I'm beginning to doubt that I'll ever actually meet him. I don't even know what he looks like. I've seen some pictures of him as a kid, but that's it." She narrowed her eyes and studied Jack. "You know, you look kind of like him."

"Do I?"

"Yeah, from what I remember. I always

thought he took after Russ, but now I guess he probably resembles your side of the family."

"Oh, there's a strong family resemblance, all right." A slow grin spread across Jack's face. "If nothing else, he is a good-looking man. It runs in the family."

"Along with humility?"

"We are nothing if not humble." He laughed, and she joined him. Then his voice took on a more serious tone. "Do me a favor, Taylor."

"Maybe."

"If you ever do meet him, give him a chance. I'd bet Russ would appreciate it."

She stared at him for a minute. Jack was turning out to be a nice guy. He seemed to really care about Russ and his son.

"I'll tell you what I'll do, Kendall. Not that I think there's any possibility of my running into RJ the fourth, but if I do, I'll try. Okay?"

"I'll take it."

"But there's one condition." She drained the last of her beer, then smiled sweetly. "I still get to knock his block off."

Where in the hell was that damn letter?

Jack couldn't remember ever receiving it, although he might have. It was what? Ten plus years ago? When he'd been in boarding school and college, all his bills had gone directly to his father's accountants. The system worked so well, and was so easy, he'd simply continued to let the accountants receive his bills and keep track of what he spent after he graduated. His father had insisted and Jack hadn't cared. He didn't realize until years later, his paper trail had been the only way his father had known where he was at any given time.

Most of his other correspondence, what little there was, had generally ended up with his bills. Occasionally letters would catch up to him, but they were usually from his father, and nine times out of ten he ignored them.

Jack pushed aside the clothes hanging in his closet to reach the back wall and the file box he'd tossed there and forgotten. He dimly remembered receiving the box from the accountants shortly after his return to Paradise Bay. Apparently, it held copies of his bills and who knew what else. He'd never actually opened it.

He grabbed the box and carried it to the bed. It weighed a ton and was covered in dust. Impatiently, he yanked off the packing tape and pulled off the lid. File after file confronted him, all neatly labeled. There were folders for hotels and airlines and Clothes and several huge files marked simply MISCELLANEOUS. He paged through them until he found one marked PERSONAL CORRESPONDENCE. It wasn't nearly as fat as MISCELLANEOUS. Not surprising. Aside from his father, he couldn't remember getting letters from anyone.

He pulled out the folder and flipped it open. Two dozen or more letters tumbled to the floor. He bent down, scooped up the letters and stood slowly, rifling through them in his hand. Most were from his dad, all were unopened, and once again he felt a twinge of regret for the lost years. He ran across a letter from a girl he'd been involved with, also unopened, a note from a guy he'd gone to school with, again unopened, and spotted the familiar return address and the name: Patricia Taylor.

He looked at it for a long moment. Would it really make any difference to read it now? Finally, he drew a deep breath and ripped open the envelope.

He scanned the two pages, a faint floral scent wafting from the paper. She was right: It was emotional and intense and colored with a young woman's passion. He wondered if she was a bit more adventurous then, or if whatever in her life made her long for safety and security had already left its mark.

He sank down on the bed. No wonder she thought he was such a bastard. Her note pleaded with him to reconcile with Russ. She pointed out that he and his father only really had each other. And she mentioned how upset his mother would have been at the rift between the men she loved. Then her tone hardened and she continued on to tell him what a selfish, insensitive jerk he was. She attacked him for everything from his lifestyle to his spending habits to his choice of women.

The letter ended with her offering to do whatever she could to help him get back together with his father, even if she didn't think he deserved a father like Russ.

He folded the letter and slipped it back into the envelope. She was right, of course. Everything she'd written was accurate, even though she had to have guessed at most of it. He didn't know if her letter had ever reached him or been forwarded directly to the accountants. It really didn't make much difference at this point.

Would it have made a difference to him if he had read it all those years ago?

Probably not. He'd been too deeply immersed in his own feelings then to pay any attention to anyone else's.

He raked his fingers through his hair. He'd thought mending fences with his dad had been tough—but at least his father had wanted to reconcile. Trish would be another story. She'd resented and, yeah, hated him for so long, there was no way she'd get over it quickly, if at all. He doubted even the fact that he was now on good terms with his dad would sway her

He'd have to work for her forgiveness, and work hard. He was certain she already liked him. Maybe if she liked Jack enough, she could get over her enmity toward RJ the fourth. But that was a big *if*.

Sooner or later she'd find out the truth about his identity. With the two of them working so closely together, it was inevitable. The revelation would be much better coming from him than anyone else. Man, if she found out on her own

173

. . . He shook his head. He'd have to pick just the right moment and ease into it. If he'd told her the truth when she'd first arrived, it would be behind them by now. Or she would have killed him. Of course, that was still a distinct possibility.

Abruptly he realized that he wanted her forgiveness. And her respect and her friendship and . . . what else? He wasn't sure, but there was no possibility of anything else between them unless he could convince her that the guy she hated didn't exist anymore. Prove to her that he had changed and was more than ready to take his place in the family and the company.

He definitely had his work cut out for him. He could see only one bright spot in this whole mess.

When the time came for her to knock his block off, he was fairly confident that her right hook wouldn't be nearly as hard to take as the disgust in her eyes.

Chapter Nine

For those preferring less aquatic pursuits, the lone mountain on Paradise Bay provides an amusing, if minimal, challenge for experienced climbers, but affords the weekend hiking enthusiast and occasional athlete a stimulating and exhilarating experience. Be aware: The hours spent in this venture are directly proportional to the skill and fitness of those involved.

However, the efforts of expert and novice alike are well rewarded with a view that is nothing short of breathtaking.

Trish leaned back in her chair and rolled her shoulders in an effort to ease the ever-present tiredness in her muscles. Still, it was a satisfying ache. Never in her wildest dreams would she have imagined the incredible amount of work a project like this demanded. The minuscule details went on forever. The potential problems stretched to eternity. Nothing was too minor to overlook. Everything had to be checked and double-checked and checked again.

She, Jack and Mo had hit the ground running and hadn't let up for a minute. Each of them was acutely aware of the months, days, hours left until New Year's Eve 1999. Adrenaline, excitement and even passion had fueled them from the minute she'd settled in the library with her laptop two weeks ago. Or was it two and a half weeks? Or more? She really wasn't sure. How could she have lost track of the date when the pressure of time was the driving force that kept them going? But the days and nights had blended together in one long marathon of work and talk and debate. Disagreements and frustration and, often, tired laughter.

Mo had brought in his personal computer and set it up on one of the tables, taking over the far end of the library. She shared Jack's computer workspace with the remaining table reserved for Mo's architectural models and an ever-expanding landscaped miniature of the site. There were moments when the only sounds in the room were the low background hum of the air conditioner, the tapping of keys on their respective keyboards and the occasional muttered "Damn" or other appropriate expletive, their individual choices as varied as their backgrounds.

Maude was an invisible but continuing presence. There was always something to eat or munch on, coffee and cold drinks waiting for them when the need arose. Trish wondered if the housekeeper-cook-Barbie had moved in for the duration. She knew Mo had taken up residence in one of the many empty bedrooms in the mansion. He was at the house all the time, anyway.

The trio had had to adapt their schedule on Paradise Bay to ESI's corporate office, where entire departments worked to expand on their ideas and refine their efforts in the battle to beat the clock. The difference in time zones dictated that they start work well before dawn. They'd come up with a three-times-a-day E-mail and fax exchange between the island and the company. But the whole idea that noon on Thursday on Paradise Bay was eight o'clock Wednesday night—the night before—in New York was a concept Trish absolutely could not grasp. It simply made no sense to her. Jack had had to print up a special conversion chart. From then on she'd given up trying to figure out the time difference and just checked the chart.

The trio lived and breathed The Inn at Paradise Bay. In fact, aside from a morning spent in town to show Trish around and let her meet more of the island's residents, the three of them had rarely left the room. They would usually call it quits just in time to catch the sunset from the porch and decompress with a cold drink, usually Maude's spiced tea. With the supply of beer at dangerously low levels, even Trish was unwilling to squander any on anything less than serious celebrations. It was an evening ritual she looked forward to more every day. Sometimes Mo joined them but, more often than not, he was too caught up in some detail he wanted to keep working on and left Trish and Jack alone. And she looked forward to those evenings most of all.

Trish raised her arms and stretched, reaching first with one hand and then the other for the ceiling. On the far side of the room, as usual, Mo was oblivious to everything except the monitor in front of him. She glanced across the table at Jack. He too was immersed in whatever he had on his screen. Trish smiled to herself. The three of them made one hell of a team. They played off each other's strengths and shored up each other's weaknesses. Each brought to the project a unique perspective and individual skills: creative and practical, realistic and idealistic.

She folded her arms over the top of her head. Funny; she'd worked with other people before, but she'd never really been part of a team until now. Oh, technically she was still in charge, but the actual working relationship had evolved to a point of mutual respect and shared leadership. Disagreements were worked out through compromise, or occasionally surrender, but what was best for the project was always first in everyone's mind. Who would have believed it? And who would have suspected the incredible satisfaction of doing a job well with others?

"My dear Patricia, I'm confident this can well be called a breakthrough."

"Really, Doctor? Do you think so?"

"Indeed. In fact, I've written it down right here." He held out a report card. *"Works and plays well with others."*

"What are you grinning about, Taylor?" Jack shot her a quick glance, then returned his attention to the monitor.

"I didn't know I was grinning." She stretched again. Pushing her laptop out of the way, she propped her elbows on the table and rested her chin on her laced fingers. "What do you think, Kendall? Do I work and play well with others?"

"I think you work well." His fingers never stopped moving across the keyboard. His gaze never left the monitor. "I really don't know how you play."

He didn't, did he? Since they'd started on the project, they hadn't done much of anything together but work. No terrifying rides on motorbikes or jet skis. No standing on the beach and seeing the world through his eyes. Not a single, solitary reason to wrap her arms around him. He hadn't even come close to kissing her again. Oh, they'd shared a fair amount of friendly affection, that annoying best-friend type, and maintained a mild level of flirtatious banter, but nothing of any significance had developed. Still, wasn't there a hint of electricity, a touch of tension lingering between them when they were alone? They'd just been too busy and ultimately too tired to do anything about it.

And she had to admit: She liked the man. Really liked him. He had a sharp mind and managed to make things that completely escaped her understandable. He was patient without being condescending and treated her like an equal, not like a pretty blonde. Or the boss's daughter. But as an intelligent human being worthy of his friendship and, more importantly, his respect. He was always straight with her and honest. All in all, he was a nice guy. But best of all, he made her laugh when she least expected it.

And he wasn't hard on the eyes either.

"That grin is beginning to scare me, Taylor," Jack said mildly, glancing up from the monitor.

"Oh, yeah?" She tried not to smirk and failed. "Good."

"You know, Trish, between us and the folks at corporate, we've been working pretty much around the clock."

"Now there's a revelation." She stifled a yawn. "I think I picked up on that one, Kendall."

"But do you realize in the last three weeks—"

"Three weeks? It's been three weeks?" She shook her head. "Are you sure?" she asked.

"Yep."

"I knew it: My mind is fried."

"Your mind is fine." He tapped a few keys.

"You've just been working the other end off. Anyway, what I was trying to say is we've reached a point where most of the preliminaries are finished. Mo's designs are nearly completed. Corporate is fleshing everything else out and finalizing all the details. Crews will arrive next week to start upgrading the island's infrastructure, then construction can begin. In short, Ms. Taylor, it's past noon and the day's long over in New York." He hit ENTER, then looked at her. "Let's get out of here."

She narrowed her eyes suspiciously. "And do what?"

"We've seen how you work. Now, let's see if you really can play well with others."

"Come on, Princess, move it."

A muttered curse somewhere below him was his only response. Jack grinned and lowered his backpack to the ground. It had taken him twice as long as it usually did to get to the top of the mountain. Trish's self-professed lack of athletic ability, not to mention desire, was even more apparent on land than it had been on water. At least she was a decent swimmer. She was definitely not a hiker.

He settled down to wait on one of the rocky outcroppings that dotted the small, flat area marking the top of the mountain. Or, rather, it was the peak of a volcano, although no one ever referred to it as that. In geologic terms this spot was once the volcano's caldera, filled in with lava through the eons and then eroded to its current shape. The mountain itself covered about half the island's land mass, but this area was maybe twenty by thirty feet—just big enough to allow a nice-sized party of hikers to relax, picnic or simply enjoy the view. It would be great for guests.

"How ya doing?" He leaned forward but still didn't see her coming up the trail. "Making any progress?"

She snapped something he couldn't quite make out and he figured that was probably for the best. To anyone even mildly athletic the trek up the mountain was no big deal. Here on the western side of the island, the slope rose at a steady but not excessively steep rate, exactly the reason he'd picked this route for Trish. The east slope, overlooking the resort site, was somewhat more rugged. There, erosion and landslides over the last few million years had carved a more challenging landscape. But even the eastern approach to the summit was at best an invigorating hike, not really a true climb unless someone chose to scale straight up the cliffs near the waterfall.

A few choice swear words drifted up to him, and he smothered a laugh. In spite of all her bitching, Trish was genuinely a good sport. She could have refused to come when he'd told her what he had in mind. Instead, she'd surprised him by agreeing with his reasoning that hiking to the top of the mountain would be one more attraction for guests and she'd better check it out.

"How could you abandon me like that, Kendall?" Trish trudged into sight. "I could have run into all kinds of problems. Don't think I've forgotten about the wild lizards and giant spiders and who knows what else lurking out here." She dropped to her knees and heaved an exhausted sigh. "You could have at least given me a hand."

Jack jumped to his feet and applauded. "Oh, bravo! Good job! Well done!"

Her lips twitched, as if she wanted to laugh but wouldn't give him the satisfaction. "Smart ass."

"Me?" He clapped his hand to his heart. "That hurts, Trish. That really hurts."

She smiled sweetly. "Not as much as I'd like it to."

"Ah-ha. Are you back to dreaming up new ways to kill me?"

"Nope. I've given that up." She got to her feet and brushed the dirt off her legs. Her very nice, very long legs. "I'd rather keep you alive."

"I'm flattered."

"Don't be." She pulled off the Detroit Tigers ball cap he'd lent her and combed her fingers through her blond hair. "Torture works much better when the victim is alive."

"Oh, well, as long as it's for a good cause." He grinned.

She replaced the hat and grinned back. She had a nice smile, but she had a great grin. More and more he'd noticed that there were a lot of great things about her.

"Did I thank you for lending me the hat? And"— she stretched her arms out wide, the fabric of her top molding against her chest. His stomach tightened—"your shirt?"

"No problem." He cleared his throat. Even though his shirts were definitely too big for her, they served as a decent compromise between Maude's clothes and her mother's. The philosopher had managed to come up with a pair of shorts that weren't quite as tight as the first ones Trish had worn. Privately, Jack thought it was a shame, although it probably was for the best, given the work they'd had to concentrate on. Until now. "Anything to get you out of those tents of Maude's mother's."

She lifted a brow, and he realized what he'd said. He started to clarify his remark, then decided against it. Besides, she looked good in his clothes. Damn good. And there was something about her wearing his stuff that he liked. A lot. Let her take his comment any way she wanted. After all, he didn't mean it the way it sounded. Did he?

"Well, I appreciate the thought." Her gaze caught his. Something wicked flashed in her eyes. Or something wonderful, whatever it was. "I just realized"—she looked around—"my report said this island was volcanic. Wouldn't that make this a volcano instead of a mountain?"

"Yep."

"Shouldn't there be a crater or something?"

"There was once." He scanned the mountaintop. "This is what's called a shield type volcano. It's like the ones in Hawaii. Basically, through the last ten million years or so, a caldera, more of a depression than an actual crater, fills with—"

"Wait, hold it, stop right there, professor." She thrust out her hand. "I don't want a geology lesson. Just the basics. Like, oh, say, is it going to explode?"

"Erupt."

"Whatever. Is it going to blow?"

"I don't think so," he said thoughtfully. "But it's not technically extinct either."

"What?" Her voice squeaked. "Define *technically*."

"Hey, I'm a computer nerd, not a geologist. Relax, Trish. It's definitely dormant."

"How do you know?"

"Well . . ." He considered his answer carefully. "The recorded history of Paradise Bay dates back about four hundred years, and there's no mention of an eruption."

"Then it's overdue, isn't it?" she said darkly.

"Give me a break, Taylor. For one thing, there's been periodic geologic testing here for the last century with no sign of volcanic activity." He laughed. "You're not seriously worried about this, are you?"

"Of course not." Her voice dripped with sarcasm. "I love the idea of standing on top of a volcano that's not technically extinct almost as much as I love the idea of spending millions of dollars to build an exclusive resort at the foot of a not technically extinct volcano to attract very rich people who can then be erupted upon."

"I don't think you can be erupted upon."

"No?" She bit her lip, but humor simmered in her sea-blue eyes. "Tell that to Pompeii."

He studied her for a minute. He never would have guessed that she was the type of woman who could laugh at herself. She wasn't anything like he'd thought she was when they'd first met.

"Come here." He held out his hand.

She narrowed her eyes in halfhearted suspicion. "Why?"

"Come on, trust me. Where's your spirit of adventure?"

She sighed, but put her hand in his. "I don't have one."

"You said you didn't have an imagination either, but you were wrong."

"Okay." She smiled at him. "I did hike up a mountain. I suppose that's pretty adventurous."

"Oh, yeah. Took a lot of courage facing down those wild lizards and all." He grinned, picked up the backpack and led her toward an outcropping on the eastern rim.

"Not to mention the nonextinct volcano."

"That too." He climbed up a few feet to the top of the rocks and a natural ledge and pulled her up behind him. "Have a seat." He waved at the island below them. "What do you think?"

What could she think? From here they could see the tops of the lush jungle foliage, a blanket of deep green falling away to the sea before them. A stream flowed toward the ocean to disappear over the edge of the cliffs and sparkled like a silver thread woven into a tapestry of nature. Beyond the cliffs lay the site for the inn and the dark, shining sands of the beach. From this vantage point the vista looked more like another of Mo's miniatures than reality. And farther on, the sea blended into the sky in a seamless mating of primeval elements.

"Pretty damned impressive," she said softly.

"Isn't it?"

"How far do you think we can see?"

"Not far." He smiled. "Probably just forever."

"I like your island, Kendall."

"I'm glad, Taylor." He stared into her eyes and decided he was wrong. They were more like the sky than the sea. Or maybe they were a bit of both. Their gazes held for a long moment. The electricity that had arced between them weeks ago returned with a jolt as strong as a punch in his gut. He realized he still held her hand, and noticed how well it fit in his. And how right it was to sit here, on top of the world, with her hand in his.

"Jack, I—"

"Trish, I—"

Abruptly, the fragile spell between them shattered. She pulled her hand from his.

"So," she said a little too brightly, looking

almost as uncomfortable as he was, "what's in the backpack?"

"Nothing much." He hauled it onto his lap and flipped open the flap, grateful to have something to do. Damn. He felt like he was sixteen again and on his first date. "I asked Maude to throw together drinks and something to munch on."

"I don't suppose you have one of your precious beers in there?" The teasing note in her voice eased the tension between them and he relaxed.

"Not a chance. They're rationed until the supply boat gets here. Besides, you've had more than your fair share," he reminded her.

"Didn't anyone ever warn you about the hazards of gambling?"

"I gotta take my risks where I can find them these days." He pulled out two bottles of water and handed her one.

"Thanks." She opened the bottle and drew a long swallow. "Actually, water tastes pretty good."

"It's not beer"—he took a drink—"but it's not bad."

"I've never been much for beer, but knowing I can't have it . . ." She shrugged and settled back against the rocks, crossing her legs in front of her.

"Anything you can't have is always more attractive than anything you can."

She stared at him for a moment and looked like she was trying to reach a decision. "If I ask you something, will you tell me the truth? Even if it'll piss me off?"

His heart thudded. Did she know about his father? Her stepfather? He wasn't ready for this. She wasn't ready for this. Oh, sure, she liked him, but a few weeks of friendship was not nearly enough to overcome years of loathing. She'd be furious. She might even feel betrayed by his failure to mention that one, tiny, practically insignificant detail. He'd tried to tell her a dozen different times, but the moment was never quite right. With every passing day, it was harder to bring up, and he grew more and more reluctant to face the consequences. Procrastination may be the coward's way of dealing with an unpleasant problem, but right now it worked for him.

He forced an offhanded reply. "Sure. Go for it."

"Okay. The truth now." She leaned toward him as if she were about to confide the secret of life. "There really isn't a supply boat, is there?"

Shock shot through him, followed by the giddy sense of reprieve and relief. He started to laugh and didn't stop until tears came to his eyes.

"I was right, wasn't I," she said smugly and leaned back against the rocks. "I'll bet there isn't a jeep on the other side of the island either."

"Actually," he sniffed and wiped his eyes with the back of his hand. "There is a boat. You just can't depend on it. Sometimes it's three weeks between visits, sometimes three months. Islanders always have enough basics stocked to last at least six months and if push comes to shove, the island can be self-sufficient."

"Oh." Her expression fell.

"There really is a jeep too, an old army-surplus type. I'm not sure how it got here, but it's on the other side of the island and always will be. It doesn't run." He chuckled, then took a swig of water. "Sorry to disappoint you."

"I just thought I had it all figured out." She gazed out over the island at the horizon and beyond. "You know. All part of my stepfather's master plan to screw up my wedding. He sends me here on a bogus assignment—"

"That turns out to be legitimate."

"Yeah, go figure. It sounded so off-the-wall in the beginning." She sighed. "Anyway, here I am. No way to escape. Literally, with just the clothes on my back. Stranded on a not-so-deserted island—"

He laughed again.

She smiled but kept her gaze fixed straight ahead. "With minimal communication with the civilized world. What better place to spend a great deal of time thinking about the rest of my life?"

"Did it work?" he asked, trying to pretend the answer didn't matter. But abruptly he realized it did matter. Maybe more than anything had ever mattered to him before.

"Honestly?"

He nodded.

"We've been so busy working, I haven't had time to think about my future or the wedding or Elliott." Her brow furrowed and he was certain she was thinking about it now.

But what? And did he really want to know?

"I know you don't like Elliott." She slanted a quick look at him. "But he's a nice guy. He's hardworking and ambitious, solid and secure and—"

"Safe," Jack said.

"Yep. I told you I had no spirit of adventure." She smiled in an apologetic way. "I like safe. And secure. It's what I want. What I've always wanted. We'll have a nice life together."

"Will you?"

"Absolutely." She nodded a little too vigorously. Was she trying to convince him or herself?

"So . . ." He held his breath. "Do you love him?"

"Sure. Of course." She downed the last of her water and set the bottle between them. "What's not to love? We've known each other forever. We have everything in common. We have the same taste. We want the same things. We know each other's likes and dislikes—"

"Favorite foods. Favorite songs. Favorite colors," he murmured.

"What's wrong with that?" She snapped her gaze to his. "You should know a lot about the person you're going to marry. You should be comfortable with each other. That's the best way to avoid problems—"

He snorted. "That's the best way to avoid life."

"It is not! How can you say that?"

"Because it's true. Think about it, Taylor. You're talking about spending the rest of your life with someone you already know like the back of your hand." He shook his head. "I can't imagine anything more boring. What's the point, anyway?"

"Not that you're any kind of marriage expert." Her brows pulled together and anger flushed her face. "But the point is going into marriage with your head on straight. Knowing what to expect. No surprises. No—"

"No excitement. No adventure. No fun."

"Yeah, okay, I admit it." She scrambled to her feet. "I'm not looking for fun or adventure or excitement. It doesn't have any place in my life or in my marriage."

"You don't think so?" He threw her bottle and his in the backpack and climbed down off their rocky perch. Anger, intense, unreasonable and totally out of proportion, surged through him. What difference did it make to him what she did with the rest of her life? Why did he care who she married or why?

The answer hit him like a bolt from above. Damn it all, he did care. He cared more than he ever thought possible. The idea of her going through with this marriage to Elliott or anyone else ripped at his soul.

He swiveled toward her. She stood on the ledge slightly above him. "What about passion, Trish? Is there room for passion in this comfortable marriage of yours?"

"Passion? What do you mean *passion?* Do you mean sex?" Fire flared in her eyes. He reached up to help her down and she slapped his hand away. "I can do it myself, thank you."

"Sorry. For a moment I forgot what an athlete you are."

She glared at him over her shoulder and started back down the rocks. "Not that it's any of your business, Kendall, but we have sex. Nice sex. No, great sex. Really, really great sex."

"Yeah, right." He glared back. "I'd bet your trust fund that you and your fiancé have never had that 'really, really great sex' anyplace other than a safe, secure, comfortable bed." She half-fell, half-slid, and he caught her in his arms and set her on her feet.

"Let me go." She ground out the words through clenched teeth.

"No!" He shook her. "Look at me."

"What?" Her gaze locked with his.

"I wasn't talking about sex." How could he get through to her? "I was talking about feelings. Emotions. The passion within you."

"I don't—"

"Passion, Trish, passion." His eyes searched hers. "Don't you get it? It has nothing to do with sex or lust or anything physical. It's emotion, feelings, plain and simple. The way your heart beats faster when she enters a room. Or the way her smile warms something deep inside you and her laugh makes you melt. It's the way you can't resist making her angry because she argues with her whole heart and soul. It's the reason you've memorized the stubborn tilt of her chin or the wonderful feeling you get when she's wearing your shirt. . . ." Her eyes widened with what? Maybe, just maybe, acknowledgment? He pulled her closer. "Or the way she makes you feel like you were a kid again about to get his first kiss."

"Are you going to kiss me?" she asked, her voice catching.

"Yeah."

"Why?"

"Because I've wanted to for a long time. Because I need to." He stared into her sea-sky eyes and wondered how she, of all people, could have come kicking and screaming into his world to lay claim to his life. "Because you want me to."

"Because I need you to," she whispered.

She raised her lips to meet his and her mouth brushed against his tentatively, as if her kiss was as stubborn as the rest of her. As if she were afraid to surrender to what they both wanted. What they both needed. Afraid to admit the inevitability of this moment. Afraid of the adventure and excitement he knew they'd find with each other. As if she was as scared as he was.

He slanted his mouth harder over hers. She wrapped her arms around his neck and responded with an ardent eagerness that stole his breath. And maybe his heart. Without warning, a longing so fierce it fired his blood swept through him, and he wanted nothing in the world but this woman in his arms forever.

He'd suspected it all along: She fit in his embrace as though they had been made for each other and only each other.

And he realized with a clarity born of the intensity of desire that swelled in his body and his soul:

When it came to the heart, wasn't passion just another word for love?

Chapter Ten

The temperate climate and dramatic tropical setting weaves a spell over even the most resistant visitor. Those committed to the active pursuit of a good time as well as dedicated workaholics will find themselves affected by the inherent enjoyment of life and appreciation of nature that permeates the atmosphere of Paradise Bay.

Few leave the island unchanged.

"If you'd take it just a bit easier, I could catch up with you," Trish called and waited for a response she didn't expect. She heaved a frustrated sigh and trudged after Jack.

Of course he didn't answer. He probably didn't even hear her. They were already halfway down the mountain, or volcano, or pile of dirt for all she cared, and Jack had hardly said two words to her. He wasn't unpleasant or nasty or anything like that; he was just withdrawn. Quiet. Maybe even brooding. And she didn't like it one bit.

When was he going to say something? Anything? Trish couldn't take much more of this silence. Didn't they have a lot to say to each other? Things they needed to discuss? Decisions to make? Damn right they did.

On the other hand, she should probably be grateful. She certainly had plenty to think about, most of which she'd conveniently avoided up to this point. This was as good a time as any to get to it.

Too bad the only thoughts in her head at the moment were centered on the man striding down the path about ten feet in front of her. The man who had totally and completely changed her life, and right now didn't seem to know she existed. What had happened to him?

What had happened to her?

In one glorious moment, when his lips had met hers, everything she'd thought she wanted in life was suddenly insignificant. All desire for safety and security and comfort disappeared and she knew she needed more than that from the man she'd spend the rest of her life with. It might have worked out well for her mother and Russ, but it wasn't right for her. Not anymore.

It was a revelation as blinding as the current of fire and light that flashed through her at his kiss. If you could call something so earth-shattering simply a kiss.

She stared at his broad shoulders up ahead. No one had ever made her feel like this. Oh, sure, she'd been kissed before, and not just by Elliott. She'd never been easy, but she was no innocent virgin either. And never, ever before had a single kiss curled her toes and boiled her blood and made her heart sing.

Made her heart sing?

She bit back a groan. What a stupid, sentimental idea. *Made her heart sing.* How crazy was that? Still . . . her step slowed. She stared at his retreating figure. As silly as it sounded, that really did describe her feelings. Giddy and exuberant and amazingly happy. She shook her head in disbelief. Who would have thought that Patricia Taylor would ever describe herself as giddy?

Did Jack feel even the tiniest bit giddy? He obviously wasn't interested in sharing his thoughts on the subject. Maybe he'd decided kissing her was a horrible mistake. Maybe he was even now trying to figure out how to escape gracefully from any further involvement. Maybe he just didn't like it.

No. That was one thing she didn't need to worry about. His body had been pressed so closely to hers that you couldn't slide a piece of paper between them. There was no way she could ignore the obvious physical evidence that he'd liked it, all right. He liked it a lot. As much as she did, if not more.

Maybe he was the kind of guy who wanted what he couldn't have and once he had it didn't want it after all.

Something you can't have is always more attractive.

Her spirits dropped a notch. Okay, he had admitted as much, but that didn't mean anything. He'd been talking about beer, after all.

He pulled farther ahead, and at the moment she had no desire to catch up. When it came right down to it, she really didn't know much about Jack Kendall. Not about his background or his life. He was related to Russ's first wife and he'd originally come to the island after some kind of trauma and had apparently followed in his cousin's footsteps for a while, but that was it. What if he really *was* a serial killer or an international jewel thief or a spy on the run? No, realistically, no matter what else he was, he was a relative, and her stepfather probably wouldn't harbor a criminal. Well, not a dangerous criminal anyway.

What if he was married?

She pushed the unpleasant thought away and wondered why she preferred the option of jewel thief. At least criminals could be reformed. And she assumed jewel thieves rarely had wives. It was possible he was married but highly unlikely. Let's face it: No woman in her right mind would let Jack Kendall out of her sight for four days, let alone four years.

He rounded a curve and she lost sight of him. No problem.

The trek down wasn't nearly as tough as the hike up. Maybe she was developing a few athletic skills after all. Besides, now that she'd finally started, she'd just as soon finish working everything out in her head while she had time to herself.

First of all, she'd have to dump Elliott. Gently, of course. But she certainly couldn't marry him now. It wouldn't be fair. Not to him and definitely not to her. Her feelings for him hadn't changed: She still loved him the same as she always had. A nice, comfortable, safe kind of love. But it was the wrong kind of love and it simply wasn't enough anymore. Now that she knew what was possible, she absolutely refused to settle for anything less.

Did she love Jack?

Maybe. Probably. She really didn't know but wanted to find out. That was number two on her list. But she'd need Jack's cooperation to do so.

Determination surged through her. She raised her chin and picked up her pace. The damn man had done it to her again. Once more he was in control. Kissing her socks off and then acting like Heathcliff stalking across the moors. Well, enough was enough. She needed to find out if she was in love with him. And if he was in love with her.

What if he was?
What if she was?

Trish hadn't the vaguest idea where they'd go from there. The whole focus of her life and future had changed radically in the course of a few short minutes and one fantastic kiss.

If this was love, it was definitely not the sex-only-in-the-bedroom kind. She grinned to herself. Now there was a benefit. When she thought about it, it really wasn't all that bad being off balance half the time. Life had never been quite as interesting before she met Jack. Maybe she needed a man who would keep her on her toes. Someone she couldn't control. Maybe she needed a few surprises in her life. And adventure and excitement. And maybe the only place to find any of that, or all of it, was in Jack's arms.

She rounded the bend and nearly tripped over him.

"About time you showed up. I was starting to think I'd have to go back and track you down." Jack lounged against a palm tree, his arms folded across his chest. A smile touched his lips but didn't reflect in his eyes.

"I was fighting off wild lizards." She frowned and studied him. "So what's going on, Kendall? I never figured you for the silent, sensitive type."

"I was just trying to work out something that's been bothering me." His jaw was set, as if he was challenging her to call him a liar. "You know, trying to get straight some of the specifics Mo mentioned this morning about the—"

"Don't give me that crap," she said, meeting his challenge head-on. His eyes narrowed. "If you're trying to figure something out, you and I both know it has nothing whatsoever to do with the inn and everything to do with what happened on top of your volcano."

"You think so?" He lifted a brow.

"I do." Fear, unexpected and swift, twisted in her stomach. If she was smart, she'd shut up right now and wait and see what happened next. She squared her shoulders and decided to be stupid. "I think that . . . that kiss affected you as much as it did me."

"Oh?" The corners of his mouth twitched.

"You think this is funny?"

"Not at all. I think it's extremely serious." The amused twinkle in his eyes belied his words. "How did it affect you?"

"It doesn't really matter how." Good God, she could never tell him that he made her heart sing! He'd laugh his ass off. And then she really would have to kill him. "It just matters that it did."

He reached out and pulled her into his arms. "And how do you think it affected me?"

"I don't know." She gazed into his eyes. They were brimming with amusement and—damn it—smoldering again. Her resolve faded. "But I know how to find out."

"Oh, yeah? How?"

She drew a deep breath, grabbed fistfuls of his shirt and pulled his head to hers until their lips touched. "Kiss me again."

He brushed his lips against hers.

She sighed. "You call that a kiss?"

"I can do better," he said, his mouth against hers.

"Prove it."

"I will." He hesitated. "Trish, we have to talk."

"Okay." She nibbled at his bottom lip and he gasped. "Now?"

"No. Have dinner with me tonight."

"I have dinner with you every night."

"Tonight it will be different."

"Then I'll be there." She pulled him closer. "Now, are you going to prove it or what?"

He did.

She couldn't wait until dinner.

"Hi, Trish. Glad you could make it. I'm fairly certain I'm in love with you and oh, by the way, my father is your stepfather. I'm the crown prince. You know, the guy you hate."

Jack groaned and rolled his gaze toward the sky. No, that was way too flip. He downed the rest of the wine in his glass, checked his watch one more time and paced across the stone pathways in the garden.

She'd be here any minute. How in the hell was he going to say this? Any of it? He heaved a deep sigh, steeled his resolve and tried again.

"Trish, my love, I've never felt this way about anyone."

That wasn't bad. It was straightforward and sincere and the truth. He raked his fingers through his hair. But in love? With the flying monkey? Why hadn't he seen it coming? He should have. The signs were all there. He'd known he liked her, maybe even cared about her, but it wasn't until he'd kissed her and she'd kissed him back that he realized the truth: He was head-over-heels in love with the flying monkey.

He still wasn't sure how he'd made it down the mountain. He probably should have been treated for shock. Hospitalized until he came to his senses. He wanted her. He needed her. He *loved* her.

And all along he'd been deceiving her.

The realization of what he'd found and how easy he could lose it kept him struggling for answers on the return hike. Telling her that he loved her was going to be hard enough. What if she didn't share his feelings? But revealing his true identity and their vague familial relationship, and why he hadn't mentioned it before, was like flirting with an active volcano.

Still, there was always the chance she'd understand.

Yeah. Right.

He strode to the gazebo, stepped onto its deck and filled his glass from the wine bottle on the perfectly arranged table. Maude had set all this up for him and then left, taking Mo with her and promising that neither of them would return until late morning tomorrow. But she sure hadn't been very gracious about it, muttering dark warnings about blond Amazons and lies by omission.

What if he told Trish about his father first, then hit her with his undying devotion? That might work.

"Trish, I'm Russ's son from his first marriage. You know, the run-around-the-world-squandering-dad's-money-worthless-shiftless-black-sheep-playboy son. But I've changed. And I love you more than I ever imagined a man could love a woman."

Pretty mushy, but not bad. He could tone down the shiftless, worthless part, but otherwise it was not bad at all. In his experience, women lapped up stuff like that. Especially if a man meant it. And God help him, he meant every sentimental word. If she cared for him even the tiniest bit, he might be able to pull this off.

If not, he exhaled slowly, maybe at least she'd let him choose the method of his demise.

"What have you done to yourself now?" Trish stepped off the veranda and walked toward the gazebo, hoping the butterflies careening around inside her stomach would settle down.

Jack smiled and picked up a goblet off a table positioned in the center of the Victorian structure. The table setting was beautiful, like something out of a magazine. There was crystal and silver, white lace and china, candles and magic.

Jack looked as if he had just stepped off of the

same magazine page. He poured a glass of wine and held it out to her.

"Where did you manage to come up with a tux?" She accepted the goblet and was surprised by the steadiness of her hand.

"You'd be amazed at what you can find in this old place." His gaze traveled over her slowly and appreciation showed in his dark eyes. "You don't look half bad yourself." He glanced at her bare feet. "Nice touch."

"Thanks. Maude managed to dig up the dress, but the only option for shoes were the grubby tennies I've been wearing since I got here." She took a tentative sip of the wine. It was red and heavy and very good. She drank again, then glanced down at the dress, a strapless ruby silk creation. It did look pretty damn good. As long as it stayed up. "I don't recall what Maude called it, but basically it's a long strip of fabric wrapped around you."

"Lucky fabric," he murmured and raised his glass in a salute.

She lifted hers. "To?"

"Us," he said firmly and drank.

"To us," she repeated, warmed by more than the wine. She finished the last swallow and held out her glass for a refill.

"Thanks." She smiled and sipped.

"Anytime." He smiled and drank.

Silence dropped like a rock. Trish took another long drink. She had to say something. Anything. There were an endless number of things they needed to talk about. How she felt about him. How he felt about her. At the very least, she had to see how he'd react to her decision not to marry Elliott. Where could she begin?

"So," she said, disgusted at her own perky tone. "It feels like the heat wave is finally over."

"Yeah." He nodded. "It's much cooler."

Oh, that went well. What was she supposed to say now? Had there ever been a more awkward moment in the history of the world? They'd never been without words before. Even when they were sniping at each other, there wasn't this strain, this tension. If she really was in love, it sucked.

"More wine?" he asked in a perfect-host voice.

"Please." No one was a more perfect guest than she. "I figured you'd break open the last of the beer for tonight. Where did you get the wine?"

He refilled her glass and handed it back. "The wine cellar."

"There's a wine cellar? Why didn't you tell me?"

"You didn't ask."

"Well, you still could have mentioned it. I wouldn't have been so eager for your beer if I'd have known about the wine." This was good. This was breaking the ice. She smiled teasingly. "What else haven't you told me?"

"What else?" An uneasy look flashed across his face.

"Jack?" Her breath caught. "You're not married or anything, are you?"

"Married?" His forehead furrowed thoughtfully. "No, no I don't think so."

"Jack!"

"Okay, I'm sure." He shook his head. "Not married now. Never have been. You?"

"No."

"But you're going to be."

"Well . . ." Now was the time to tell him. She could just blurt it right out. But what if he didn't care? Worse—what if he was disappointed? She turned away from him and wandered a few steps down a path, stopping by a large hibiscus. "About that . . ."

"What about that?"

"You remember what you said about excitement and adventure in a marriage?"

"Yeah?" His footsteps sounded behind her.

"I've decided you were right." She held her breath.

"Was I?" His voice was close.

She nodded. "I'm not going to marry Elliott."

"Good."

"Good?" She swiveled to face him. "Why?"

His gaze searched her face for a long moment, as if he was trying to reach a decision.

"Jack! What's good about it? Why do you care?"

"Damn it all, Trish, because, well, I think I love you." He heaved a sigh of surrender.

"You think you love me," she said slowly.

"No, I don't think I love you." A decisive look passed over his face. "I'm sure of it. Positive. I definitely love you."

"Really?" She tried not to smile, but he looked so sincere. Besides, her heart was singing again. "I'm not positive, but I think I might possibly love you too."

"Possibly?"

"Don't take it so personally."

"It is personal." He huffed. "I'm positive. Why aren't you positive?"

"I wish I knew," she said softly and sipped her wine.

"You think about me all the time, don't you?"

"You are so egotistical."

"Trish?"

"Okay, okay." She laughed. "I think about you all the time."

"I thought so. Do you miss me when I'm not around?"

"You're always around." He raised a brow. "Yes, I miss you."

"Now we're getting somewhere." He took her glass, moved to the gazebo and placed their goblets on the step.

"Hey, give that back!"

"I need your hands free."

She clasped her hands behind her back. "Why?"

"Trish, we're trying to determine something here." He gave her a scolding look. "But if you're not going to cooperate . . ."

"I'm cooperating." She whipped her hands out in front of her. "What now?"

"Now." He stepped to her, placed her arms around his neck and slipped his around her waist.

"This is love?" she said skeptically.

He flashed her a wicked grin. "No, but it's very nice."

She shook her head. "You are really something."

"So are you." His expression grew serious. "Okay, here's the real test. Do you want to be with me? Every minute of every day? See me the first thing in the morning and the last thing at night? Can you envision your life, your future, tomorrow without me?"

"Whoa, Kendall." She tried to lighten the mood. "That's a lot—"

"I mean it, Trish." He looked into her eyes, his gaze trapping hers. "That's how I feel about you. And I think—no, I'm positive that's love." He paused, and apprehension flickered in his eyes. "What about you?"

"Me?" She swallowed hard, knowing she couldn't settle for safe and secure was one thing; admitting she was in love with this man was something else altogether. As stupid as throwing herself into a volcano. Still, the way down would be wonderful. "Yes, damn it, that's exactly how I feel. I love you too."

"You're positive?"

"I'm positive."

"Good." He pressed his lips to hers, and any lingering doubt washed away in a wave of sweet longing for more. If she had socks on, they'd be knocked off by now. If this wasn't love, she didn't know what was.

She pulled away to catch her breath and his mouth brushed the side of her neck and trailed kisses to the curve of her shoulder. Her eyes closed and a sigh came from somewhere deep inside.

"Trish," he whispered against her skin, "we have to talk."

"Didn't we just do that?" She tilted her head to give him better access to . . . anything he wanted.

"There are still things . . ." His hands slipped down the slick silk of her dress past the small of her back and lower.

"Yeah . . ." She ran her hands over the front of his shirt. The muscles of his chest tightened beneath her touch. ". . . things."

"I have to . . ."

She pulled his tie free and popped the studs at his collar and down his shirt, lower and lower, one by one, until his shirt gaped open.

". . . tell you . . ."

"Tell me." She pressed her lips to the hollow of his throat and he shuddered and pulled her tight against him. "What?"

"Later." It was more a groan than a word. He pulled her face to his and his lips crushed hers with a determination that sapped her will, weakened her legs and called to hidden, secret places in her body and her soul. She wrapped her arms around him, her fingers raking through the hair at the back of his neck.

His one hand splayed across her back, the other wandered in an agonizingly slow movement up the side of her hip to her waist and higher, until his thumb grazed the underside of her breast. She shivered and clutched at his chest, her mouth opening to his, welcoming, wanting. He brushed his thumb over her nipple, already hardened and sensitive through the thin fabric.

She drew in a deep breath and held it, every fiber of her existence focused on his touch. He pushed the cool silk down and a breeze played over her naked breast. He bent his head and his tongue circled her nipple, teasing until she thought she'd pass out from anticipation. He took her breast in his mouth and her hands tightened around fistfuls of his hair. Pleasure shot through her. He pushed aside the fabric covering her other breast and moved to take it with a greed she recognized. A greed she shared.

She wanted him. *Naked. Hot.* "Oh God, Jack." She tried to push off his jacket. *Now.*

"Trish."

His mouth returned to cover hers, his tongue hard and demanding, his urgecy matching her own. He peeled off the jacket and tossed it aside. She tugged his open shirt from his pants and pulled it down his arms, then leaned forward to

212

nip at his bare shoulder. His skin, still warm from the sun, tasted lightly of salt. And passion.

Impatiently, he tore his shirt free and let it drop. His hands slipped to her back to pull her close to him. Her bare breasts flattened against the solid planes of his chest and she reveled in the feel of rough hair on tender flesh.

His hands caressed her skin, slipping to the small of her back and easing her dress down over her hips. The silk slid to the stone walkway, a puddle of red around her feet, and she stood naked in his arms. He cupped her buttocks and she ground her hips against the hard evidence of his erection beneath the smooth texture of his pants. He groaned. The low, primitive sound vibrated through his body into hers.

His hands covered her breasts and he shifted his attention to the pulse point at the base of her throat. His mouth, his teeth, his tongue tasted and teased and wandered lower in an expanding exploration down, between her breasts and lower still to her navel. He sank to his knees before her. She couldn't breathe. Couldn't move. Every muscle tensed, every nerve quivered, every atom of her being hungered for his touch.

His hands skimmed down her sides, her hips, the outsides of her legs. Then around and up, slowly, to her inner thighs. His lips caressed her stomach lightly, as if he sensed her spiraling desire, her need for more. She gripped his shoulders until her knuckles whitened. And still she waited. The setting sun warmed the tan of his

213

skin to a golden glow and gilded his dark hair. Never had she known anything so erotic, so glorious. She stood naked before a half-clothed man who basked in the final moments of the day and looked for all the world like a Greek god kneeling before the mere mortal he would have as his own.

His fingers slid upward between her legs and he opened her to him. She dropped her head back and arched her back. A whimper sounded deep in her throat. She throbbed with a sweet, awful ache. He bent forward and flicked his tongue over her hot flesh. Pleasure, intense and exquisite, shot through her. A sharp gasp escaped her lips and her body jerked forward, doubling her over his back. At once Jack stood, threw her over his shoulder and strode toward the house.

"What are you doing?" She could barely choke out the words. "Where are we going?"

"Bedroom," he muttered in a hoarse voice.

"No!"

"No?" He stopped. "What do you mean, *no?* You don't want—"

"Oh, yes, I want." She groaned with frustrated desire. "I want a lot."

"Great." He started toward the house.

"No!"

"Trish." He stopped again. "Don't confuse me. I hate being confused at a moment like this."

"We can't have bedroom sex, Jack." A tinge of panic sounded in her voice. "We just can't!"

"Bedro—okay. Sorry. I get it." He paused for a moment. "Let me think."

"In the meantime"—she raked her teeth across his back—"the blood is starting to rush to my head."

"Sorry." With a quick move, he flipped her off his shoulder and into his arms. "Better?"

"Much." She slid her arms around his neck and nibbled on the lobe of his ear. "I like being naked in your arms."

"Me too." His gaze scanned the grounds. "There's no lawn out here, just these damn gardens." He sighed in frustration. "Wait. I know—the gazebo." He stepped toward it.

"No room with the table." She traced a line down his chest and circled his nipple. He shuddered. "We really, really need to find someplace." She leaned forward and replaced her finger with her tongue. "Soon."

"We do as long as you keep doing that."

"What about the veranda?" she said against his chest.

"There's really nothing to . . . I've got it." Once again he started toward the house. "Close your eyes."

"Why?"

"I want to surprise you."

She squeezed her eyes shut. He climbed the porch stairs, and she heard the door open and close. The feel of the air against her nude body changed from the cool breeze of the garden to

215

the warm stillness of the house. She sensed his start up the main stairs.

"Am I getting too heavy for you?"

"Getting?" She could hear the laughter in his voice.

"Watch it, Kendall."

He climbed to the second floor and continued to the third. She hadn't been up here before. He pushed open a door and fumbled with something, then dropped her lightly onto a soft, comfortable surface that conformed to her body and propped up her back and head. A chaise, maybe? "Jack, I don't—"

"It's not a bedroom." There was a rattle and a thunk. "Keep 'em closed," he growled.

The noises continued, moving in a semicircle around her. Then she heard the unmistakable sound of a zipper opening and her blood quickened.

He sat down next to her. His tongue grazed the tip of one nipple, then the next, and she sucked in a hard breath.

"You can look now."

She opened her eyes. The world around her glowed a deep, dusky pink with the final moments of sunset. Shutters framing long, wide windows were folded back. There was no glass, no screens, and aside from a high, pointed ceiling and the wall behind her, they could have been outside. "It's the room in the tower, isn't it?"

"Yep." He stared into her eyes. "Do you like it?"

"It's . . ." She brushed his lips with hers. "Perfect."

"I've always wanted to make love here." He nuzzled her ear. "High above the island and the rest of the world. With the shutters open to the sea and the sunset."

"Then go for it, Kendall," she whispered.

"You're the lord and master." His hand drifted across her breast and over the flat of her stomach to the curls between her legs. "What can a loyal minion do but obey?"

"Works for me," she murmured and lost herself to the sheer pleasure of his touch.

He stretched out beside her, his naked flesh next to hers, his need matching her own. His hands caressed and teased and taunted until every part of her strained toward him and tension curled tight within her. She demanded his touch and demanded to touch him. With lips and teeth and tongue, she discovered his taste, his scent, his heat. She wanted to sob with the delicious yearning that swept away all lucid thought until she knew nothing but the feel of his flesh on hers. And still she needed more.

Until finally his legs straddled hers and she arched up in welcome. He entered her with a sure, easy motion, and her breath caught. He was hard and hot, and sensation acute and exquisite coursed through her. He moved within her and she matched her actions to his. She joined him in a rhythm as natural as the sea, as right as the stars.

She urged him faster and he drove her higher until they melded body and soul and the world consisted only of pleasure and passion and need. Her heart throbbed against his, with his. The blood in his veins pulsed against her, through her. And when she knew she couldn't survive the unbearable joy that surged like molten lava in her blood and didn't care, her body erupted with a force of which she'd never dared dream. Her nails dug into his back and she clung to him to keep from careening over the edge of the world. Or to drag him with her. His breath came short and fast and he shuddered once and again. And for a second or a lifetime she marveled at the miracle of touching this man's life with her own.

He lay on top of her for a long moment, then rolled them both to their sides. She stared into his eyes, which even in the fading light smoldered, now with satisfaction and contentment and . . . love.

He pressed a light kiss on her forehead. "What are you thinking about?"

"I'm thinking that you were right." She brushed her lips across his. "There's a lot to be said for surprises and adventure."

Chapter Eleven

The lack of industry and minimal use of motorized vehicles combine with trade winds to provide a virtually pollution-free environment and ideal climatic conditions for relaxation. Visitors to the island rarely report anything but enjoying an excellent night's sleep.

Newcomers to Paradise Bay almost invariably awaken refreshed and invigorated.

What a wonderful morning. No. Trish grinned. A *magnificent* morning. Exactly as the travel guide promised. Better. Maybe it was even the best morning in the history of the world. She pulled the sheet tighter around her, tucked the end in and started down the main stairs. First, she'd find her dress in the garden, then she'd track down Jack. It was still fairly early, but he wasn't beside her when she'd awoken in whatever bedroom it was they'd ended up in. In an effort to dispel the stigma of bedroom sex, they'd felt compelled to try out as many different bedrooms as possible.

She reached the bottom step and the library door opened. Jack stepped into the hall and gazed up at her.

Her knees weakened at the sight of him. "Good morning."

"Hi." A smile lifted the corner of his lips.

She crossed to him and stepped straight into his arms, pulling his head down to meet his lips with hers. His touch was tentative at first; then he drew her tighter against him, his mouth demanding and hard. Her sheet slipped lower. Desire swept through her and she wondered wickedly how foyer sex would be. Or library sex. There was still a lot of magnificent morning left and maybe a few more stigmas to dispel, and with only a sheet between them . . .

She drew back and gazed into his eyes, trying to catch her breath. "Very nice, but I have an even better way to start the day."

"Do you?"

"Um-hum." She nibbled on the lobe of his ear, noticing out of the corner of her eye a set of beautifully matched teal-colored luggage stacked inside the entry to the parlor across the hall. She had a set exactly like it. Of course, she'd probably never see her luggage again. It was on that damn boat somewhere in the South Pacific. Actually, there was a lot to be said for not having clothes available. "Do you want me to show you, or can you figure it out for yourself?"

"Oh, I have a pretty good idea." He drew a deep breath and gently pushed her away. "But first—"

"First, Jack?" Surprise widened her eyes as realization dawned on her. "That's my luggage, isn't it? Why didn't you tell me?"

"I didn't have the chance."

"Yes!" She whooped and punched the air with her fist, grabbing her sheet just as it started to slip. She hobbled into the parlor to the first suitcase and ran her hand lovingly over its suede finish, resisting the urge to open it right there. Oh, what the hell.

"Look, Jack, Christmas!" She knelt down, adjusted the combination on the lock, and threw open the lid. "No. Better than Christmas. These are all things I *want*." She picked up a silk tank top and hugged it to her chest. "My clothes! Stuff that actually fits me. I really thought I'd never see any of this again."

She tossed the shirt on the folded garments and pawed through the bag. "And shoes, Jack, shoes!" She grabbed one of her barely scuffed designer athletic shoes and held it up triumphantly. "Have you ever seen anything so wonderful?"

She looked up. Jack leaned against the doorway of the parlor, watching her. "It's great."

"You could be a little more enthusiastic." She dropped the shoe back in the suitcase, snapped the lid closed and scrambled to her feet. "Can you help me bring these upstairs? I can't wait to—"

"Trish." His expression was guarded. "We have to talk."

Her heart stopped. Oh, God, had he changed his mind about loving her? Wanting her? Worse, had he simply come to his senses? "What is it? What's the matter?"

"I've been trying to tell you—"

"No, wait." She clapped her hands over her ears. "I've never been happier in my entire life than I was a split second ago. First you and everything we did last night and did again this morning, and I was kind of hoping we would do again maybe now. Second, I have my clothes back. So if you're going to tell me something that will burst my bubble, like how you've realized you don't love me after all, I don't want to hear it. Not right now anyway."

He pried her hands away from her ears. His gaze locked onto hers. Sincerity shone in his eyes and sounded in his words. "I love you, Trish. Don't doubt that for a second. No matter what happens."

"What do you mean, 'no matter what happens'? What could happen?" Her voice rose. Fear clutched at her stomach. At once everything became clear to her. She hadn't taken the possibility seriously, but it made sense. It was the only answer. Whatever had sent him to this island in the first place must have been illegal after all. And the supply boat had brought more than her luggage. "It's the police, isn't it, Jack? They're here to arrest you, aren't they?" She looked around the parlor quickly.

"What?" Jack drew his brows together.

"You don't have to pretend with me. I'll stand by you. No." She threw her shoulders back. "I'll help you escape. There's got to be some way to get off the island. Maybe a fishing boat or a canoe or—"

"Trish, it's not—"

"Russ will help. I know he will. Everything will be fine. Don't underestimate the power of wealth. All we have to do—"

"Trish, listen to—"

"Well, Trish, I knew you didn't have your bags." There was the sound of a door opening and then a familiar voice sounded from the hall. Her breath caught. "But I did think someone would have found something for you to wear by now."

Her eyes widened. She thought she'd hyperventilate. No, a heart attack would be more appropriate. She'd know that droll tone anywhere. Still, she could be wrong. She stared at Jack hopefully. "Police?"

He shook his head. "Hardly."

She choked out the question she dreaded, "Elliott?"

Jack nodded. "Elliott."

Trish turned slowly and composed her shock-frozen face into a semblance of a smile. "Elliott. What a surprise."

"Good. I wanted it to be a surprise." He strode forward and enfolded her in an affectionate embrace. "I missed you, Trish." He planted a quick kiss on her forehead and whispered in her ear. "Why in the hell don't you have any clothes on?"

"Why?" Good question. She wished she had a good answer.

"Yes," he hissed.

"Well . . ." Only one answer came to mind and she didn't think this was exactly the right time to tell him how she'd spent her night and how she now wanted to spend the rest of her life. And with whom. "Well, my luggage wasn't here yet and what I was wearing needed to be washed and I couldn't find anything else and . . ."

He drew back and stared down at her. He was as tall and as blond and as attractive as ever, in spite of the suspicion in his blue eyes. He flashed a quick look at Jack then his gaze returned to hers. "Is there something going on here I should know about?"

"Yes," Jack said in a hard tone.

"No," she said quickly. "At least nothing important. We can talk later."

She hated lying to him. But, aside from everything else, he was her best friend and he deserved to hear the complete truth about their soon-to-be cancelled wedding and her feelings

Thrill to the most sensual, adventure-filled Romances on the market today...

FROM  LOVE SPELL BOOKS

As a home subscriber to the Love Spell Romance Book Club, you'll enjoy the best in today's BRAND-NEW Time Travel, Futuristic, Legendary Lovers, Perfect Heroes and other genre romance fiction. For five years, Love Spell has brought you the award-winning, high-quality authors you know and love to read. Each Love Spell romance will sweep you away to a world of high adventure...and intimate romance. Discover for yourself all the passion and excitement millions of readers thrill to each and every month.

Save $5.00 Each Time You Buy!

Every other month, the Love Spell Romance Book Club brings you four brand-new titles from Love Spell Books. EACH PACKAGE WILL SAVE YOU AT LEAST $5.00 FROM THE BOOK-STORE PRICE! And you'll never miss a new title with our convenient home delivery service.

Here's how we do it: Each package will carry a FREE 10-DAY EXAMINATION privilege. At the end of that time, if you decide to keep your books, simply pay the low invoice price of $17.96, no shipping or handling charges added. HOME DELIVERY IS ALWAYS FREE. With today's top romance novels selling for $5.99 and higher, our price SAVES YOU AT LEAST $5.00 with each shipment.

AND YOUR FIRST TWO-BOOK SHIP-MENT IS TOTALLY FREE!

IT'S A BARGAIN YOU CAN'T BEAT! A SUPER $11.48 Value!

Love Spell  A Division of Dorchester Publishing Co., Inc.

GET YOUR 2 FREE BOOKS NOW—AN $11.48 VALUE!

Mail the Free Book Certificate Today!

TWO FREE BOOKS

Free Books Certificate

YES! I want to subscribe to the Love Spell Romance Book Club. Please send me my 2 FREE BOOKS. Then every other month I'll receive the four newest Love Spell selections to Preview FREE for 10 days. If I decide to keep them, I will pay the Special Member's Only discounted price of just $4.49 each, a total of $17.96. This is a SAVINGS of at least $5.00 off the bookstore price. There are no shipping, handling, or other charges. There is no minimum number of books I must buy and I may cancel the program at any time. In any case, the 2 FREE BOOKS are mine to keep—A BIG $11.48 Value!

Offer valid only in the U.S.A.

*Name*_____

*Address*_____

*City*_____

*State*_____ *Zip*_____

*Telephone*_____

*Signature*_____

If under 18, Parent or Guardian must sign. Terms, prices and conditions subject to change. Subscription subject to acceptance. Leisure Books reserves the right to reject any order or cancel any subscription.

A $11.48 VALUE

Get Two Books Totally
FREE —
An $11.48 Value!

▼ Tear Here and Mail Your FREE Book Card Today! ▼

PLEASE RUSH
MY TWO FREE
BOOKS TO ME
RIGHT AWAY!

Love Spell Romance Book Club
P.O. Box 6613
Edison, NJ 08818-6613

AFFIX
STAMP
HERE

for Jack when they didn't have 'the other man' as a witness. She shot Jack a sharp glance and prayed he'd keep his mouth shut.

"So, did you miss me?" She gave Elliott her brightest smile and stepped back.

"Of course." Speculation lingered in his eyes but his tone was neutral. "That's why I came. It's been a month since I've seen you and with the wedding getting closer, there are things we need to discuss."

"Sure." The last thing she wanted to talk about was wedding plans.

"I managed to convince Russ to let me come and see firsthand how everything's going. He said it wasn't necessary but I wouldn't take no for an answer. Like I said, I missed you."

"When did you get here?"

"A good half an hour ago. The man who runs the supply boat would only help me with the bags as far as the road at the bottom of the drive." He frowned in annoyance. "I would have preferred to ride but he said there was only one car here and it was—"

"On the other side of the island," Trish finished.

"At any rate, I brought your luggage up to the house, renewed my acquaintance with Jack"— Elliott nodded politely at Jack—"and went back to get my bags. Not that I have nearly as many as you."

She glanced at her sheet, tucked it a bit tighter and forced a light laugh. "I certainly need them."

"So I see." Elliott's gaze flickered over her. She couldn't tell if he believed her story about her clothes being in the wash, but he apparently wasn't going to push it. At least not at the moment.

He glanced around the parlor with mild interest. "I've heard about this house, but I've never been here. It's nice, but a little old fashioned for my taste."

"I like it," Jack said flatly.

"You would." Elliott pointedly turned to Trish. "I'm hearing great things about this resort project of yours, Trish."

"Thanks." Unexpected satisfaction washed through her. "Jack is a big part of it."

"Oh, Jack used to be a big part of everything." Elliott's tone wasn't as amicable as his smile. "Something of a surprise though. I never expected him to turn out to be quite so—I don't know—responsible?"

"Elliot," Trish said, shocked. "What's this all about?"

"Sorry. Childhood rivalries die hard." Elliott's gaze met Jack's and the two men stared at each other for a tense moment.

"If they die at all," Jack said softly.

Elliott ignored him. "Russ has mentioned, over and over frankly, how pleased he is that his children are working so well together and doing such a good job.

"Elliott," Jack said in a low warning tone.

"His children?" Trish pulled her brows together. "You must have heard wrong."

"Yeah, Elliott." Jack's eyes narrowed. "You must have heard wrong."

"Once maybe, but not again and again." Elliott shook his head. "No, Russ thinks it's terrific that his stepdaughter and his son have made such a great team for the company."

"What are you talking about?" Trish stared in confusion. "His son? What son?"

"Shut up, Elliott," Jack growled.

Elliott's gaze slid from Trish to Jack and back. Realization dawned on his face. "You don't know, do you?"

"Know what?" Trish snapped. "If you have something to tell me, why don't—"

"Trish." Jack stepped to her side. "Listen to—"

"Trish," Elliott said quickly, "Kendall is Jack's mother's maiden name. He's used it for years, but his real name is Evans."

"Evans?" For a split second Elliott's words made no sense. Then the truth slammed into her like a fist in the stomach.

"I can't believe he didn't tell you." Elliott smirked. "Trish, allow me to introduce Russell Jonathan Evans the fourth."

"Russell Jonathan . . ." The color drained from her face. "Russ's son? The crown prince?"

"Trish," Jack said cautiously, "I can explain."

"Russ's son!" Her eyes were wide and she stared at him for a long stunned second. Myriad

227

emotions crossed her face. Disbelief. Hurt. Anger. The hand clutching her sheet shook slightly.

"Trish." Jack stepped toward her

"Hold it, Jack." She drew a deep breath and smiled a bit too pleasantly. "Don't worry about it." Wasn't she going to yell at him? Try to rip his throat out? She was calm. Cool. Terrifying. "It's no big deal. Forget it." He had obviously underestimated just how mad she'd be. A heavy weight settled in the pit of his stomach.

She turned to Elliott. "Has the boat left yet?"

Elliott shook his head. "I believe the captain, such as he was, mentioned something about leaving later today. Midafternoon, I think he said."

"Good." She nodded firmly. "Your timing couldn't be better. There really isn't anything left for me to do here that I can't finish just as easily at home, so I might as well leave with you."

"Great." A wide, triumphant grin stretched across Elliott's face as he spoke. Jack wanted to slug him. "I was hoping I could talk you into coming back. Your mother is doing a fine job pulling things together, but it is our wedding, after all, and it's only three months away."

"It is, isn't it," Trish said and shot Jack a pointed look.

"We have to talk." Jack moved toward her again, and she stepped back.

"I don't think so. We *had* to talk. Past tense. We should have talked. Also past tense."

"Is it?" Elliott murmured. "I thought it was past perfect."

"No, wait," Trish said. "I take that back."

"Good," Elliott said under his breath. "Because I'm certain it's past perfect."

Trish ignored him. Her voice was still collected, but fire flared in her eyes. "*You* had to talk. *You* didn't."

"I tried." Jack raised his hands in a helpless gesture.

"Not hard enough."

"What was I supposed to say?"

"You were supposed to tell me the truth," she said through clenched teeth. Great. She was finally showing her anger. This was a little more like the Trish he knew. The knot in his stomach eased.

"I did." Even to his own ears the protest sounded weak.

"Sure, as far as it went!"

"You know . . ." Elliott's gaze shifted uneasily between the two of them. "This might be my fault. I probably put the wrong spin on the whole thing. So he didn't mention his relationship with Russ. It's really not that important, is it?"

"Yes," she hissed.

Jack stared at him with surprise. "Thanks."

"No, I owe you an apology." Sincerity underlaid Elliott's words. "I really have put old rivalries aside. It was just for a moment there, well, I've been hearing so much about how well you

229

two have been working together. It's not always easy to listen to your fiancée's stepfather rave about her accomplishments with another man. Especially when that man is the same one you never felt you quite measured up to as a kid. Add to that the fact that she's alone with him in a place called Paradise Bay. And when you show up, she's practically naked—"

"I have a sheet on!"

"Anyway," Elliott shrugged sheepishly. "It got to me, I guess."

"I can see where it would. No problem." Maybe Jack was wrong about Elliott. That admission of his wasn't an easy one to make. Maybe he had changed. After all, Jack wasn't the same headstrong, rebellious kid he'd been when Elliott's mother was married to Russ. If Jack could grow up, why couldn't Elliott? "It takes a lot to admit something like that. I really appreciate it."

"Are you two through bonding now, or should I turn my head so I won't see the secret handshake?" Trish glared.

"Who's bonding?" Maude stepped into the parlor and glanced at Trish's attire. "Nice look. The dress didn't work out?"

Elliott's eyes lit up and an appreciative smile curved his lips. "Good morning." He stepped toward Maude and held out his hand. "I'm Elliott Hunt. And you're?"

"Maude. Maude Wellington." She pulled off

her glasses with one hand, then placed her other hand in his. "You're the fiancé."

"Among other things." Elliott grinned. "I like your shirt."

"Thanks." Maude grinned back. She wore one of her endless supply of T-shirts proclaiming some obscure philosophical quotes. Today's read: TRUTH: SOMETHING THAT IS STRANGER THAN FICTION BUT NOT AS POPULAR—ANONYMOUS. Given her comments before she'd left yesterday, it wasn't hard to figure out that this particular message was aimed at Jack. "Anonymous is one of my favorite philosophers."

Elliott's smile widened, if that was possible. "Me too."

Elliott still held Maude's hand, and she stared up at him as though she had never seen a tall, blond corporate flying monkey before. Still, Jack had to admit that the man wasn't ugly; some women might even find him attractive. Maude obviously did. And he could apparently be quite charming. Elliott looked down at her with a stunned and, frankly, stupid expression on his face. There might be real possibilities here. Far be it from Jack to hinder any potential for romance between his best friend and a semi-relative who might not be nearly the jerk he'd always thought he was.

"You know, Elliott"—Jack nodded at Maude—"she's a genuine philosopher."

Trish groaned and collapsed onto a blue velvet Victorian sofa. "Aren't we all?"

Maude smiled sweetly at her. "But I have a doctorate to prove it."

"A doctorate?" Disbelief washed across Trish's face.

Admiration shone in Elliott's eyes. "In philosophy? How impressive. I've always loved philosophy."

"She cooks too," Trish muttered.

"And I love to eat," Elliott said eagerly.

"Maude." This was good. This was very good. Jack moved to the couple and directed them toward the door. "Elliott has never been here before. Why don't you show him around the island?"

"I don't think that's such a good idea." Trish pulled herself to her feet and managed to hold on to her sheet in the process. "I don't want to miss that boat and be trapped here for—"

"There's plenty of time." Jack ushered them through the doorway.

"Don't worry, Trish, we'll make the boat," Elliott called over his shoulder, his voice growing fainter. "So, Maude, where do we start on Paradise . . ."

Jack chuckled with satisfaction. Maude would keep old Elliott busy. There was an unmistakable attraction between those two. Now, for the bigger problem. He braced himself and turned toward Trish. Her arms were crossed over her chest, the gesture nicely lifting her breasts a bit while slightly lowering her sheet. What would she do if he swept her into his arms and ravished her right there in the parlor?

"Why did you do that?" She almost spit the words at him. On second thought, ravishing her might not be the best move right now. "Why did you send Elliott—my fiancé, mind you—off with South Seas Barbie?"

"South Seas Barbie?"

"Okay, Philosopher Barbie. Ph.D. Barbie. Gourmet Barbie. Whatever. In case you haven't noticed, that is one good-looking woman and you practically threw her at Elliott."

"Hardly. Did you see the way they stared at each other? Another minute and they'd have been rolling around on the floor. Besides, he didn't seem to mind."

"Well, I do. He was obviously distracted by the reading material stretched across her perky, well-developed chest."

"Trust me. He'll enjoy the distraction." Jack grinned.

"You think?" She stalked across the room, then swiveled to face him. "Why didn't you tell me she was a little more than a housekeeper and cook?"

"It didn't come up?" Damn. He wished that hadn't come out like a question.

"Wrong answer." Her eyes narrowed. "Is there anything else I should know that you've conveniently neglected to mention?"

"No," he said with a defensive glare.

She looked unconvinced.

"Not that I can think of." He sure as hell wasn't going to spill his guts about even the most innocent incident in his past unless he absolutely had to. Who knew what fell into the category of what she should know? "Come on, Trish, you're not really mad at me about Maude. You're mad that I didn't tell you who I was."

"Yes, that's at the top of the list."

"It's not like I actually lied to you. You never asked me if Russ was my father. I just didn't mention it. So technically, in the strict definition of the word, I never lied."

"I asked you what your connection was to the family."

"And I told you I was related to Russ's first wife."

"Yeah." Fire flashed in her eyes. "But you didn't say she was your mother."

"Okay. Whoops. My mistake." He smacked his hand against his forehead. "I'm sorry. I shouldn't have kept my mouth shut, but it seemed like a good idea at the time. And what would you have done if I'd told you, anyway?"

"For one thing, I would have belted you."

"If it will make you feel better, you can hit me now."

"I wouldn't give you the satisfaction," she said loftily.

"I swear I won't be satisfied. It's perfect, Trish. Sock me. Get it out of your system and then we can live happily ever after."

"In your dreams." Her eyes narrowed. "Just

how far does this conspiracy go, anyway?"

"What conspiracy?" he asked cautiously.

"Oh, get off it, Kendall or Evans or whatever you call yourself now. Don't even try to deny it." She punctuated each word with a jab from her finger. "Russ sent me here because he didn't want me to marry Elliott and you were obviously in on the plan. How perfect. Father and son working together at last.

"How could you? I trusted you. I spilled my guts to you. And all the time you were probably laughing at me."

"No, Trish, I swear I—"

"I thought you were a good guy. I thought you were honest. I thought you respected me." Her eyes glittered with anger and maybe even unshed tears. She sniffed and paced the room. "I can't believe this whole thing. Like father like son. You both deserve to be boiled alive—" She pulled up short and whirled to face him. "Did he tell you to seduce me too?"

"No!" He shook his head. "Jeez, Trish, that was my idea."

"Ad-libbing, were we?" Anger battled with hurt in her eyes. "Daddy will be so proud."

He held up his hands. "I didn't mean it like that."

"It doesn't matter how you meant it." She jerked her chin up. "It didn't work."

"I thought it worked great," he murmured.

"Not that."

"Then what are you talking about?" he said carefully.

"This whole scheme of yours and your father's. Well, I'm going home." Triumph flashed in her eyes. "And I'm marrying Elliott."

"That's ridiculous. Aside from the fact that Elliott's not the man you really love, I didn't see him looking at you the way he looked at Maude."

"He likes philosophy."

"Yeah, right. Besides, you can't marry Elliott just to get even with me."

She snorted. "Don't flatter yourself. And don't forget, I was engaged long before I ever heard of Paradise Bay. Or you. Whoever you are."

He studied her for a moment. He could understand her anger, but now she was being unreasonable. "Trish, I love you."

"Love me? Hah. You lied to me. How can you expect me to believe this isn't just another part of your plan?"

"I don't know." Frustration surged through him. "But it's the truth. Trish, you know I could never lie about this." He moved closer and reached out to put his arms around her, but she jerked away and scrambled to the other side of the sofa.

"I don't know anything anymore. And don't touch my sheet." She pulled it closer around her. If she didn't stop doing that, he'd have to rip the damn thing off of her. "Don't you ever touch my sheet again."

"Come on, Trish." He circled the sofa. "I love you, you love me—"

"What makes you think so?" She matched him move for move.

"Last night. This morning. Now." He changed direction.

So did she. "That wasn't love, that was sex. Great sex, but sex. And nothing more than that."

"Sure it was. Remember? You said you loved me. You said you think about me all the time—"

"I'd think about lice all the time too if I had them," she snapped.

"You admitted you couldn't see your life, your future without me."

"I'll be fine. I'll have Elliott."

"Don't count on it. From what I just saw of Elliott—"

"I'll get a dog, then. You can trust a dog. Dogs don't conspire to run your life and control you. And dogs don't lie."

"Technically, I didn't—"

"Technically, do you know where you can shove it?"

"Trish, damn it." He pounded the back of the sofa with his fist and she jumped. "You love me and you know it."

"Wrong! I *don't* know it. You defined the terms for love. I simply met your conditions. You told me I was in love. But technically or not, you lied to me about at least one really significant item!" Her voice rose and her eyes sparked. "So how

237

am I expected to know now what was the truth and what wasn't?"

"I love you, Trish." The volume of his voice matched hers. "That's the absolute—swear to God—bottom-line truth. And I won't ever lie to you about anything again." He heaved a deep sigh. "Even though, you have to admit, by strict definition, I didn't lie, I just didn't—"

"Tell it to the IRS. I'm sure they hear that one all the time." She strode toward the door. "I'm out of here."

"I promise!"

She stopped short in the doorway, then turned, suspicion in her eyes. "You promise?"

"Cross my heart and hope to die."

"That can be arranged." Her gaze swept over him. "Okay, then tell me this."

"Anything." Relief flooded through him. She'd forgive him and they'd go on from there. She was already dressed to make up.

"Tell me, Russell Jonathan Evans the Fourth, have you ever slept with Philosopher Barbie?"

Oh, damn.

"I'm waiting."

He was doomed. No matter what he said, he was a dead man.

"Well?"

"Well, if you're specifically asking about sleep—"

"That's what I thought." Her voice was grim.

"Not recently," he said, hoping timing would

make a difference and knowing full well it wouldn't.

She gave him one of those withering looks generally reserved for people with no noticeable table manners or politicians caught with their pants down and leaned against the doorframe. "You know there's one more thing that really pisses me off about all this."

"Just one?" He couldn't help the sarcasm in his voice, but he was fast approaching the pissed-off stage himself. She wouldn't even listen to him.

"You had the nerve to call *me* Princess. To tease me about being the boss's daughter, when all along you were—"

"Okay, I admit it. Anyway you want to look at it, I've been a real jerk. What else can I say? It doesn't mean I don't love you."

"Hah!"

"And you love me."

"Double hah!"

"And you can't settle for a nice, safe, comfortable bedroom life with Elliott."

"Watch me." Defiance rang in her voice.

"I won't let you," he said quietly.

"You can't stop me." She gathered her sheet around her and swept out of the room with the dignity of a queen. A very angry, very stubborn queen. A queen about to issue orders for mass executions.

He stared at the empty doorway for a long second.

"Don't bet your crown on it . . . Princess."

Chapter Twelve

"Well, I'd say you were right about one thing." Maude crossed her arms and lounged against the walnut wardrobe. "You are a jerk."

"Thanks, pal." Jack threw another shirt into his suitcase. "I can't believe you're taking her side. I didn't even think you liked her."

"I don't actually dislike her." Maude shrugged. "She's okay. You're the one I'm concerned about."

"Don't be." He crossed the large bedroom he'd occupied for the last four years to a tall dresser matching the wardrobe and yanked open a drawer. "I can take care of myself."

"Right." She watched him for a minute. "I warned you to tell her the truth."

"Hey, I tried." Rolls of balled socks stared up at him from the drawer. Where did they all come from? He hadn't realized he owned so many socks. "More than once."

"Apparently you didn't try hard enough."

"Apparently." He grabbed a sock ball, turned and fired it toward the suitcase on the bed. It sailed over the bag and the bed and hit the far wall. "You know, this morning I really understood why she was so mad. I'd probably feel the same way. She honestly thinks my dad set this whole thing up and she's half right. Plus there's that little problem about her hating my guts. But I don't know how to get through to her about the rest of it. About us." He shot another ball of socks. It bounced off the headboard and rolled toward the suitcase.

"You're getting closer."

Jack ignored her. "I thought promising never to lie to her again, even though, technically I didn't lie in the first—"

"Jeez, Jack, get over it." Maude shook her head. "You can hedge all you want, but this was definitely a lie of omission. Like it or not, it counts."

"Okay, okay." He flung another ball. This one flew in a straight shot right out the open window. He flexed his arm. "I'm really out of practice."

"And off the subject."

"Yeah, well, the point I was trying to make was that I'm getting a little angry myself. Plus, I feel like an idiot." He exhaled a long, heartfelt breath. "I never thought of myself as a hopeless romantic, but I must be. I really believed that because I loved her and she loved me, everything would work out."

"She does love you. Any fool can see that. That's probably your biggest problem."

"What do you mean?"

"Have you considered the possibility that a woman in love with Jack Kendall"—Maude pinned him with a steady gaze—"might not have the same feelings for Russell Jonathan Evans the Fourth? A man she's always detested? At the very least it's got to be a little confusing."

His heart sank. "Damn." His voice was grim. "I hadn't thought of that at all." What if Maude was right? "Well, there's only one way to find out."

"You're going home."

"Yep."

"It's about time." She smiled. "You've changed a lot since I met you, Jack. You've gotten your life together. You know who you are, and I think, finally, you like that person. You've made peace with yourself." She tilted her head and considered him. " 'A man cannot be comfortable without his own approval.' "

He raised a brow. "Aristotle? Descartes? Nietzsche?"

"Better." She grinned. "Mark Twain."

He chuckled, pulled the drawer out of the dresser, walked across the room to the bed and dumped the contents in the suitcase. He caught Maude's gaze. "I'm not giving up on her."

"I didn't think you would." She moved around the room, gathering the misfired sock balls. "Any plan of attack?"

"Right now, she swears she's going to marry Elliott." He paused to pull together the vague idea hovering at the edge of his mind. "It seems to me, if Elliott is who she wants"—abruptly the thought crystallized in all its magnificent glory— "Elliott is who she'll get."

"What?" Maude's expression was a portrait of concern. Apparently Maude and Elliott had hit it off even better than he'd thought.

"Relax. I'm not handing her over to Elliott—"

"Good." Maude huffed. "I think he deserves better."

Jack snorted. "And I deserve Trish?"

"You two deserve each other."

"Thanks. I think."

She sighed. "You know what I mean. As volatile as your relationship is, you're both in love. Elliott loves her but"—she thought for a moment—"it seems more like a comfortable, friendship type of love than a grand passion."

Jack stifled a grin. "You two had quite a little chat this morning."

"Uh-huh." A soft smile spread across her face. "I liked him. I liked him a lot."

"I kind of liked him myself. He's definitely not the Elliott I remember." He held up his hands like a catcher's mitt and she tossed him the socks she'd collected. "I figure once I get to New York and start functioning in the real world, she'll see I can be just as stable and secure as Elliott. And in a side-by-side comparison, I'll win."

"You're definitely number one on the arrogance scale." Maude scoffed. "I'm almost afraid to ask, but what makes you think you'll win?"

"Names, for one thing."

She laughed. "What?"

"Elliott is a nice name, but let's face it: It's the name of the guy who loses the girl. Maybe the hero's best friend. He's a secondary character at the most."

"Not in my story line," she murmured.

"But Jack, now that's the name of the hero." He grinned his best hero-type grin. "That's the guy who saves the world, beats the bad guys, gets the girl and does all that other heroic stuff."

"You've been reading too much Tom Clancy. So tell me this: Where does Russell Jonathan the Fourth fit in?"

"First of all, he sticks with Jack." He dropped the socks in the suitcase. "And puts all his money on the power of love." He snapped the lid closed. "The company helicopter is picking me up"—he glanced at his watch—"in ten minutes. Can you pack the rest of my things?"

"I'll have my mom do it."

"Great. Send them with Mo. The helicopter will be back for him the day after tomorrow. I already talked to him about it."

"I know. I talked to him too."

"We figured he needed to meet with the folks in New York in person." He hauled the bag off the bed and headed for the door.

"Absolutely. It makes perfect sense to me. I can hardly wait."

He stopped in his tracks. "You're coming?"

"Sure. I haven't been back to the States in almost four years. And I'd really like to see Elliott again."

"I don't know if that's such a good idea."

Maude grinned wickedly. "I think it's a great idea."

He set down the suitcase and chose his words carefully. "Remember when I said I told Trish I'd never lie to her?"

"Yeah?" She drew the word out slowly.

"Well, the first thing she asked me was if you and I—"

"And you told her? How could you, Jack?" Maude groaned. "She'll tell Elliott. He'll think I'm some kind of tramp."

"Oh, I don't think—"

"Did you tell her it was just fun? Recreational? And over a long time ago?"

"I didn't mention the recreational part," he said under his breath.

"That's something anyway." She paced the room. "We'll have to think of what to tell her to get out of this."

"I won't lie to her," he said loftily.

"Now is not the time to develop scruples. Besides, this is for her own good." She stopped and

245

stared at him. "You know, for the international-playboy, girl-in-every-port reputation you had, you don't know anything about women."

"I know a few things."

"Hardly. Listen and learn." Her voice and her gaze were firm. "Women do not understand recreational sex unless they are the ones having it. And if you can have it just for fun in the past, you can have it just for fun in the future. Understand?"

"You're trying to say she won't trust me." The knot in his stomach returned.

"That's a distinct possibility." She considered him for a second. "Would it go against your new-found moral standards to let her believe there was more between us than sex? That's something she could understand and get past. Tell her it's all over now, of course, except for friendship, but in the beginning we thought maybe it was love."

"That would be a lie."

"Would it?" Her gaze bored into his. "Honestly, Jack, would it?"

"Honestly, Maude." He stared into her blue eyes. There *had* been a moment, before they'd realized they each needed a friend more than a lover before they'd recognized that the two of them couldn't be both. "Maybe not a complete lie."

"Good." She heaved a sigh of relief. "Now get out of here."

He gave her a quick hug, picked up his bag

and took off through the broad hallway and down the ornate staircase. He paused at the bottom of the stairs in the grand foyer and tried to absorb the peace of the place. He'd miss this great old house that had been both home and sanctuary, but it was time to move on. He drew a deep breath, pushed open the heavy carved door and wondered when he'd return.

A memory flashed in his mind of the last time he'd left the island. The scene played out in his head: a ten-year-old-boy, two loving parents and an understanding that the world, his world, would always be a place of wonder and joy.

He wasn't the same innocent kid and hadn't been for a long time. Life had seen to that, but abruptly he realized that long-ago sense of optimism, of hope, of faith in the future was back. Maude was right: He knew who he was and what he wanted. But he was right too: No matter how crazy it sounded, no matter how it had happened, he was a hopeless romantic.

Because what he wanted most was Trish.

Russ tapped his pen on the desk and stared unseeingly across his office. He certainly hadn't expected anything like this. All he had wanted was to stop Trish's wedding. Now, according to Jack, she was more determined than ever to marry Elliott. And Jack was just as determined to stop her.

It was great to see his son again. And better still to see him right here where he belonged, ready to take his place in the family and the company. He and Jack had been down a long, rocky road together, but the end result was well worth the trip.

Very little ever threw Russ for a loop, but this business about his stepdaughter definitely did. The possibility of a relationship between Trish and Jack had never crossed his mind. He simply wanted them to work together and, hopefully, develop a friendship—all with the ultimate goal of persuading her not to ruin her life with a marriage he was convinced wouldn't last.

Still, the more he thought about it, the more he liked the idea of a union between Jack and Trish. Although it certainly wouldn't be smooth sailing. He'd never suspected Trish's loyalty to him would result in dislike for his son. Hate, actually, was what Jack had called it.

And, apparently, she was furious at both father and son. Her mother probably wouldn't be any happier. Evelyn wasn't going to be thrilled at the idea of canceling the wedding of the century.

Of course, at this moment the wedding was still on. It was just to the wrong man.

Marjorie rapped on the open door and entered with her usual air of efficiency.

"Jack mentioned a hotel, but I assumed you'd want him to stay at your house. Your driver is taking him there now. You might want to call Evelyn and warn her." Marjorie raised a brow.

"Correct me if I'm wrong, but they've never met, have they?"

"I forgot about that." Trust Marjorie to remember tiny but important details. Damn, he would miss her. Her scheduled retirement was less than six months away.

Marjorie glanced down at the pad in her hand. "I'd suggest we place him in that vacant office across the . . ."

He wondered what she'd do when she wasn't making sure his professional life, and often his personal life, ran smoothly. She'd be fine financially. Even without her pension, investments he had helped guide ensured that she would be quite well off. In fact, if income was the only consideration, she could have quit years ago. She'd once mentioned something about traveling, and Russ had stored away that rare insight into Marjorie Caplan. He suspected, upon retirement, the prim, capable lady would take a trip somewhere pleasant but not too far, maybe a tour of the Grand Canyon or the Ozarks. Then she'd settle in Florida or someplace equally appropriate.

He realized with sudden insight and more than a twinge of regret that he'd never really thought much about the personal side of his right hand. She'd always been a fine-looking woman, and even now, in her sixties, looked far younger than her years. Did she have relationships in her life? Had there been men, or were there still men vying for the attention of the efficient Marjorie Caplan?

". . . and your stepdaughter should arrive sometime tomorrow, possibly even later, depending on connections and the weather. I believe there are typhoon warnings in some of the areas they may have to travel through." Marjorie looked at him expectantly.

"That gives me time to breathe at least." Even though Jack had left the island after Trish and Elliott, he'd radioed to arrange for both the helicopter and the corporate jet, leaving the other two to fend for themselves with last-minute commercial transportation. *Commandeer* was probably a more accurate word than arrange. Regardless of what surname he used, Jack was an Evans, all right. Russ looked at his assistant. "You know what's going on with Jack and Trish, don't you?"

"I know everything, Russ." She smiled. "It's my job."

"In that case, any advice?"

"May I speak freely?"

"Can I stop you?"

"No, but I do like to ask first." She paused, not out of fear—she never hesitated to speak her mind with him—but obviously to pull her thoughts together regarding the best course. He didn't always like her advice, but often regretted the occasional times he didn't take it. At any rate, it was always well considered.

"Well, I would suggest you butt out."

"What?"

"Butt out. Leave them all alone. Let the two—
or rather the three—of them work it out."

"But—"

"No buts, Russ." Her brows pulled together in
an exasperated frown. "Don't you think you've
done enough?" There was that look of hers
again.

"I haven't done anything," he said with a touch
of indignation.

"No?" She tucked her pad under her arm and
ticked the points off on her fingers. "You sent
Trish to that island with the express purpose of
breaking up her wedding. You didn't warn her
that Jack was there before you sent her. You
didn't tell her Jack was your son and, frankly,
after they began working together there was
plenty of opportunity for communication."

She retrieved her pad and waved it at him.
"How on earth do you expect her to believe
Jack's relationship with her wasn't part of some
sort of diabolical scheme you cooked up?"

"It does sound bad when you put it that way,"
he murmured.

"It is bad." She huffed. "For heaven's sake, the
very least you can do is let them muddle through
this mess on their own."

"You really think that's best?" He didn't need
to ask. She was right and he knew it.

"Indeed I do." She straightened her shoulders.
"Now, is there anything else?"

"No, that's pretty much it."

"I should think so." She turned and walked toward the door.

"Marjorie," he called, "what are your plans for retirement?"

"My plans?" She turned back to him. "Why do you ask?"

He shrugged. "I was just wondering."

"Very well." She smiled slowly. "Russ, I'm going to travel to every odd and unique spot on the face of the globe, keeping an eye open for adventure and whatever else I can find. Excitement. Maybe romance. Possibly even danger. I'm going to write about everything I see, maybe for publication, maybe just for my own enjoyment, and eventually, after many, many years, I plan to end my days in a place I haven't found yet, one where I can dance naked on a beach in the moonlight."

His jaw dropped open.

"I'll be in my office if you need me." She nodded, turned on her heel and walked out, shutting the door behind her with a crisp snap.

And for the second time today, Russell Jonathan Evans the Third was caught completely by surprise.

Trish stepped into the elevator in the lobby of the ESI building, grateful there was no one she knew in the confined space. She didn't want to smile. She didn't want to make small talk. And she didn't want to be here.

It had taken two full days to recover from the

journey from hell. Actually, that was probably too generous a description for her trip home from Paradise Bay with Elliott. Thanks to some kind of massive screwup with the company jet, they'd spent hours waiting for commercial planes in tacky, over-bright, uncomfortable airports—only to end up on flights that were crowded and delayed by maintenance problems or weather. More than once Trish had wondered if some island god had cast a curse on her. Elliot had seemed preoccupied during most of the trip and unusually quiet. Fine. She'd been in no mood to talk anyway. Especially since anytime he did open his mouth it was to ask a question about Maude. And Maude was definitely number two on her top-ten list of topics she did not want to talk about. Still, it did ease her guilt to realize he was hot and bothered over the diminutive philosopher. It was also incredibly irritating.

She stepped off the elevator on the penthouse floor, the exclusive domain of ESI's top corporate officers. For the first time in years she wondered if she had earned her place here by virtue of her work or the good graces of her stepfather. No. She'd worked damn hard for this company, and the plans for The Inn on Paradise Bay were solid evidence of that. In spite of who she'd worked with.

She pasted a smile on her face, hoped it looked relatively natural and said hello to Marti, her secretary, who greeted her with an enthusiastic welcome and a volley of messages involving who knew what. Trish barely heard her. She escaped into her perfectly decorated office, dropped her briefcase and laptop on the sofa, then sank into the cushy, soft suede chair behind the oversized Victorian partner's desk and heaved a deep sigh.

This was the last place she wanted to be. She hadn't talked to Russ since she'd returned home and had ignored her mother's messages as well, but she'd bet anything Jack had fired off an E-mail with his own version of the sorry mess. She had no desire to face Russ or her mother. Russ was both her stepfather and boss, and this disaster affected both those relationships. She was still furious with him. But she no longer wanted his execution, even though the idea of slow torture was still pretty appealing. All she really wanted now was to forget the whole thing and pretend it never happened.

Not that she could. Not that she didn't think about it—no—him every minute. Not that she hadn't given forgetting it her best shot. Her first twenty-four hours home had been spent in a battle between anger, guilt and major self-pity that included a fair of amount of weeping, half a gallon of peanut butter cup ice cream straight from the carton and a few useless purchases on a cable shopping channel. Of course, if she ever seriously decided to take up rug weaving that loom she'd bought would come in handy. She'd realized recovery was going to take more than an ice-cream and shopping binge when she'd found herself rereading the entire *Paradise Bay Visitor's Guide*. Three times.

There was a quick knock on the door and Marti poked her head in.

"Mr. Evans would like to see you in his office. He said any time in the next half-hour, but I got the impression sooner would be better than later."

"Okay. Thanks."

Marti nodded and shut the door.

Great. Obviously she couldn't postpone the inevitable any longer, whether she was ready or not. And she wasn't ready, even though, by her second day back in civilization, she'd decided that she needed to think long and hard about everything that had happened. There was a tiny possibility that she'd overreacted, at least when it came to the extent of Russ's involvement. She had no doubt he would have taken any help he could get in the effort to stop her wedding, but he'd always been protective of her, and it was a stretch to assume he'd encourage anyone to seduce her. Even his own son.

His *son*. That revelation still shook her, but she should have realized the truth on her own. Jack had his father's smile and eyes. Why didn't Jack just tell her who he was when they'd first met? It wouldn't have made any difference to her.

No, that was as big a lie as his. It would have made a huge difference. She would have said everything to him that she'd always wanted to say. She probably would have gone out of her way to avoid him after that. Avoid his company and his friendship. And she definitely would have avoided his bed—or beds, as the case might be. But at the very least, whatever might have still happened between them, she would have walked into it with her eyes open.

Absently, she rifled through the mail piled on her desk. Marti would have taken care of anything important. Only uninteresting personal items were left. Mostly bills.

Russell Jonathan Evans the fourth.

She shook her head. He had a bad-boy reputation when it came to women and everything else in life. He was daring and adventurous. He drove too fast, played too hard, lived life on the edge. There was nothing he wouldn't try. Nothing he wouldn't do. It was all detailed in the scandalous rumors she'd heard about him for years, beginning when he was still in boarding school.

She'd dismissed him from her mind after she'd written him all those years ago and he'd ignored her. She just hadn't been particularly interested anymore, although she'd been vaguely aware of his existence in the years that followed. Now that she thought about it, his disappearance from the international lifestyle of the rich and spoiled probably dated back about four years.

She knew he'd come to Paradise Bay after

some kind of major crisis in his life. Was the story he'd told about "Jack's" previous life actually that of RJ the fourth's? Why hadn't she asked him? She'd had the perfect opportunity to find out more about him, but she'd blown it.

No, she'd had to ask him about sleeping with South Seas/Philosopher/Gourmet Barbie. For God's sake, the man had been on the island for four years with that beautiful midget as his best friend. What normal, healthy man in his right mind wouldn't sleep with her? It wasn't like he was in love with her or anything. Besides, that was long before they'd met. She hadn't exactly been pure and innocent before meeting Jack either. In fact, she was still engaged to another man. Technically, anyway. She groaned. She was as bad as he was. Well, almost. At least he knew she was engaged to another man.

She pushed her chair away from the desk, got to her feet and started toward the door. It really didn't matter. She could make all the excuses she wanted for him, but the bottom line was that she didn't trust him. She wanted to believe his declaration of love, but she couldn't. And as lousy and heartbroken as she felt, she was no longer one hundred percent sure that what she felt for him was love. But what else could possibly hurt so much? At the very least, she knew that whatever it was she had felt for Elliot, it couldn't hold a candle to the torrent of emotions she felt toward Jack.

Trish plastered her best corporate smile firmly

in place, stepped out of her office and walked briskly down the long corridor to the CEO's suite. It was time to get back to the real world. She had pulled herself together, more or less. Enough to appear in public prepared to discuss the inn with a professional demeanor, anyway. And she had every intention of going on with her life exactly as she'd planned before her tropical exile.

Except for her wedding. Whatever she'd felt for Jack or with Jack, she couldn't marry Elliott now. She wouldn't do that to him, or herself. She'd thought she'd be happy with the comfortable affection they shared, but now she knew just how wrong she'd been. She suspected Elliott knew it too. They definitely had to talk, but at the moment she didn't know when or where—and didn't want to think about it either.

At any rate, she was back where she belonged and Jack was half a world away. Where he belonged.

Trish pushed open the glass doors guarding the foyer of the executive suite and greeted the two sentrylike secretaries flanking the outer doors to Russ's inner sanctum. The pleasant woman on the right smiled and waved her on to Ms. Caplan's domain through the walnut double doors. To reach Russ's private office, friends, family and foes alike had to run this gauntlet of protective employees from the private lobby through Ms. Caplan and finally, if you made it alive that far, into Russ's presence.

Ms. Caplan looked up from her computer screen and a smile of genuine pleasure curled her lips. "Welcome back, Trish. I understand you've done some very creative work. Your stepfather is extremely proud."

"Thanks." Trish returned her smile. Praise from this paragon of corporate competence always lifted her spirits. Trish never failed to wonder what secret life lurked behind that woman's totally together façade. She nodded at the second set of doors, a mirror image of the ones she'd just passed through. The doors between Russ's office and his assistant's were open as often as not, but this morning they were closed. "Should I—"

"Certainly. He's expecting you."

Trish started toward the door.

"Wait, Trish." The older woman considered her for a second. "Are you all right?"

Did she know? Trish stared. Of course she knew. Ms. Caplan knew everything. Trish raised her chin. "I'm fine."

Ms. Caplan looked doubtful.

"Really. I'm okay." She smiled, touched by the woman's concern.

"Very well." Ms. Caplan paused, as if there was something she wanted to say, then shrugged slightly and gestured at the door. "Good luck."

"Thanks." How weird was that? The unflappable Ms. Caplan actually appeared uneasy. Trish stepped to the door, knocked twice, then braced herself and walked in. "Good morning."

Russ leaned against his desk, arms crossed

259

over his chest, deep in conversation with someone who sat in one of the high-backed leather wing chairs facing it. She could tell by the legs that it was a man, but from this angle she couldn't see his face. Russ's gaze met hers and he smiled with affection.

"Trish." He strode toward her and pulled her into his arms for a fatherly bear hug. He was the only father she'd really ever known, and it was hard to stay mad at him when she knew his intentions were good, even if his actions were misguided. He stepped back and gave her a quick once-over. "You look wonderful."

"I look like hell and you know it. And feel free to blame yourself," she said quietly and for his ears alone. There was no way she wanted some stranger to hear this. "If I were any paler, I'd be dead. My eyes are puffy. And you'd see how red my nose is if I didn't have a ton of makeup on."

"Great." His voice was a touch too loud and way too enthusiastic. He put his arm around her shoulder and walked her toward the desk. "We were just talking about you, Trish, and the Paradise Bay project. You two will be working together."

"How nice." She forced a smile. The last thing she wanted today was to meet someone, anyone, she'd have to work with in the future. The stranger in the chair stood and turned to face her.

He was taller than she was. His hair was fashionably short, his designer suit impeccable. His square jaw was clean-shaven. His gaze met hers.

His brown eyes smoldered.

Her breath caught in her throat.

"Trish," Russ said, "you know Jack."

Chapter Thirteen

"Hi, Trish."

A slow, cautious smile spread across Jack's face. His smooth, great-looking, clean-shaven face. No beard. No mustache. No hair.

"What am I saying?" Russ laughed awkwardly. "Of course you know Jack. You two have worked closely together for about a month now."

"Haven't we, though?" Her heart thudded in her chest and she willed herself to calm down. "But can one person ever really know another?"

"I think so," Jack said, his gaze challenging hers.

"You would," Trish snapped. "What are you doing here anyway?"

"Jack is here to work on the Paradise Bay project, initially at any rate." Russ's tone was abruptly all business. Stepdaughter and son were now co-workers, and personal relationships carried little weight at ESI. He circled his desk and settled into his chair. "Sit down, Trish. Jack."

Sitting here, next to Jack, across from her stepfather, was the last thing she wanted to do. She ignored the urge to flee and perched stiffly on the edge of the chair next to Jack's, little more than a foot separating her armrest from his. A small leather-topped table occupied the space between them.

Russ leaned back and picked up a gold filigree pen. He aimed it at her. "I wanted to tell you, Trish, how impressed I am—how impressed the entire staff is—with the work you and Jack and Mo turned out on Paradise Bay." He smiled and shook his head. "I honestly did not doubt the talent I had thrown together, but frankly all three of you were untested in terms of a project of this magnitude. The creativity your team exhibited on both an esoteric and practical level has almost guaranteed the ultimate success of The Inn on Paradise Bay."

A warm glow of pride flushed through her and she sat up a bit straighter. Out of the corner of her eye, she noticed Jack glance at her but refused to return the look.

"I've already told Jack all this—"

"When?" Trish frowned and leaned forward.

"I got here on Tuesday," Jack said.

She turned toward him. "How in the world did you do that? You were still on Paradise Bay when we left. Granted, we had to take commercial flights that were totally screwed up, even though Elliott swore he had arranged for the corporate jet. But apparently there was some kind of confusion and . . ." A nasty suspicion popped into her head. "How did you get here?"

A sheepish expression crossed his face. "Corporate jet."

Trish's eyes widened. "I went through travel hell because you—"

"Trish," Russ said sharply. "You and Jack can discuss your transportation conflicts later. Right now I want to talk about where we go from here."

"I know where I'd like him to go," she said under her breath.

Russ continued as if he hadn't heard her, but she was pretty sure Jack had. Good. It served him right. Beard or no beard, hunk or not, he was still a deceitful hulking beast. What she wouldn't give for a good tribe of cannibals right now with a pre-heated pot and—

". . . so ultimately you'll continue coordinating your efforts, here of course, instead of on the island itself. Trish . . ." Russ shifted his gaze to meet hers. "I have to tell you, at this stage I seriously considered placing the leadership of this project completely in Jack's hands—"

"What?" Her stomach reeled. How could he?

"However, I think the two of you make one hell of a team, and Jack agrees."

"Damn decent of him," she said through clenched teeth. *Especially since this project was mine from the beginning.*

Jack didn't say a word. She had to admit, the man knew when to keep his mouth shut. On second thought, that was what had caused the trouble between them in the first place.

"Trish." Russ's voice was firm. His pen tapped a steady staccato beat on the desk. "This was not a choice of Jack over you because of performance or family connections or anything else. It's true that Jack will be in this chair one day, running ESI. It's his heritage and it's what I've always planned. And I believe he's starting to realize it's what he wants, as well.

"But there is room at the top of this company for both of you if that's what you want." He paused. "I've never had the impression you did. Am I wrong?"

She started to protest, then shook her head. She had no desire to run the company. She liked public relations, but she wasn't sure that was how she wanted to spend the rest of her life. What *did* she want to do? She'd spent so many years trying to prove herself in the job she had, she'd never stopped to consider whether it was the career she truly wanted. She was nearly thirty and, confronted with Russ's question, she realized that she had no idea what she wanted to be when she grew up.

"Okay. Then that's settled." Russ nodded with satisfaction. "The two of you will share the responsibilities, the decisions and, ultimately, the success or failure as co-directors of The Inn on Paradise Bay development project."

"Great." Jack grinned and got to his feet.

"Swell." She smiled weakly and stood.

"In the meantime . . ." Russ gave her his *now-then-young-lady* look; she'd first seen it when he'd married her mother, and it was still effective. She stifled a sigh. "Your mother is planning a family dinner tomorrow night and she expects to see you there." Russ paused. "And Elliott, of course."

"Of course." Had this fiasco with Jack convinced Russ that she'd be better off with Elliott, after all? Probably not.

"You too, Jack," Russ said.

"I'm looking forward to it." Jack slanted a quick glance her way. "Do you think Evelyn will mind if I bring Mo—"

"Mo's here?" Relief washed through her. If they were all going to work together, as they had on the island, Mo would make a great buffer.

"He got in yesterday, but he's only going to stay for about a week."

"Absolutely, Jack. I've always been fond of the Wellingtons." Pleasure colored Russ's words. "Besides, they're practically family, and two more is no problem. It will be a welcome-home party."

"Two more?" Trish looked from Russ to his son. "You mean Mo and Elliott?"

She was close enough to Jack to notice him swallow uneasily, like a man whose tie was too tight.

"Well, no," Russ said. "I meant Mo and Maude. She came too."

Or a man with his neck in a noose.

"Really?" South Seas Barbie was in town? Great. "How nice."

Russ nodded. "Jack tells me that she's an accomplished gourmet cook. With her knowledge of island specialties, food availability, that sort of thing, he figured her input would be invaluable in planning the food offered at the inn."

She glared at Jack. "I'm sure input is the least of her invaluable offerings."

Jack smiled with an annoying innocence.

"And one more thing." Russ got to his feet and walked around his desk to join them. "Evelyn suggested, and I agreed with her, that we throw a big welcome-home party for Jack now that he's back to stay."

Trish glanced at him sharply. "You're back for good?"

"Yep." His dark gaze trapped hers. "I realized the island just couldn't give me what I wanted, what I needed, anymore."

"Oh?" Why was her mouth suddenly dry? Without thinking, she licked her lips. His gaze dropped to her mouth and back to her eyes. Now that she knew who, and more importantly, *what* he was, she knew it was a seductive trick. He'd used it on her before and it had worked then. His eyes smoldered. And God help her, she thought as her insides melted, it worked now.

"I finally figured out you can't hide from life. You can't settle for what's safe and secure and comfortable." Was he still talking about himself? "Life isn't worth living without a little excitement, adventure"—he paused—"passion. That's all worth taking a risk."

"Is it, Jack?" Without warning, tension ran between them like a cable stretched too taut. "From what I've heard, you used to take a lot of risks for the sake of excitement."

"Skiing a glacier, hang gliding in the Alps, physical risks are just as much a way of hiding from life as, oh"—he shrugged but his gaze never wavered from hers—"marrying the wrong person."

"As I was saying"—Russ cleared his throat— "Evelyn wants to have a party, probably in a couple of weeks. That's still at least two months away from the wedding, so we can squeeze everything in." He put an arm around each of them and walked them toward the door. "It's great to have you both home."

"It's great to be home," Jack said simply.

"Yeah." Trish sighed. "Great."

She walked into Ms. Caplan's office, Jack one step behind her. The moment she heard him close the door to Russ's office, she wheeled to face him.

"Look, Jack—or do I call you Russell the fourth now?"

"I've always been Jack."

"Okay, *Jack*, we have to work together. We apparently have the occasional social obligation where we will be forced to be in each other's presence, but that will be the extent of our relationship." She poked her index finger at his chest. "Do you understand?"

"Oh, I understand, but I don't think you do." He grabbed her hand and leaned toward her until they were nearly nose to nose. "I've had a lot of time to do a lot of thinking in the last few days. I made a mistake when I didn't tell you who I was. I admit it. But it wasn't because of some grand design to screw up your plans, no matter how much they need somebody to screw them up."

"My plans are none of your business." She tried to pull away, but he held tight to her hand.

His voice was low and firm. "Oh, but they are. You see, whether you believe me or not, I am in love with you. I've never been in love before and I'm discovering it's a real good news/bad news kind of thing."

"Sorry to inconvenience you."

"Yeah, right." The muscle on the side of his jaw clenched. She'd never seen his jaw without his beard before, and she had a ridiculous impulse to touch it. "I'm warning you right now, Trish, there was a time when I would have shrugged at this point and let you go your own way. No hassles, no sweat. But now, I know what I want, I know how I feel and I don't intend to give up until you admit you feel the same way I do."

"Well, brace yourself, Jack, you're in for a long wait. Besides I'm getting married." She didn't even flinch at the lie. After all, *technically*, she was still engaged. And who would understand *technically* better than Jack?

"I don't think so." A slight, smug smile curved his full, sensuous lips. Before he'd shaved, she'd never noticed how . . . well, inviting they were. "I don't think you could ever marry Elliott or anyone else when you love me."

"Except that I don't love you."

"Now, who's lying?" He raised his voice. "What do you think, Ms. Caplan, is she lying?"

Trish sucked in a hard breath. Heat rushed up to her face. She jerked away from Jack and turned toward Ms. Caplan. "I am so sorry and I'm so embarrassed." She waved at Jack impatiently. "It's his fault. He was driving me crazy and I'd forgotten you were here."

"That's one of the things that makes me so good at what I do." The executive assistant's gaze slipped from Trish to Jack and back. "Another is poor hearing. Did you two say something?"

Jack grinned. "It's amazing how you still manage to know everything with that kind of impediment."

Ms. Caplan raised a brow, then turned back to her monitor.

Jack laughed and glanced at Trish. "Would you like me to pick you up for dinner tomorrow?"

"No," she snapped. "My fiancé will take me."

"Suit yourself." He winked at Ms. Caplan and left.

Trish stared after him. She had to talk to Elliott. Unless he was really heartbroken at the idea of splitting up—and only an idiot would fail to realize with Maude on the scene he wouldn't be—she'd like to stay engaged a little longer. Just to show Jack whoever-he-was he did not have the upper hand here. No way. She was in control.

"Trish." Ms. Caplan's gaze didn't waver from her screen. "He was right, of course.

"You *were* lying."

The doorbell rang and Trish groaned.

She should have known, sooner or later, someone who'd left one of the well-intentioned messages filling her answering machine would show up in person. It was too much to expect that everyone would just leave her alone for a while. No, Russ and her mother had each left messages urging her to talk to them.

Elliott had called several times, saying they needed to talk. No kidding. He wasn't stupid. Given the state of undress he'd found her in on the island, plus her refusal to mutter more than a curt response on their trip home, she'd bet he'd figured out their wedding wouldn't go exactly as planned. Add to that his obvious attraction to Maude and she wouldn't be surprised if he was about to beat her to the punch and call it off himself.

And of course Jack wasn't letting her forget his presence for a moment. She'd made some stupid excuse about jet lag and left the office right after their meeting with Russ, but Jack had called nonstop since the minute she'd stepped in the door. Trish now refused to pick up the phone and, after losing count of his calls, had simply turned the sound off on the machine. She didn't want to talk to him. Not now and possibly not ever. She braced herself for the worst, stepped to the door and yanked it open.

"Trish Taylor?" A delivery man stood in the hall holding a vase filled with a large arrangement of flowers.

"Yes?"

"These are for you." He thrust the flowers at her and she had no choice but to accept them.

"Oh. Thanks." She struggled to balance the heavy offering in her arms. "Just let me get my purse."

"It's been taken care of." The man—boy actually, he couldn't have been more than twenty—grinned and strode off down the hall.

She closed the door, placed the vase on an antique table in the tiny area that served as an entryway then stepped back and glared. She had to admit the arrangement was gorgeous. It had half a dozen enormous hibiscus blossoms and at least that many birds of paradise. *Paradise?* Of course. There was no card but this had to be from Jack. Well, if he thought a few tropical flowers were going to—

The doorbell rang again.

Jack! Returning to the scene of the crime probably.

She stalked to the door and flung it open.

The delivery man was back, the same grin plastered across his face, a brown-paper-wrapped box in his hands.

"Trish Taylor?"

She bit back a sharp reply. After all, he was just doing his job. There was no need to treat him like Jack's henchman. "Yep, *still* me."

"This is for you." He handed her the box, nodded and once again walked away.

She closed the door and hefted the box. It was way too heavy to be something like jewelry, but that probably wasn't Jack's style anyway. What was he up to? Of course, there was always the possibility it wasn't from him at all. It could be an early wedding present. Just the thought clenched her stomach. She had to call the wedding off before she had to face returning gifts along with everything else.

She walked into the living room, sank into the overstuffed sofa and plopped the weighty package on the low butler's tray that served as a coffee table. For a moment, she studied it, wondering if she really wanted to know what was inside. Then, with a few misgivings and more than a little curiosity, ripped away the paper and pulled off the lid.

Nestled inside layers of tissue was a six-pack of beer.

Trish stared in disbelief. She reached in the box, hooked the plastic rings binding the cans, and pulled out the six-pack.

It was still cold.

Oh, Jack was good. He was very good. Any other man would have tried to worm his way back into her good graces with something ostentatious and terribly expensive like a huge, perfect emerald or a foreign sports car. It wouldn't have worked and he probably knew it—although it would have been nice if he had tried. Still, a reluctant grin tugged at her lips. If nothing else, she had to give him points for originality.

The doorbell pealed once more.

Trish wiped the smile from her face, got to her feet and squared her shoulders. Forgiving him for lying to her and making her feel like a fool would take a whole lot more than a couple of beers and a vase of exotic flowers.

She drew a deep breath and opened the door.

Cases of beer stacked a good six feet tall confronted her.

"What in the—"

"Trish Taylor?" The delivery henchman peered from behind the boxes.

She absolutely didn't want to see the humor in this. She didn't want the tiniest bit of laughter to break down her defenses, but it was tough to keep a straight face.

"Bring them in." She stepped to one side and waved the smirking delivery guy into the foyer.

"Where would you like these?" He wheeled the cases on a handtruck past her.

"Just leave them here," she said with a sigh of resignation.

"Okay." He worked the cases off the dolly and turned to leave.

"I assume this has been taken care of too?"

"Sure has." He grinned. "It looks like you're going to have one hell of a party. If you need another guest, I'm free toni—"

"She doesn't." Jack lounged in the doorway. "It's a very small party. By personal invitation only."

"And I don't recall inviting you," she snapped, ignoring the annoying way her heart leapt at the sight of him.

The delivery henchmen's gaze jumped from her to Jack and back. He shrugged. "Okay, but you don't know what you're missing." He pushed the dolly through the doorway. "Have fun."

"Oh, we will." Jack stepped into the apartment and closed the door behind him.

"We will not." Any amusement at his clever tactics vanished at the smug note in his voice. "What are *you* doing here?"

He stepped past her, skirted the stack of cases

and walked into the living room. "You wouldn't answer my calls."

"I have nothing to say to you," she said in as lofty a tone as she could manage, then trailed behind him.

"Too bad, because I have a lot to say to you. I hate one-sided conversations, but if that's the way you want it." He looked around the living room, scanning the mix of stylish traditional pieces and antiques with an approving eye. "Very nice. Not exactly what I expected."

"Oh? Exactly what did you expect?"

"I just figured everything would match. Perfectly. This is very eclectic. I like it." He flashed her a grin. "It shows me a whole new side of you."

"Well, I'm happy if you're happy." Her voice dripped with sarcasm and she crossed her arms over her chest. "I assume there's more to your visit than an assessment of my taste. What else did you want?"

"I wanted to talk and"—he wagged his brows lecherously—"kiss and make up."

She snorted. "Don't hold your breath."

"To quote your friend in the hall: You don't know what you're missing. I kiss and make up well. I have a real knack for it."

"Which one of you?" she said with an oversweet smile. "The crown prince or the computer nerd?"

"Ouch." He cringed and clapped his hand over his heart. "That hurts. Trish, that really hurts."

"Not as much as I'd like it to."

"Okay, if you don't want to kiss and make up, the least you can do is offer me a beer."

"I'd like to but"—she shook her head mournfully—"it's my beer. This is all I have. I'm rationing. You understand."

"Yeah, if you're careful it will last to the turn of the next century."

"That's the goal. Now, if there's nothing else . . ."

"There is." He settled down on her sofa as if he belonged there. She had to admit he looked pretty good tonight in jeans just tight enough and a yellow, Henley-style shirt. "We have to get some things settled."

"I think we settled everything on the island."

"We didn't settle anything." He reached forward, pulled a beer from the six-pack and offered it to her. "It's still cold."

"I know." She rolled her eyes toward the ceiling and waved it away. "Go ahead and have it."

"Your generosity is equaled only by your charm." His gaze traveled over her. "I didn't think you were the work-shirt-and-cutoffs type either."

She'd prefer to have been wearing something far more presentable for her next confrontation with Jack than a ten-year-old frayed denim shirt with a cartoon character embroidered over the pocket and cutoffs too beat up to wear out of the house, but it couldn't be helped. "It's comfortable. Now, are you going to tell me what you want?"

He popped the top of his beer, his tone as laid-back as his attitude. "Aren't you going to sit down?"

"I prefer to stand."

"Suit yourself." He took a long drink from the can. "I told you today, I've had a lot of time to think about us."

"There is no *us*."

"Whether you want to accept it or not, there is definitely an *us*."

"No, there isn't." She kept her voice as casual as his. It was no mean feat given that her heart was pounding a million miles a minute. "I suppose there was a moment, one brief shining moment, when there was the potential for *us* but, right now there is no *us*."

"Because I didn't tell you the truth?"

"Because you lied."

"Well, technically I didn't. . . ." He sighed. "Call it what you want, I am sorry."

"You said that on the island."

"And I probably mentioned it again today and I'll keep saying it until you forgive me or get over it or whatever."

"Then you'll be saying it forever, because I'm never going to forgive you or get over it." No matter how forcefully she said it, she knew it was a lie. He probably knew it as well as she did; she'd forgive him and she'd get over it. Eventually. Maybe she already had.

"Of course you will." His gaze caught hers. His eyes smoldered and she steeled herself against the familiar aching sensation they triggered within her. "You love me."

"In your dreams."

"And yours."

"Only my nightmares. Now, if you've said what you came to say—"

"I haven't." He pulled a deep breath. "I love you and I want to marry you."

"Sorry, too late," she said quickly, her words spurred by a strange shot of what could only be panic. "I'm already engaged. To Elliott."

"That doesn't count. You don't love him—"

"I do too."

Not in the way that matters."

"Technically." She held out her left hand and waved her ring finger at him. Her engagement ring flashed in accompaniment to her words. "I'm committed."

"Oh, hell, Trish." He smacked his can onto the table, grabbed her outstretched hand and pulled her down on the sofa and into his arms. "I should be committed for this."

"What are you doing?" She struggled in a half-hearted way.

"Kissing and making up." He nibbled on her neck.

"I don't want to make up," she said, hating the complete lack of conviction in her voice.

"Really?"

"Really." Even as she said the word she knew

279

she did indeed want to make up. Wanted this. Wanted him. She wrapped her arms around him and closed her eyes. Her head dropped back and she savored the delicious feeling of his mouth caressing her flesh.

His lips whispered against her throat. "Are you sure?"

"Oh, yeah." She sighed.

"Positive?"

"Uh-huh," she murmured, unable to concentrate on anything but his touch and the sheer wonder of being back in his arms.

"If that's the way you want it." He shifted abruptly and she rolled off his lap, landing with a thud on the floor.

She blinked hard and stared in stunned disbelief.

He smiled and got to his feet. "Then I guess I'd better be going."

"What was that all about?" She glared up at him with frustration.

"That, Princess, was to prove a point." He picked up his beer, drained the can and set it back down.

"What point?"

He reached out to help her up and she slapped his hand away. He shrugged and stepped around her.

She scrambled to her feet. "What point?"

"You want me as much as I want you. Another minute or two and you would have proven it."

He smirked and once again, she wanted to slap the smile off his face.

"That wouldn't have proven anything other than basic animal lust. Desire. Passion. Whatever. I'm a normal, healthy female and you know the right buttons to push." She fisted her hands on her hips. "Let's face it, we had one hell of a great night on Paradise Bay, but that's it."

"We had one hell of a great night because it wasn't just lust. Or desire. Or passion." His gaze bored into hers. "It's love, Trish. Deny it all you want, but you love me. We belong together. Your future is with me."

"My future is all planned, thank you very much. Exactly how I want it. And you're not in it."

He walked toward the door with a swagger that could only be described as arrogant. "Now who's lying?" He disappeared around the stacked cases and called back to her. "See you tomorrow."

"I don't want to see you tomorrow," she yelled. "I don't want to see you ever again!"

His laugh drifted back and she heard the door open and click shut.

Damn the man anyway. He was right even if she refused to give him the satisfaction of admitting it. She did want to see him tomorrow and the day after and the day after that. She wanted to be in his arms, in his bed, in his life. She wanted him to sweep her off her feet, kiss her senseless, dissolve her defenses—

No! Abruptly, all traces of desire vanished. This was exactly the kind of thing that happened when you let throw-me-on-the-floor-and-screw-my-eyes-out passion mess up your mind. You forfeited control of your life. You happily handed over your future. You let someone else make your decisions.

And even her imaginary shrink would agree she'd come much too far to allow anyone to run her life ever again.

"Well said, Patricia."

"Thank you, doctor."

"Still, I am disappointed. I had hoped identifying the underlying cause for your need for control would help you manage those feelings."

She squirmed uncomfortably. "You think I overreacted?"

"What do you think?"

"It's possible, I suppose."

He raised a brow.

"Okay, okay, I overreacted. He does that to me. So what do I do now?"

"What do you think you should do?"

She gritted her teeth. "Just this one time would you give me your opinion?"

"My opinion is your opinion." He removed his glasses and tapped them against his chin thoughtfully. "And in my opinion, you might consider that, with this particular man, it may not be the possibility of his controlling your life that scares you.

"It's rather the possibility of his sharing it."

Chapter Fourteen

"Another glass of wine?" Jack directed his words to Maude, but his gaze kept straying to the arched living room entry and the foyer beyond. If he shifted a bit to the left, he could keep an eye on the front door.

"Oh, don't worry about a glass," Maude said. "Just bring me the bottle."

"Okay." Where was Trish anyway? She was late. Was she always late? Was this a habit of hers? Man, he was nervous. She was supposed to be here by seven. It was at least—he glanced at his watch—seven-fifteen. Maybe she was so mad at him about yesterday, she wouldn't come at all. It was damn hard to leave her like that, but he'd wanted to make a point. And he had, even if the resulting frustration had kept him tossing and turning all night.

"That way it won't have to be refilled."

"Right." Where was she? She should be . . . He looked down at Maude. "What did you say?"

"Nothing." She studied him curiously. "I've never seen you like this before."

"Like what?" He took a sip of the scotch and water in his hand.

"Tense. Nervous. Apprehensive. Uneasy. On ed—"

"Okay." He grimaced. "I get the message."

"I bet it's not easy being the prodigal son." She swirled the wine in her glass. "Is it strange coming back? To this house?"

"Actually, it's different, but it's kind of nice being home."

Maude nodded at Russ and Evelyn talking to Mo on the other side of the spacious living room. "How's it going with the stepmother?"

"Pretty well." Evelyn was a shorter, rounder version of her daughter. "The first few minutes were a little awkward, though. Apparently, she didn't know I was coming, so when she found me in the library checking out things I hadn't seen for years—"

"Checking out?"

"You know. Picking up, oh, a paperweight or a vase, stuff like that. Anyway, she thought I was casing the joint." He grinned. "She threatened me with a lamp."

"That's gutsy." Maude stared at Evelyn with

admiration. "She's as short as I am. And you tower over me by more than a foot."

"Plus, I still had the beard. She told me later, the beard was what really worried her."

"You do look a lot more civilized without it." She struck a pose. "How do I look?"

"Nice." He nodded approvingly. Her dress was made of some kind of shiny black material, very low-cut, very short, very tight. "Very nice. New outfit?"

"Yep." She brushed her long dark hair away from her face. Her eyes sparkled behind her glasses. "I bought it today. It cost a small fortune, but I figured it was worth it. Besides, now that I'm a genuine ESI employee, I thought, why not?"

"It looks good." He checked the foyer again and resisted the urge to look at his watch. "Anyway, Evelyn has really made me feel welcome. She and Dad have been married for about thirteen years now, and I think he made a good choice."

"I guess she's not holding your little problem with Trish against you."

"I don't think she knows." Jack took another swallow of his drink and savored the hard-wood taste of the liquor. "I'm pretty sure she hasn't talked to Trish yet, and I know my dad's keeping his mouth shut."

"Wise man." Maude glanced at the entry. "Well, I think your princess is here."

"She's not my princess." Jack's gaze followed hers. Trish and Elliott exchanged a few words with the butler, then stepped toward the archway. He drew in a hard breath. Except for the slightly bedraggled suit she'd worn when he first met her, whatever business thing she'd had on yesterday and her cute, but grubby, outfit from last night, he'd never seen her in anything other than the scraped-together outfits she'd been stuck with on the island. He'd thought she looked good then, and better still wearing nothing but a crisp white sheet, but she was dressed to kill tonight. She'd done something different to her hair. It was curly and floated above her shoulders like a blond cloud. A slinky black dress caressed her like liquid silk, and dark lace hose covered shapely legs that seemed to go on forever. She looked like an angel in black. A very hot, very sexy, very luscious angel. "Yet."

"Trish!" Evelyn hurried over to embrace her daughter and then Elliott.

Jack had to admit that Trish and Elliott did look good together, if a little too much alike. He studied the couple. Two blondes should never be paired together, he decided. There should be some kind of law against it. They looked like brother and sister. Practically inbred.

He pulled his brows together in annoyance. At first glance, all he'd noticed was how terrific she looked. But that slick black dress clung to every delicious curve and barely covered her lovely butt in the process. And those tiny little straps would obviously give way any minute. Not that it would make much difference. The so-called dress already revealed far more cleavage than was necessary. You could practically see down to her navel. Adult or not, how could her mother let her dress like that?

"Oh, she's going to be thrilled to see me," Maude said dryly.

"What do you mean," Jack said absently. Trish glanced around the room and her gaze met his. For a split second he thought he saw something welcoming in her eyes, but then her gaze fell upon Maude. Her eyes widened and disbelief swept across her face. She shook her head, then turned her attention to Russ.

"You can be such a man." Maude sighed. "She might forgive me for you someday, but she'll never get over this one."

"I don't get it." Was he surrounded by women these days who made no sense? "What are you talking about?"

She shook her head and rolled her eyes toward the ceiling. "Look at me, Jack. Look at my dress."

"Yeah. It's black." He shrugged. "I said it was nice."

"Trish probably thinks so." Maude emphasized every word, as if she was talking to a little kid. "She's wearing the same dress."

"So are you still mad at me?" Russ grasped Trish's elbow and steered her out the French doors and onto the terrace.

"Mad?" She smiled sweetly. "Why would I be mad?"

"You tell me." He leaned back against a stone retaining wall and took a sip of his drink. "All I know is what Jack—"

"That would be your *son* Jack?"

"That's the one. I am sorry about this mess, Trish. He should have told you who he was when you first got to Paradise Bay."

"You think?" She couldn't keep the sarcasm from her voice.

"It wasn't my idea to keep the truth from you. But Jack figured you might feel the whole family was ganging up on you if you knew he was my son. His reasoning seemed to make sense at the time." His tone was cool. "He said you thought I'd sent you to the island to rethink your wedding plans."

"Did you?"

"I sent you to do a job."

She raised a brow.

"Okay." He shrugged in a casual way. "I confess. I didn't think giving you a little time to consider your future was such a bad idea."

"Thanks for admitting it." She sipped her wine thoughtfully. "Can I ask you something?"

"Anything, you know that."

"What's up with you and Jack? The last I knew, you hadn't seen him or spoken to him. *Estranged* was an understatement when it came to your relationship. Or at least I thought it was."

"Jack grew up. And I suppose, in some ways, so did I. It's as simple as that."

"A little too simple."

288

Russ swirled the liquor in his glass and stared at it as if the past floated there amid the ice cubes. "Four years ago, Jack had an accident. A bad one. It shook him up and gave him time to look at his life. Where he was going and where he'd been. He didn't like what he saw.

"That's when he went back to Paradise Bay to get his act together. He's always loved the island. It's a very special place."

"I know," she said softly.

"And that's when we started talking again, and worked out our differences. I know Jack and I both regret all the years we lost, but I guess it's the price we had to pay. We're closer now than we were when he was a kid."

"And you've forgiven him?" Trish asked.

"And he's forgiven me," Russ said pointedly. "The problems were on both sides. He took his mother's death really hard and blamed me—"

"How could he blame you?" she asked quickly. "I thought she was sick."

"She was, but that doesn't negate the fact that I wasn't around as much as I should have been. He resented me for that, blamed me for her death almost as much as I did myself. I could never really fault Jack for feeling the way he did." He paused, and a wry smile lifted his lips. "Add to it basic father-son conflicts, typical youthful rebellion . . . I went through the same thing when I was a kid, although it didn't last as long.

"Remember too, Trish, I'm not perfect. I can

be overbearing and stubborn and inflexible. In fact, I believe I recall a certain young woman once telling me to stop trying to run her life."

"Fat lot of good it did," she muttered.

He chuckled. "I said I wasn't perfect. My belief in my own infallibility—"

"You do think you're always right."

"Don't we all? But the bottom line is, my problems with my son were as much my fault as they were his."

"And now you two are living happily ever after," she said slowly.

"That's as good a way to put it as any. You know"—he shook his head—"there were times when I didn't think he'd survive. When he'd be climbing a mountain somewhere, or partying with an international set that thought nothing of mixing alcohol and drugs and God knows what else, or racing a car at unbelievable speeds. It wasn't easy."

Sympathy for a father worried about his son stabbed her.

"But he's landed on his feet." A hint of amazement sounded in his words, as if he couldn't quite believe it himself.

"He's become the man I always hoped he would be. I'm not entirely sure how it happened, but I'm damn proud of him."

"He's okay, I guess." She shrugged, trying to appear noncommittal.

"Just okay?" He raised a brow. "That's it?"

"What else?"

"I don't know. I got the impression from Jack that he thinks you're more than just okay."

"Russ." She drew a deep breath. "I know you're trying to help, but that's off-limits. I don't want to talk about Jack and me. Besides, there's nothing to talk about."

"Okay, if that's the way you want it."

She studied him suspiciously. It wasn't like Russ to simply say "okay" and let it go at that. Chances were he wasn't going to let this go for long. She'd bet he was already planning something. On this subject she couldn't trust the father any more than she trusted the son. She'd have to stay on her toes.

"So." He took a long sip of his drink. "Did you think about your future while you were on the island?"

"That's another subject that's off-limits." She absolutely refused to give him the satisfaction of knowing his plan had worked, and his instincts about her relationship with Elliott were right. He'd know soon enough.

Let him and his son continue to wonder if she was going to marry Elliott. It would serve them both right.

As torture went, it was pretty mild. It wasn't the kind of pain and suffering she'd originally had in mind for either of them. But it was the best she could do.

At least for now.

Chapter Fifteen

How had her life gotten so screwed up in such a short time?

Trish took a long swallow of her wine and wondered if she'd had too much alcohol or not nearly enough. She stared across the blue glow of the pool at Elliott, deep in conversation with Maude—in her dress no less—probably continuing the discussion they'd started at dinner on the relative merits of one obscure philosopher versus another and their definitions of morality. Who knew Elliott had even a passing interest in philosophy, let alone could hold his own with an expert? All through dinner, Maude had bewitched Elliot with her apparently astute comments on existentialism and other deadly topics

Trish didn't understand and didn't want to.

Dinner, in general, would have made a condemned prisoner's last meal look like a festival of fun, although Trish was probably the only one to think so. Elliott, sitting beside Trish, had hung on Maude's every word. Jack, next to Maude and across the table from Trish, had sported an annoying smile of amusement through most of the meal, except for those moments when he was trying to charm her mother. At the head of the table, Russ wore the speculative, assessing expression he usually donned when a big business deal was in the making. Her mother, when she wasn't busy being captivated by Jack, always the perfect hostess, expertly kept conversation going for those not intrigued by the vagaries of philosophy. And Mo was apparently oblivious to everything except the pepper steak with brandy cream sauce and the champagne sorbet. For her part, Trish thought she'd shown admirable self-control not to scream out loud during the horrifically long meal—not even once.

She drained the last of her wine. She would have preferred to leave immediately after surviving dinner, but Elliott wanted to stay, and protesting would have just made things worse. So here she was, sitting alone, exactly the way she wanted it anyway, watching her not-yet-dumped fiancé get visibly closer in body and soul to Ph.D. Barbie—and probably closer to — dumping her—it was not exactly the way she wanted it. The rest of the party chatted at the end of the terrace closest to the house.

How could everything have gotten so messed up in one little month? First, her wedding was definitely off, even if she hadn't made it official yet. From the look of things, Elliott would be thrilled. Second, she'd realized she had no idea what she really wanted to do with her life when it came to a career. Oh, sure, her mother had floundered during the long years after her parents' breakup and her father's death. Not until Evelyn had married Russ had she discovered what she did almost as well as spend money was make it for charity. Still the idea that Trish was a late bloomer like her mother when it came to a vocation in life wasn't especially comforting.

She raised her glass to her lips, then held it at eye level, surprised to find it empty. It figured.

And then there was Jack. She could deny it all she wanted, but even Ms. Caplan knew she was in love with him. But loving Jack, and all that went along with it, was tantamount to throwing herself head first into a whirlpool without so much as a life preserver to keep her head above water. No security. No safety. No control. It was terrifying, and she wasn't sure her feelings for him were worth it. Whatever those feelings were. It was hard to reconcile what she'd felt for Jack with what she'd always felt about Russ's son. It was all damned confusing. Especially whenever he kissed her.

"This was a very good year." Jack's voice sounded beside her.

She sighed. "Not so far."

He laughed and with a flourish, presented a bottle of cabernet.

"I meant the wine."

"You just never give up, do you?"

"Never."

"I didn't think so." She held out her glass and he refilled it, then dropped into the wrought-iron chair beside hers and set the bottle on the matching patio table in front of them.

"That looks like it's going well." He studied the couple across the pool.

Her gaze followed his. "They share a common interest. That's all."

"Yeah, but I don't think it's philosophy."

"I think it's the dress," she said ironically. She took a sip of her wine. Realistically, it was useless to protest. It didn't take a genius to see that Elliott was enraptured by more than Maude's doctorate.

"When are you going to tell him?" Jack asked.

"When am I going to tell him what?"

"When are you going to tell him you're not marrying him?"

She kept her gaze on Maude and Elliott, but she knew Jack was staring at her. Probably looking for any chink in her armor. "What makes you think I'm not going to marry him?"

Jack heaved an exasperated sigh. "Come on,

Trish. Even if you weren't in love with someone else—"

"Which I'm not."

"Fine, even if you won't admit you're in love with someone else—"

"Much better," she murmured and suppressed a smile.

He paused for a long moment, as if trying to decide exactly what she meant. Good. It would keep him on his toes.

"Go ahead. You did have another point to make, didn't you?"

"I think so." He shook his head. "What I was about to say is, you can't marry somebody who has obviously fallen for someone else."

"Why not?" She propped her elbow on the table and rested her chin on her fist. "I mean, what I was—what I am—looking for in marriage hasn't changed. I want something secure and comfortable and—"

"Boring."

"There's a lot to be said for boring." She stared at him thoughtfully. "For example, with Elliott—"

He glanced at Elliot and Maude pointedly.

"Or someone like Elliott, you would never be confused about what he felt or what you felt. You'd never have to wonder what was true and what was a lie—"

"Well, technically—"

"And you'd never have to worry about throw-me-on-the-floor-and-screw-my-eyes-out-passion affecting everything else in your life."

He grinned. " 'Throw me on the floor and screw my eyes out'?"

"Yep." She leaned toward him. "It's just a description, Jack, not an invitation."

"Oh, yeah?" His voice was low and heavy with undercurrents that reached out to wrap around her soul. She caught her breath. Between the underwater lights from the pool and the subtle indirect lighting discreetly hidden in the plantings beside the terrace, the overall effect was vaguely magical, like a forest glen where fairies danced in the starlight. For a moment she felt like an enchanted princess waiting for the handsome prince to take her in his arms and break the wicked spell that held her captive. Or maybe cast a spell of his own.

And even here his eyes smoldered. "Trish—"

"Let's take a walk," she said quickly and got to her feet. "I'll show you around the rest of the terrace and the gardens."

"The gardens would be nice." He rose in that slow, easy way he had. "I'd love to see the gardens in the starlight. With you."

I'll bet. She groaned to herself. She'd walked right into that one. "On second thought, I prefer the terrace. It has much better lighting, and I'd hate for us to trip over anything in the dark."

"I think I'd prefer the gardens." He grabbed her hand. "And I promise to catch you if you fall."

Why did every comment sound like so much more than just the words he said?

"No." Her protest was weaker than she'd intended. She drew a deep breath. "The terrace. Or we could join Elliott and Maude."

"Definitely the terrace." He led her around the pool in a route that would avoid the other couple even though they probably wouldn't notice anything anyway. Jack still held her hand, and the smart thing to do would be to pull away. Hadn't she sworn to keep her distance? But his fingers entwined with hers so naturally and the gesture felt so right—why not?

"Mom will probably have your party on the terrace. She loves entertaining there, especially in the spring. There are a whole series of French doors that lead from the solarium—"

"I know, Trish." He chuckled. "Remember, I grew up here."

"That's right. I had completely forgotten. Sorry." They reached a turn and abruptly the lighted pool vanished behind artfully planted evergreen shrubs and shaped yews. In front of them, the flagstone walk opened up to a huge terrace, similar in size and shape to the area they'd just left without the pool. The French doors were dark tonight, but hidden fixtures along the edge of the stone cast puddles of light. And magic. "I've always liked it here. It's a great place for dancing."

"Dancing?"

She stared at him increduously. "Don't tell me

the infamous RJ the Fourth doesn't know how to dance."

"It's just been a long time, that's all."

"I can't believe you and Bar—Maude didn't dance now and then."

He drew a deep breath. "About Maude, Trish. I really—"

"No." She held out a hand to stop him. "Don't say another word. It's none of my business. And even if it was, it was over a long time ago, right?"

"Right."

"That's what I thought. Besides—again, not that it's any of my business—but it wasn't a big deal anyway, right?"

"What do you mean?" he asked cautiously.

"I mean, it's not like you were in love or anything."

"No?" he said slowly. "Absolutely not," he repeated with more enthusiasm, and strangely enough, with what might have been relief. "Not at all. Just for fun. Recreational, really."

"Oh?" Maybe a little too much enthusiasm.

"I don't mean it to sound, um—we did like each other. And there might have been the chance, a slim possibility—"

"Okay, okay, that's enough." She laughed. "I meant it when I said it wasn't any of my business. Just like my past isn't any of your business. Agreed?"

"Maybe. We'll have to see about that." He grinned and pulled her hand against his chest, wrapping his other arm around her waist. "In the meantime, are you going to help me brush up on my steps?"

"I think your steps are already pretty polished," she murmured. "I hate to be practical and down to earth, but what about music?"

"I already have music." He stared down at her. "You make my heart sing."

Her breath caught in her throat, and for once she couldn't think of a sharp comeback. Jack swayed to music only he could hear and Trish followed his lead without thinking.

"Believe it or not, this is the first time I've ever danced on the terrace."

"Really?" She might as well surrender right now. Once again, the man had her in the palm of his hand. And Heaven help her, it wasn't bad being there. "How come?"

"I went to boarding school when I was thirteen and haven't stepped foot back in this house until now." He smiled wryly. "Nearly sixteen years."

"Are you kidding?" She stared up at him. "I didn't know it was so long."

"You never noticed my absence around the table at Thanksgiving? The lack of a stocking at Christmas?"

"Well, sure. Mom married Russ when I was a junior in high school. Your name came up now and then, usually around school vacations, but Russ always said you were busy or had plans. I got the feeling they talked about you mostly when I wasn't around." She paused to remember. "I know it bothered them both and bothered Russ a lot. That's why I wrote to you."

"I never opened the letter. I don't even remember getting it." He sighed and Trish felt his warm breath on her shoulder. "In those days I tended to ignore anything that might be from home.

"I did manage to find it after you told me about it." He smiled down at her. "It was very sweet."

"Sweet? I thought it was pretty self-righteous." Strange, she hadn't thought of it that way until right now.

"That too. But the thought was sweet. Trish"— he said, hesitating. "About my father and me . . ."

"Don't. I had a long talk with Russ." If Russ could get over it, well, so could she. "I think I understand what you and he went through."

"So do you still want to sock me?"

"Not about that."

"About yesterday."

"Maybe, for the moment I'm saving myself."

"For marriage?" He grinned.

She ignored him. "As I was saying, then I went to college, and frankly I just didn't think about whether you were here or not." Guilt stabbed through her. "Sorry. I was pretty self-centered as a kid."

"Who wasn't? Besides, you're wrong. Self-centered kids don't write heart-wrenching letters on their stepfather's behalf." He twirled her in a quick, intricate step she matched without effort. "Very good."

301

"I don't think you need much practice." Had she really changed? Wasn't she just as self-absorbed now as when she'd been sixteen? Just as selfish? "I knew the split with your dad was major, but I didn't realize you never saw him."

"Oh, we got together now and then. He'd arrange to meet me in Nice or Florence or wherever. We'd be fine for the first ten or fifteen minutes, and then the battle would begin again." Jack gazed into the night, as if looking into the past. "We've fought in most of the capitals of Europe, and to be honest, nine times out of ten it was my fault. I egged him on." A wry smile curved up the corners of his mouth. "I was really a royal pain in the ass for a long, long time. I don't know why he put up with me."

"Maybe because you were his son and he knew you'd turn out okay."

"Have I?" He stared down at her.

"I'm still trying to decide." She swallowed hard, looking into his dark eyes.

"And what about you, Trish? You've got my life's story. All of it. What's yours?"

"Pretty typical, really." She shrugged in his arms. "My parents split when I was seven, but my father wasn't around much even before that. There was a huge, nasty custody battle. My mom wanted me and my father didn't want her to have anything." Even now, the thought of those days sent a shiver of helplessness through her.

"Then he died in a car accident, and he hadn't made any provisions for his ex-wife or his daughter. I always thought we were rich, but it turned out his money was actually his family's. He had access to some kind of trust, but that was it. The ironic part was that he could have arranged for us to have the same kind of access if he died. He just never got around to it. I guess he just didn't care enough." She didn't want to meet Jack's gaze. She didn't want to see anything approaching pity.

"I'm sorry," he said simply.

"It was a long time ago." And it still hurt. "My mom's family has some money and they helped as much as she'd let them. You probably wouldn't realize it to look at her, but she has a fierce independent streak. She was madly in love with my father in the beginning and married him in spite of her parents' objections. Ultimately, he broke her heart. She hated to admit that her family was right, so she tried to make it on her own."

"Sounds tough."

The sympathy in his voice startled her and she looked up at him. "Don't get me wrong, we weren't starving in the streets or anything. It was just . . . different. For both of us, of course, but I was a kid so it wasn't that bad. She tried so hard, but she could never seem to find her niche: you know, figure out what she liked doing and what she was good at.

"When she met Russ, she was working in a museum in the gift shop. She married him and the rest is history." Trish laughed softly. "A couple of years later she was back at the museum, coordinating some of their big fund-raising efforts."

"She'd found her niche?"

"Yeah." A vague suspicion crystallized in her mind. Was history repeating itself? Her mother had been the same age during the divorce as Trish was now. And Trish had just realized that she had no idea what her niche in life was. Evelyn had married Russ for security and safety, but her first marriage had been about passion. Excitement. Adventure. Love. And look how that had ended.

Panic, harsh and swift and overwhelming, rushed through her and she pushed out of his arms and stepped back. "You don't need any more practice, Jack. You're a great dancer and you know it. Besides, there isn't any music."

"There is for me." The intense tone of his voice tugged at her heart, but she ignored it.

"I have to go. Elliott will be wondering where I am."

"I doubt that Elliott even knows you're gone."

"I don't care." Her voice rose. "I have to go. Now. And I can't see you anymore. Not like this. Don't show up at my apartment. Don't send me beer or flowers or anything else." She backed up. "It's just business between us from now on."

"Trish." He stepped toward her. "I'm sorry about not telling you—"

"No!" She thrust her hand in front of her. "It's

okay. It doesn't matter anymore. This has nothing to do with that."

"Then what—" He sounded so helpless, she thought her heart would break for him. And for her.

"I can't, Jack. It won't work. I just . . . I can't." She turned and ran back toward the pool.

"Trish!" His voice echoed behind her, and she steeled herself against the urge to turn around and throw herself into his arms. She would absolutely not repeat the mistakes of the past.

No matter how tempting they might be.

Chapter Sixteen

"It's driving me crazy. She hasn't said one personal word to me in three weeks. Three weeks!" Jack paced the width of Russ's office like a frustrated lion. "I'm around her every day and she is strictly business. The only time she broke the code of silence was to threaten to sue me for harassment! Harassment!" He stopped and glared. "Can you believe that?"

"It's incredible." Russ fought to kept his expression serious.

"Wait, can she do that?" His son's brows pulled together in concern.

"I'll have Legal check on it. But I believe that since you two are equal directors on this project,

and neither has the power to fire the other,
you're safe."

"Good, but I sure wouldn't put it past her." He
paced again in silence, then swiveled toward his
father. "Have you noticed that she hasn't called
off her wedding yet?"

"I've been surprised by that."

"What is she waiting for? I know she's not going to marry Elliott and I'm pretty confident that
with Maude in the picture, he doesn't want to
marry her."

"That is a problem," Russ murmured.

"No kidding. And it needs to be taken care of
soon. Do you realize her wedding invitations go
out in two weeks?" He paused. "Evelyn told me."

Russ nodded. "I thought maybe she would."

"I just don't get it." He sighed. "Tell me one
thing. Why is it that even with you, her mother,
probably Elliott, definitely Maude and possibly
Ms. Caplan on my side, I'm no closer to . . .
to . . ."

"To what?" Russ raised a curious brow.

"To . . . I don't know." Jack threw his hands in
the air and looked at his father. "Getting the girl.
Winning the hand of the fair Patricia. Whatever."

"Winning the hand?" Russ studied his son.
"Are you talking about marriage?"

"It's come up." Jack grimaced. "I've never really thought about marriage before Trish. In

spite of your example, it's always seemed so permanent."

"Watch it, son." Russ narrowed his eyes. "I made one mistake in marriage, but it wasn't your mother and it wasn't Evelyn. I'd say two out of three isn't bad."

"Sorry." Jack collapsed into a wing chair. "I guess the answer is yes. I want marriage. Kids. A dog. The whole bit. Now I just have to convince her."

"Trish always has been stubborn."

"The word *stubborn* doesn't cover it." He rested his head against the back of the chair, narrowed his eyes and stared into space. "If I could just get her to talk to me. She won't answer her phone. I tell you, I've never talked so much to an answering machine in my life. I'm afraid she'll shoot me if I show up at her apartment again. She makes sure we're hardly ever alone. I don't know what to do next."

"Well, your homecoming party is just three days away. Maybe you can talk to her there. Sometimes you can be more intimate in a crowd full of people than you can alone."

"Right. In a crowd, she can't kill me." His voice was grim. "Hopefully."

Russ laughed

"You'll come up with something."

"I'd better. I can't take much more of this." He smiled ruefully. "Love really does bite, doesn't it?"

Russ grinned. "It always has."

Jack left a few minutes later. Russ stared thoughtfully at the open door. Marjorie had told him to butt out, but his children needed help. "Marjorie," he called out.

His assistant appeared almost immediately. The woman seemed to know when he needed her before he did.

"He needs to get her alone," Russ said.

"I take it this means you're not going to mind your own business?"

"Nope. You think it's a mistake?"

"I did initially, but Trish seems to be really holding her ground. At this stage, some sort of divine intervention is probably called for."

"Any suggestions?"

"Well . . ." She tapped her chin thoughtfully. "They could go back to the scene of the crime, I suppose."

"Paradise Bay?" He shook his head. "She'll never go. Not unless we tie her up and throw her on a plane."

"Drastic and unnecessary, but you're right. Trish will never go willingly, especially if she knows Jack is going too."

"At least it's nice to see you admit that I'm right once in a while," he muttered.

"However . . ." Marjorie lowered her head and gazed at him over the rim of her glasses. "Trish will be on the next plane or ship or canoe if she thinks there's a problem with the inn. In case you haven't noticed, she's obsessed by this project."

"I've noticed." He picked up a sterling fountain pen and tapped it absently on the desk. "I'm not sure if that's good or bad. Trish has always been a hard worker, but her behavior here worries me a bit."

"It's perfectly natural, Russ." Marjorie smied patiently. "The more she puts of herself into the inn, the less there is left for anything else. Or anyone else. Also, I believe your stepdaughter has finally found her calling in life—exactly as you planned."

"As I planned?" He tapped the pen a bit faster.

"Everyone knew Trish wasn't the appropriate person to send to Paradise Bay in the first place, not if you were serious about developing a resort."

"And I *was* serous," he said quickly.

"You and I both know that public relations is simply a job for her. And while I'm sure she derives some satisfaction from it, it's not anything she has a great deal of passion for. Am I correct?"

"Absolutely." Russ nodded. What on earth was she getting at?

"However, Trish does seem to have a certain knack—call it a natural instinct, if you will—for this kind of work. Plus, she obviously enjoys it."

He nodded slowly. "It's perfect for her."

"So you've achieved one objective." She paused thoughtfully. "I'm rather surprised she hasn't called off her wedding yet, but I expect that announcement any day."

He heaved a heavy sigh. "She's awfully stubborn."

"So is Jack." Her expression was serious, but a smile lurked in her eyes. "He does come by it genetically."

Russ laughed. "That's the nicest thing you've ever said to me."

"Enjoy it." She started to leave.

"Marjorie?"

She turned. "Yes?"

"What kind of problem?"

She gazed at him tolerantly. "Something that would realistically be a threat to the success of the project, of course. At the moment, Trish is putting all her effort, energy and soul into this project. She wants it to succeed so bad that she can taste it."

"Good idea." He picked up the tempo of the tapping. "I don't suppose you have any specific thoughts . . ."

"No." She smiled pleasantly.

"Well, if you come up with something . . ."

"You'll be the first to know." She nodded and left the office.

"Problem, huh? Hmm. What kind of problem?" he muttered to himself.

Absently, he turned to his computer and pulled up the Paradise Bay file. Maybe there was something there. He scanned various subfiles until he found one marked MEDIA. It consisted primarily of news articles from publications around the world dealing with the South Pacific, the International Date Line and the millennium. He glanced at a few: one about the predicted computer chaos, another on efforts to attract tourism, a third on ecological concerns. He closed the file and leaned back in his chair.

Russ picked up the pen and tapped it slowly and rhythmically on the desk, staring at the starfield screen saver. Something he'd read . . .

Inspired, he grinned and reached for the phone. It wouldn't be divine intervention, but it would be damn close.

"I'm going crazy, Mom." Trish paced the length of her mother's dressing room. They still had a good half an hour before the guests would arrive for Jack's party. "I don't know what's the matter with me. I can't sleep. I can't eat." She glanced at a full-length standing mirror. The red sequined gown, with its low-cut halter and practically nonexistent back, fit her with no room to spare. "Okay, maybe I can eat a little."

"You look fine, dear." Evelyn sat at her dressing table trying on earrings.

Trish turned toward her mother. It was impossible to get any decent advice without spilling all the facts, but Trish wasn't ready to talk to anyone about Jack. "What am I going to do?"

Evelyn met her gaze in the mirror. "I thought you were getting married."

"Oh. Yeah." Trish wrinkled her nose. "It slipped my mind."

"That's not a good sign, Trish. I suspect marriage slips many people's minds, but not just a few weeks before the wedding." Evelyn tilted her head first one way and then the other. Clusters of diamonds flashed on her ears. "What do you think?" she asked.

"Very nice, Mom." Trish drew a deep breath. This was ridiculous. She had to talk to somebody. "There's something I need to tell you."

"No. These won't do." Evelyn shook her head and took off the diamonds.

"Mother—"

"Trish, sweetheart"—she pawed through the enameled Japanese box on the table—"if you're trying to tell me you aren't going to marry Elliott, it's not necessary."

"It's not?"

"Not at all." Her mother held up another selection. "What do you think? Emeralds, maybe?"

"Yeah, whatever." Trish stepped closer. "Why isn't it necessary?" she asked impatiently.

"Trish, it's painfully apparent that Elliott is enamoured with that lovely little intellectual. Personally, I have no idea what they're saying most of the time, although I did get the chance to sample her paté. It was very good." Evelyn dropped the earrings on the table and turned to her daughter. "And it's just apparent that he is not the right man for you."

"It is?"

"No question about it, although I certainly thought that he was in the beginning." Evelyn sighed. "I didn't realize how wrong I could be until you met the right man—"

"The right man?"

Evelyn's delicate brows drew together in annoyance. "Don't be dense, darling. Jack is definitely the right man for you."

Trish sank onto the chaise next to the dressing table and stared. "How do you know?"

"Isn't it obvious?"

"Not to me."

"It is to everyone else in the world. Why, the man's heart is in his eyes every time he looks at you. And you have refused to look at him at all." Evelyn turned back to her earring selection. "That spells love in my book."

Trish's stomach clenched. "I'm not in love with him, though."

"Of course you are," Evelyn countered.

Of course I am. Trish heaved a heartfelt sigh, stood, crossed her arms and resumed pacing. "I suppose I should talk to Elliott—"

"You haven't talked to Elliot yet?" Evelyn's eyes in the mirror widened in surprise. "What are you waiting for?"

"I don't know, Mom. As long as I was engaged, I had this nice illusion of safety." Not that Jack paid any attention to a little thing like an engagement. Apparently, it wasn't bothering Maude and Elliott either.

"I guess we'll cancel the wedding."

"Over my dead body."

Trish pulled up short and stared at her mother. "Why not?"

"I've spent way too much time and far too much money to cancel what your stepfather so lovingly calls the wedding of the century." Evelyn's mouth was set in a firm line and a stubborn light gleamed in her eye. "I've planned your wedding from the day you were born. I never had a real one myself, so yours will have to do. I love weddings. Big, showy, expensive, ridiculous, extravagant celebrations. I want six-foot-tall cakes, flowers adorning everything from the aisles in the church to the bathrooms at the reception, and I want doves."

Trish groaned. "Not doves. I thought we'd decided against doves."

"Doves." She shot her daughter a no-nonsense glare. "You're nearly thirty, Trish, and this may well be my last chance. And yours. I don't give a hoot in hell who the groom is, but there *will* be a wedding."

"Mother!"

"All right." Evelyn huffed. "I'm sorry. I do care who the groom is. And I do think we both know exactly who that should be. Besides, there's plenty of time if we want to cancel it altogether. There, are you happy now?"

"Thrilled." Trish grimaced. "I can't marry Jack."

"Why on earth not?"

"He's not at all safe and secure and comfortable. He makes my stomach churn, and it's hard to breathe around him and . . ." *He makes my heart sing.* She shook her head. "It's way too scary. I don't want that. I want a marriage like yours."

Evelyn swiveled around to face her. "What do you mean 'a marriage like mine'?"

"Well, you married Russ for safety and security and—"

"You think I don't love Russ? That I married him for safety's sake?" she asked slowly.

"Oh, I'm sure you were fond of him—"

"Fond of him?" Her mother's eyes widened. "Fond of him?"

"Sure." Trish shrugged.

"Oh, my God." Evelyn buried her face in her hands and her shoulders shook.

"Mom!" Trish rushed to her side and threw her arms around her mother. "I'm so sorry. I didn't mean—"

Evelyn raised her head and laughter bubbled from her. Tears filled her eyes and spilled onto her cheeks.

"Mom?" Trish straightened up and stared at her.

"Pass me the tissues." Evelyn sniffed and waved at the box on the table. Trish handed it to her. Her mother grabbed a tissue and dabbed at her eyes. "Oh, that was too, too funny. I haven't laughed that hard in a long time." She glanced at the mirror and made a face. "I'll have to touch up my makeup, but it was worth it."

She nodded at the chaise. "Sit down, sweetheart. We need to clear up a few things."

Trish perched on the edge of the seat, apprehension stiffening her spine. "What's so funny?"

"There are things I probably should have mentioned to you years ago, but they never came up, and at the time I didn't really think they were your business." She reached out and took Trish's hand. "I had no idea you were modeling your relationships on mine. And I never imagined you saw my relationship with Russ as a marriage of convenience."

"Not exactly 'convenience,' but—"

"Trish." She stared into her daughter's eyes. "The moment I met Russ, my heart thudded and my breath caught and my stomach leapt, and in all the years since that has never stopped. I had no idea if he had two pennies to his name. And I didn't care. I fell madly, deeply, passionately in love with him that moment and I still am. And that very first night I met him, we made love like wild bunnies." Her eyes sparkled wickedly.

"Mother!" Trish jerked her hand away.

"Jackrabbits, really."

"Stop that!"

"Or minks. Minks are very prolific, you know."

Trish jumped to her feet and backed away. "You're right; this is none of my business. I don't want to know this."

"Well, that's just too bad." Evelyn stood and shook her finger at her daughter. "It became your business when you decided your mother was some fortune-seeker just looking for a man to take care of her and her child."

"That's really not exactly what I thought," Trish said uneasily.

"I hope not." Evelyn's tone was firm. "My marriage to your father was a horrible mistake. He was handsome and reckless and I was very young and very stupid and just *thought* I was in love. It was a very juvenile kind of love." A small smile quirked her lips. "You were absolutely the only good thing that came from that.

"Russ is the love of my life, Trish. Mad, passionate, steal-your-breath, knock-you-off-your-feet love isn't anything to be afraid of." Her mother studied her for a long moment before continuing. "The real fear, my darling daughter, is not grabbing it when you find it."

"So, Patricia, it appears your rationale for avoiding passionate involvement with your young man is no longer valid."

"I suppose, doctor. Logically, I realize now that my whole outlook was based on false perceptions." She sighed. "But I still don't know what to do."

"My job is to guide, not lead you by the hand. However . . ." He shrugged. "In your case I'll make an exception. First, my dear, trust yourself. Listen to your heart. And second, listen to your mother."

Trish leaned against one of the additional tables set up around the terrace and scanned the crowd of dancers for Jack's tall figure. She'd seen him a couple of times tonight, but he was never alone. Usually, he was stuck in some polite conversation with people who had known his father or her mother for years, or occasionally someone who'd known his mother and remembered him from his childhood. He also apparently had been roped into a dance or two with various unmarried friends of the family, but he was obviously just being polite by dancing with them.

"Here you go." Elliott offered her a glass of champagne. "Nice party."

"Isn't it?" Trish took a sip. "My mother certainly knows how to throw 'em. Of course, you know the wedding will make this look like a tea party."

Elliott hesitated. "About the wedding, Trish . . ."

"Wait. Before you say anything." She drew a steady breath. She'd put this off for way too long. Jack had called Elliott a wuss when they first met, but she deserved the title more than he did. She'd been too much of a coward to face Elliott or her own feelings. Trish put her glass on the table and twisted his diamond off her finger.

"Here. You might need this for someone else," she said. She took his hand, placed her ring in his palm, folded his fingers around it and met his gaze. "I'd say I was sorry, but I know you're going to be much happier without me."

"You know about Maude, don't you?"

"It's pretty hard to miss."

"I guess I owe you an explanation." He blew out a long breath. "Remember how you thought Russ sent you to Paradise Bay to give you time to think about marrying me?"

"Yeah."

"Well, I had time to think too. And the more I did, the more I realized, as much as we care for each other, there was something missing."

"Passion? Adventure? Excitement?"

He grinned wryly. "D: all of the above. When I showed up on the island, I really came to talk to you about us. About calling off the wedding."

"I see."

"You're not upset are you?"

"Crushed." She smiled. "But just my ego. And only a little."

"Good. You know, I thought you and I had it all perfectly planned out. Simple. Straightforward. No big surprises. But from the moment I met Maude, I knew it wasn't enough." He shook his head in amazement. "Imagine, someone like her with someone like me."

"She's very lucky."

"What about you, Trish?" His gaze searched her face. "What are you going to do?"

"Who knows?" She shrugged. "Actually, my mother refuses to cancel the wedding, so I've got about two weeks before the invitations go out to fill in the blank next to the spot marked groom." She grinned and released his hand. "You'd better hope I come up with a name, or you're going to be stuck with me after all."

He laughed. "I can think of worse fates." He glanced across the terrace and she followed his gaze. Jack stood next to his father, laughing at something. Her heart tripped. "That looks like a good candidate to me."

"Does everyone in the world know about Jack and me?"

"Oh, not everyone." Elliott grinned. "I think there are a few people in Michigan, in the north woods somewhere, who don't."

"I wouldn't be surprised." A comfortable silence fell between them, and Trish realized that there would have been a lifetime of comfortable silences with this man. Was that so bad?

As if in answer to her question, Jack's gaze met hers and he smiled. A feeling of utter weakness that wasn't at all comfortable but wonderful anyway washed through her. She smiled back, and his eyes widened slightly.

"What do you think would have happened to us if we hadn't met them?"

"A lifetime of bedroom sex," she murmured.

"What did you say?"

"Nothing." She laughed and sipped her champagne. "Go find Maude."

"Thanks, Trish." He leaned forward and kissed her lightly on the cheek. He started to leave, then turned back. "By the way, if Jack tries to tell you there was something beyond a good time between him and Maude, don't believe it."

"Oh?"

"She said she told him to say it was more than just fun and games between them. She figured you'd take it better if you thought they had a relationship." He shook his head. "It's the first illogical thing she's said to me."

"Don't worry, I understand completely. It's a female thing." She gave him a little push. "Now go."

Elliott grinned and made his way through the crowd. Trish smiled to herself. Any lingering jealousy she might have felt toward Maude vanished.

"You smiled at me." Jack's voice sounded behind her.

She turned around and widened her eyes. "Are you sure?"

"Very sure." His voice was solemn. "You definitely smiled at me."

"It must have been some sort of horrible mistake." She shook her head mournfully. "I don't know what I was thinking."

"Trish—"

"I remember now." She gazed up at him. "I was wondering what it would be like to dance with you when everyone can hear the music."

"We can find out." He took her hand and led her into the crowd of dancers. "But I don't need music." He took her in his arms. She'd almost forgotten how good it felt to stand in his embrace.

"Neither do I," she said softly.

He narrowed his eyes suspiciously. "What are you up to?"

"There's something I need to tell you."

"Oh?"

She nodded. "It's kind of a confession."

"Ah-ha. Confession is good for the soul, you know." His expression was serious but his eyes twinkled.

"I don't like mysteries. I'm not very good at them."

"I see. You're one of those people who reads the end of the book first, aren't you?"

"Sometimes. I'm not all that wild about surprises either. I like having all the facts."

"Now there's a revelation."

"And I can be very self-centered. For example"—she drew a deep breath—"I asked you once why you were on the island, but I never really pursued it. I knew it was something traumatic, some kind of crisis, but it didn't really affect me, so I didn't really care."

"And now?" His dark gaze trapped hers.

"Now I do," she said simply.

He held her a bit tighter. "In hindsight, it doesn't seem like that big a deal. I was in a skiing accident. A couple of friends and I were heli-skiing in British Columbia—"

"Heli-skiing?"

"Yeah." He looked almost embarrassed. "A helicopter drops you off in a remote area and picks you up later."

"Sounds, um, fun."

"It is, usually. But we were screwing around. You know, stupid, risky, dangerous stuff. We thought we were invincible. The details aren't all that important and I still feel like an idiot when I think about it. We were really lucky." His eyes took on a faraway look. "There was an avalanche and two of us were hurt. The other guy's injuries weren't so bad, but I was in a coma for a couple of days."

"Oh, my God." Her heart stuck in her throat.

He smiled. "No permanent damage, but it did scare the hell out of me. I took a long look at my life and it sucked. I had no focus, no purpose. I was basically a worthless, spoiled rich kid trying to make up for whatever it was I thought was missing in my life by risking my neck every chance I got. The only problem with that kind of adrenaline high is that when it wears off, if you survive, there isn't much of anything left."

"You sound pretty together about it now."

"I am. Now. Thanks to Paradise Bay and my dad." His voice was thoughtful. "We'd visited the island a couple of times when I was a kid and I'd loved it there. It seemed the perfect place—the only place, really—to get my life back together. My dad came right away, and for the first time in years we talked, really talked about our relationship and my mother and her death. We made peace with each other, I guess. After a few months, he brought a computer. He said he thought I needed a hobby."

Jack chuckled. "One thing led to another, and

I discovered a fascination and a talent for programming. I also discovered a balance in my life. It took a long time, but the island worked its magic on me.

He gazed down at her. "I'll always be a risk-taker, Trish, in one way or another. I'll always enjoy a good adventure and excitement, but it's not like an addiction anymore. Does that make sense?"

"I think so."

"What about you?"

"I've never been much for adventure. I've always wanted everything laid out precisely, with nothing left to chance. I'm not big on fear. I probably wouldn't recognize adrenaline if I were swimming in it, no matter how much of a rush it was. And I've never really taken a risk." She swallowed hard. "Until now."

"Now?"

She nodded. "Jack, I—"

"Pardon me, sir." A waiter tapped his shoulder and handed him a phone.

Jack shrugged ruefully and accepted the phone. "Jack Evans . . ."

Jack Evans? That would take some getting used to. So would adjusting to the tremendous risk of loving him. Just like jumping into the volcano to appease the gods. Terrifying and exciting and one amazing adventure. No guarantees of safety or security. And no turning back. As soon as he got off the phone, she'd tell him she'd broken up with Elliott. And she'd tell him she loved him.

What was he talking about, anyway? His expression grew concerned.

". . . yeah. Right away. Thanks for calling."

"Jack?"

Jack snapped the phone closed. "Sorry, Trish." He took her elbow and guided her toward the house. "That's one of the downsides to finally getting an earth station and real phone capabilities on Paradise Bay. That was Mo. We've got problems."

"What kind of problems? Construction? Labor? Weather?" Her voice rose. "What?"

"Accidents," Jack said grimly. "Mo thinks it's sabotage."

"Sabotage?" She stopped and stared. "Are you kidding? Who would want to do something like that?"

"Think about it. There are dozens of other islands along the International Date Line. Paradise Bay isn't the only place where you can be the first in the world to greet the dawn of the year 2000. The potential for tourism is unlimited. There are very big bucks involved and some major investments in the South Pacific. While we're aiming for a very specific market, it's not inconceivable that some other operation on another island would see us as a real threat.

"Look." His gaze searched her face. "As much as I think we were having the most important conversation of our lives, it's going to have to wait. I have to go back to the island."

"What?"

"This is my first big project with ESI. I can't—"

"Wait a minute." He didn't really think he could leave her behind, did he? "I'm co-director of this operation. I care as much about it as you do. And my butt is just as much on the line as yours. I'm going with you."

"I don't think so. You said it yourself. You don't like adventure. You don't like excitement. You don't take risks."

"Well, apparently I'm learning." She crossed her arms. "I slept with you, didn't I?"

He ignored her. "Frankly, Trish, this could actually be dangerous. I'm not going to let you come."

"You're not going to *let* me?" Angry heat flushed up her face. "You can't stop me."

"Stop you from doing what?" Russ joined them. "What are you two arguing about?"

Jack quickly filled him in.

"This is a problem." Russ thought for a moment. "Marjorie is around here somewhere. She'll make the arrangements for the jet and whatever else you need. It will take a few hours, though."

"Good," Trish snapped. "I need a little time to throw some things in a bag. A carry-on that doesn't leave my sight."

"Tell her she's not coming. Tell her this could be dangerous." Jack clenched his teeth. "Tell her she doesn't do adventure."

"Well, maybe it's time I try a little!" She planted her fists on her hips and glared at him.

"Tell her, Dad." He glared back. "Tell her she can't come."

"I wish I could." Russ shook his head. "I can suggest to my stepdaughter that she should reconsider. But I hate to tell you, Jack, as head of this company I can't discriminate between two employees with equal responsibilities. If you go and she wants to go—"

"And I do!"

"—she gets to go." He shrugged.

"Great." She couldn't resist a smug smile. "I'll see you at the airport." She turned on her heel and started off.

"If you're late, I'll leave without you," he called after her.

"Don't worry about it," she yelled over her shoulder. "I'll swim if have to."

She glanced at her watch and made her way through the guests. She'd make it. She wasn't about to let him take over this project. Her project. If there was a problem and he needed to be there, then so did she. The Inn on Paradise Bay was the biggest thing she'd ever done and the most satisfying. And nothing was going to screw it up. Not tourism terrorists and certainly not Jack Evans.

She must have been insane to think even for a moment that everything would work out between them. She was willing to deal with the risks of love, but she wasn't about to let anyone run her life and make her decisions, and she didn't give a damn what her all-too-sensible, non-existent shrink said about it. Once again, Jack was trying to take control.

And once again, she was determined to take it right back.

Chapter Seventeen

"So now what?" Mo's gaze traveled from Jack to Trish and back. "Any ideas?"

"Security guards?" Trish said.

"The construction chief has already set up something," Jack said. Trish looked at him curiously. "I didn't talk to him without you, if that's what you're thinking. Mo told me."

"That's what I figured." She gave him a forced smile.

The three of them stood near the base of the waterfall on a natural terrace. Their plans called for expanding the space for an outdoor bar and casual grill restaurant while retaining the feel of a spot carved out by nature instead of man. A picture postcard setting and a spectacular view.

And the perfect place for a good look at the construction site spread out below them.

"I can't believe all this was accomplished in five weeks." Trish stared at the scene. "It's amazing."

Mo grinned. "Anything's possible if you have enough money and are willing to spend it."

The site swarmed with activity. Even though Jack was well aware of the number of people involved, some local, most imported, there was a big difference between numbers on paper and seeing it all come to life in person. Jack could vaguely equate the drawings and Mo's models with what he saw now. Already, the resort's foundations were laid out.

There would be a central hub to include a lobby, a spa, a workout facility, a few specialty shops and offices connecting to a main restaurant, a mini conference center and guest rooms. Most of the lodging would be in wings that spread north of the main building, giving every suite an ocean view and allowing each guest to be one of the first in the world to see the dawn of every new day. It was a brilliant marketing ploy. They'd even incorporated Mo's slogan: *Where the day begins.* Russ deserved credit for the original idea, but it was Trish who'd realized that the new millennium would come only once; Mo's slogan would keep visitors booked long into the future.

The goal right now was simply to get the bulk of the guest rooms plus the main building and the restaurants completed by the end of the year.

Everything else could move a little slower—but not much. Russ wanted a private, by-invitation-only kickoff for the inn. The first of the last New Year's Eve parties of the 1900s. His dad didn't worry about not being open for general business at that point. After all, they had one more year until the actual start of the twenty-first century, which technically began on January, 2001. On that date, they'd have another big blowout celebration for people who had more money than they knew what to do with and would cheerfully spend it for the experience of a lifetime.

"Are we going down?" Trish nodded at the construction site.

"Think you can make it?" Jack asked innocently.

"No problem. It's just a path."

"Yeah, but it's fairly steep, and I know what a great athlete you are." He returned the same forced smile she'd given him.

Mo shot an exasperated gaze at the sky. Jack and Trish had been sniping at each other since they'd arrived. "Play nice, you two. Put your hard hats on and let's go."

Trish followed Mo and Jack trailed a few steps behind. She had on a pair of not-too-short shorts and a not-at-all-tight shirt, and he thought with regret of the days when she'd been forced to wear Maude's clothes. Of course, today's view still wasn't half-bad.

If he'd thought she drove him crazy when she wasn't talking to him, it was even worse now.

She wanted to be included in every discussion, every decision, everything. He wasn't sure how exactly, but he knew deep down inside, in some convoluted way, this was all his fault. In the last twenty-four hours he'd gone over their last conversation word by word.

He was fairly certain she'd forgiven him for just about everything, including the mistakes of his youth and keeping his identity from her. He was also certain she'd been ready to let go of whatever hangups had pulled her back from him before and admit again that she really did love him. And then Mo had called and she'd gotten all pissed because he didn't want to take her with him. Hell. He shook his head. She'd said she didn't like adventures or surprises, and this situation had the potential for both. Plus, he wasn't about to let her get hurt confronting saboteurs. All he was trying to do was protect her.

To make matters worse, when he'd shown up at the plane, Maude and Elliott were there too, with Ms. Caplan. Privately, the efficient woman had explained to Jack that Russ thought it was a good idea if the other couple came along. It made sense, he supposed. Maude had a stake in the project and, like it or not, there had been no official declaration of a broken engagement for Trish and Elliott. Thank God Ms. Caplan had had no desire to accompany them to the island, although he suspected the executive assistant was probably very handy to have around in dangerous situations. But she had simply gone over a few travel details and wished them well.

"Jack." Mo waved him forward and Jack hurried to catch up. Mo and Trish stood talking to a tall, tan, efficient-looking man. "Jack Evans, Ben Gibson. Ben's in charge of construction."

"G'day." Gibson's gaze was direct, his handshake firm, his accent definitely Australian. "I've done some work for ESI in the past. It's a good operation."

"Thanks. I think so." Jack liked him at once and figured he could be trusted.

"Can you tell us what's going on?" Trish asked.

Gibson glanced at Mo and shrugged. "Sure. For starters, we've had trouble with some of the equipment. When we leave it up by the road at night, there's no traffic you know, and . . ."

Twenty minutes later, the impromptu tour was finished, but there was something that Jack couldn't quite put his finger on that nagging at the edge of his mind. They'd seen the evidence of sabotage, or tampering or whatever. Most of it was already fixed, and all of it was minor. Trish asked Gibson a question and he responded with a disgustingly charming grin and launched into a monologue that was as much flirtation as explanation. Jack pulled Mo aside but kept his gaze on Trish. He didn't want her to overhear him.

"Okay, Mo, what in the hell is this all about?" he asked quietly.

"I wish I knew." Mo shook his head. "There have been all kinds of prob—"

"Cut the crap, pal." Jack studied his friend suspiciously. "There's nothing here to warrant you calling us back. You haven't shown us anything that can't be attributed to accidents or mistakes or just plain bad luck—and certainly nothing I'd consider serious."

"Nothing at all?" Mo said hopefully.

"Nothing. Zip."

"Are you sure?" Mo glanced around. "Maybe if you looked a little harder—"

"Mo."

"I knew I couldn't keep my mouth shut. I told them, 'You don't want my help,' but no . . ." Mo blew out a long breath. "It wasn't my idea."

"What wasn't your idea?"

Mo looked like he'd rather be anyplace but where he was. "Look, when the head—I mean the absolute top guy of a major international corporation—"

"My father?"

"That's him, all right." Mo glanced at Trish. "Your father called and said you and the goddess—"

"Goddess?" Jack bit back a grin

Mo's face darkened. "Okay, flying monkey."

"We're all flying monkeys now, Mo. What did my dad want?"

"If captured and tortured, you didn't hear this from me, right?"

Jack heaved an impatient sigh. "I think my father gave up torture years ago."

"I wasn't worried about *him*." Mo looked pointedly at Trish.

"You're scared of her?"

"Petrified. She was okay when we were all working here together, but since you two returned . . ." He shuddered. "Fortunately, you're her main target. I'd like to keep it that way. Besides, she's a good head taller than I am. She could squash me like a bug if she wanted to."

"Okay, I promise to protect you. Now what's up?"

"He said you and Trish needed time together, preferably here, but she'd never come back on her own, so he thought—"

"He thought she'd come if there was a problem," Jack said. "Damn, he's good."

"That's probably why he's the boss. I've got to admit, getting this off my chest is a real relief. And now that you know"—Mo held up his hands—"I'm out of it."

"No problem." Jack watched Trish, who was still talking to Gibson. His father's idea to get them back here together wasn't half-bad. He had told his dad that he needed to be alone with her. Of course, Russ's insistence that Maude and Elliott come along made no sense . . . unless he thought Elliott should be handy when Trish was finally ready to dump him. At least Maude could keep him busy. Jack smiled to himself.

Trish laughed at something Gibson said. Jack narrowed his eyes. The Australian might be just a shade too good-looking, a touch too tan and more than a bit too flirtatious.

"Let's keep this just between us for now." Jack directed his words to Mo, but his gaze remained fixed on Trish. "Don't mention anything to Trish."

"You're not going to tell her?"

"Not quite yet."

Mo groaned.

Elliott dropped into the chair next to Trish's on the front porch of the mansion and handed her a beer. "I never thought I'd hear you ask for a beer."

"It's kind of like forbidden fruit." She popped open the top. "I acquired a real taste for it when I was here. Now, at least, it's no longer in short supply. I also acquired a taste for this." Trish nodded at the view. From here she could see the village down below, the bay and the ocean beyond that. The last rays of the sun filled the sky to her right, and the first of the evening stars twinkled to her left.

"I can see why." He was silent for a minute. "So, any thoughts on this sabotage business?"

"Not really." She shook her head. "Tell me this, though. I don't know a lot about construction, but these incidents just don't seem like all that big a deal to me. There's nothing that can't be rationally explained. I got the distinct impression that Gibson feels the same way. I guess I could be wrong and we could have a serious problem here, but my gut instinct says otherwise."

"I suppose it's possible Mo overreacted," Elliott said. "I'm not quite as high-profile as you are. I'll see what I can find out if you want."

"Thanks."

"Have you mentioned this to Jack?"

"Nope." She took a long swallow of beer.

"Shouldn't you?"

"Maybe. Probably." She shrugged. "But I'm not going to."

"I know I'll hate myself for asking, but why not?"

"I want to figure it out myself. Then I'll present it to Jack as a fait accompli."

"I get it." A wry smile curved his lips. "A little game of one-upmanship?"

"Something like that."

"At least this will give me a legitimate purpose here." Elliott stared out across the island, over the village and to the sea. "I'm not quite sure why Russ wanted me to come. I haven't worked on this project at all. All I can figure out is that maybe he thought you'd like to have your fiancé along."

Trish snorted. "Yeah, right."

Elliott laughed. "I always figured that he wasn't wild about us getting married." He looked pointedly at her. "I gather you haven't told him we've called it off yet?"

"Not yet." She propped her bare feet on the porch railing. "I haven't told Jack either."

"What are you waiting for?"

"I was about to tell him when Mo called and I discovered what a domineering, macho, control-freak jerk he is."

"Domineering, macho control freak?"

"Don't forget jerk. Would you believe he didn't want me coming along? This is as much my project as it is his—more, really—and he told me I couldn't come. He practically ordered me to stay home. He said I didn't like adventure or excitement—"

"And that's inaccurate because. . . . ?"

"—and he said it might be dangerous. That's just what I need. Somebody to run my life, tell me what to do, take control—"

"Trish." Elliott's brow furrowed. "He was trying to protect you. He cares about you, and your safety."

"I know that. Now." She sighed. "I also know he was right about the adventure and excitement business. And honestly, I hope these problems turn out to be nothing. It scares the hell out of me to think someone's doing this on purpose."

She paused and thought for a moment. "You want to hear something crazy?"

"Always."

"I thought I was completely satisfied with my life before I came to Paradise Bay. But since I set foot on this island I've discovered that I'm not all that wild about my life or, for that matter, about myself."

"Come on, Trish."

"No, really." She gazed out over the island. "I often overreact. I always feel the need to be in control." She paused. "I was going to marry you because I thought we'd have a nice, secure life. I thought it'd be something I could control." She smiled in a sad apology. "Sorry."

"Don't be." He took a swig of his beer. "I felt pretty much the same way."

"Add to that my tendency to be a real bitch. I only think of myself most of the time and I'm something of a wimp."

"And those are your good qualities," he said. She shot him a sharp glance, but he laughed. "I'm kidding."

"I'll bet."

"You're being too hard on yourself."

She shook her head. "I don't know, Elliott. I feel like I need to prove something, especially with this project. It's representative of what I need to do in my personal life, you know what I mean? I need to stand up to my fears, try a tiny bit of adventure; stop wanting everything to be planned with no questions, no unknowns, no excitement—no passion." She caught his gaze. "I need to prove myself, I guess."

He nodded. "To Jack and your stepfather."

"Not really." She took a long, cool sip. "To me."

* * *

"Nice setup." Elliott wandered around the perimeter of the library, stopping here and there to check out a book or examine an odd item added to the array of knickknacks collected by generations of Evanses. He picked up an antique pistol from a velvet-lined case and turned it over in his hands.

"Thanks." Jack scanned the room. "I like the atmosphere here. The contrast of tradition and high-tech: antique books and state-of-the-art computers."

Elliott replaced the gun and moved to a row of old leather-bound volumes. "Some of these look pretty rare." He pulled out an aging copy of H. G. Wells's *The Time Machine* and flipped it open. "This is a first edition."

"There are a lot of first editions on those shelves." Jack studied him for a moment. "Why do I have the feeling you're not here to talk about literature?"

"Because I'm not." Elliott snapped the book closed and replaced it on the shelf. "I want to talk about Trish."

Jack blew a long breath. "I figured this was coming."

"What are you going to do about her?"

"Are you asking if my intentions are honorable?"

"Yeah." Elliott settled into a chair. "I guess so."

"Kind of a strange question for a fiancé, isn't it?"

"Trish and I have kind of a strange and wonderful relationship." Elliott hesitated, as if trying to decide what to say next. "She and I will always be friends. Beyond that"—he shrugged—"I wouldn't make any bets."

"I wasn't." In spite of his confident words, a surge of relief washed through Jack.

"Look, Jack." Elliott leaned forward, his forearms resting on his legs, his hands clasped. "I've known Trish for a long time. Our engagement was something that sort of evolved through the years. We just expected to marry each other."

"Sounds like a match made in heaven."

"Not exactly, but we do love each other in a nice, comfortable sort of way."

"So I've heard."

"She and I are a lot alike. Up until she came here, we both wanted the same things out of life." Elliott shook his head. "We each still want the same things, I think, but those things have changed for both of us. And who we want them with has changed." Elliott's gaze met his. "Does that make any sense?"

"Not really."

Elliott sighed and pulled himself to his feet. "Let me see if I can explain." He paced the room, his forehead furrowed.

"In my entire life, I've never felt this way about anyone before. I think about her all the time. I want to be with her every moment. I want to talk to her and I want to listen to her. I want to touch her. I want her to touch me—"

"Wait a minute." Jack rose to his feet, feeling confused and angry. "Didn't you just say you and Trish have that nice, comfortable type of love?"

"Yeah." Confusion crossed Elliott's face, then his eyes widened and he laughed. "Oh. I didn't mention I was talking about Maude, did I?"

"No, you sure as hell didn't."

"Sorry." Elliott ran his fingers through his hair. "I'm not thinking as clearly as I used to, probably because Maude is on my mind every minute. She's like nothing I ever imagined and everything I never dared to dream of."

"And"—Jack grinned—"she's one incredible cook."

Elliott grinned back. "All wrapped up in a great-looking package."

A weird thought flashed through Jack's mind: This must be what it was like to have a brother. A guy to talk out your problems with and share your good times and your bad. He met Elliott's gaze and saw his own thoughts reflected in the other man's eyes.

"You know," he said slowly, "I was kind of a smartass as a kid."

"Yeah, well, I was kind of a weasel."

"Good thing we've grown up." He leaned against the desk and crossed his arms. "Any chance we can be the kind of brothers now we couldn't be then?"

"If we're brothers, that would put Trish in the sister category—and while I don't mind that, I don't think you want to go there."

Jack laughed, crossed the room to the mini-fridge, pulled out a couple of beers and tossed one to Elliott.

Elliott raised a brow. "It's not quite noon yet."

"It's evening in New York. Besides"—Jack shrugged—"we're on vacation."

"No, we're here to find out . . ." Elliott watched him thoughtfully. "I was at the construction site this morning. Trish was right, wasn't she?"

"Right about what?"

"She suspects these accidents aren't sabotage or anything other than bad luck."

"Damn." Jack popped the top of his beer and took a long drink. "She's too damn quick."

"Trust me. Don't ever underestimate her. She's smarter than even she realizes. But she's a lot like an untapped natural resource." Elliott sat back down in his chair. "I didn't realize it before Paradise Bay, and I don't think she did either, but she hasn't really figured out where she's going in life." He lifted his can in a toast. "Once she does, look out."

"She's done an amazing job on this project."

"So the alleged sabotage . . ."

"My dad more or less set it up to get us back here. The accidents were just accidents, and pretty basic stuff. He just took advantage of them."

"What are you going to do now?"

"I have a plan."

Elliott chuckled. "I figured you did."

"Do me a favor: Don't tell Trish. At least not right away."

"Well, now here's a moral dilemma." Elliott's brows drew together. "Do I owe my allegiance to Trish, or should I do what I think ultimately will lead to her happiness?"

"You think I can make her happy?"

"I think she feels about you the same way I feel about Maude." Elliott sighed in surrender. "It's amazing how quickly one's loyalty changes."

"It's a guy thing." Jack grinned. "It's us against them. Men and women are natural enemies. Men are on the same team. We have to stick together."

"Should we grunt now?"

"Later. After we crush the cans on our heads."

Elliott shook his head and laughed. "Do you need any help with this plan of yours?"

"I don't think so. Basically, I just need to get her alone. I figure a night of watching over the building site will do it. Just the two of us, a bottle of wine, a starlit sky, total and complete repentance on my part for anything I've ever done or ever will do. Maybe a little groveling. Probably a lot of groveling. That's about it."

"Good luck. But if you don't mind a little advice . . ."

"You've known her longer than I have."

Elliott paused for a moment. "Her biggest problem with you not telling her who you were was probably the feeling that you and Russ were plotting to run her life. If she figures out she was lured back here on false pretenses, regardless of who instigated it, she's going to see it exactly the same way. Especially if she knows you knew about it."

"And then we'll be right back where we started." Jack heaved a heavy sigh. "And this time she really might kill me."

Chapter Eighteen

As is common for most South Pacific locations, the clear night skies are well suited for the viewing of stars, planets and other celestial bodies. Long appreciated by amateur and professional astronomers alike, the star-filled heavens will not fail to enrapture even the most jaded visitor.

An evening under the stars on Paradise Bay is invariably magical.

Trish leaned the scooter against the metal prefab hut that served as a construction office and smiled with satisfaction. It hadn't taken long to figure out how to drive the thing, and when she'd zipped along the road from the house to the inn, she'd actually increased her speed. Gradually, cautiously, she'd given the bike more gas until she'd imagined she was flying. Of course, when she'd hit a bump and actually been airborne, she'd had to fight the immediate urge to panic, but she miraculously landed upright. By the third bump, panic no longer threatened, and by the time she'd arrived she'd actually sought out a few rough spots for both the exhilaration and the challenge.

Talk about a dramatic change. It hadn't been that long ago that this little Tinkertoy had scared her to death. Maybe it wasn't much, but riding the scooter was a perfect example of facing her fears. Jack was next on her list. Elliott was right about Jack having only wanted to protect her. She'd been confusing concern with control. She definitely needed to lighten up

But right now, she wanted to get to the bottom of these accidents. She knew Elliott had come over this morning, but she hadn't had a chance to talk to him. He and Jack had been together in the library when she'd left, probably bonding again. She shook her head. Who would have thought those two would end up friends? They had nothing in common—except maybe her. And Maude.

The door to the office swung open and Ben Gibson stepped out.

"Well, hello there." The construction worker gave her a big grin and his eyes lit up.

"Hi." She smiled back. There was nothing like

a man's eyes lighting up to give a female a lift. Even if the man in question was a major flirt, thought he was God's gift to women and treated her like she didn't have a brain in her head. She knew what was going on here, and if Gibson thought to keep it from her, he had another thing coming. She'd planned on pinning Mo to the wall to find out if her suspicions were correct, but Gibson presented too good an opportunity to pass up. "How's everything going?"

"Great." He looked out at the half-constructed resort with the air of a king surveying his domain. "We're still ahead of schedule."

"I'm so glad." She heaved an exaggerated sigh and gazed up at him. "I have to tell you, I've been kind of worried. Scared, really. I mean"—she bit her bottom lip as if she was trying to hold back tears—"the idea that there might be some lunatic psycho lurking around here, watching us, just waiting to . . ." She covered her eyes with her hand and shook her head.

"Oh, hey, are you all right?" Concern sounded in his voice. He really ate this stuff up.

"I'm fine." She kept her eyes covered and sniffed. "It's just so frightening."

"It's okay. Really."

She lifted her head and sniffed again. "Really? I mean, how can you be sure?"

"Look." He glanced to one side, then the other, and lowered his voice confidentially. "I'm not supposed to say anything, but the problems we've had are standard issue on a project like this. I don't know why exactly, but that architect, Wellington, said somebody in New York wanted you guys to think there was the possibility of sabotage. He said it was some kind of security test. Which sounded pretty stupid to me, but hey"—he shrugged his massive shoulders—"they pay the bills, so I do what I'm told."

"So there isn't any real reason to be concerned?" she said hopefully.

"Not a thing for you to worry your pretty little head about."

She bit back a groan. Ugh. Had he really said *pretty little head*? "Thank you. I feel so much better." She shot him what she hoped was a grateful smile.

"You know"—his grin returned—"it's Friday and we're ahead of schedule, so we get tomorrow off. A couple of helicopters will be picking me and the rest of the crew up this afternoon for Fiji. We'll be back Sunday." He flicked his gaze over her. "You want to come?"

"Thanks, but I'll pass."

"It's a great place. They call it a honeymooners' paradise."

"I'll wait until my honeymoon, then."

"Suit yourself." If possible, his grin widened. "There's always next weekend."

She laughed. He was a bit of a chauvinist and way too easy to manipulate, but he wasn't a bad guy. He waved and walked off.

Triumph surged through her. Between confirming her suspicions and her victory over the motorbike, she was having a pretty good day. Now, like in any good conspiracy investigation, it was time to find out who knew what and when they knew it.

She pulled open the door and stepped inside. Mo sat at a portable table at the end of the room with a laptop in front of him, surrounded by oversized sheets of paper.

He glanced up and froze, his eyes widening. "Trish."

She smiled sweetly. "Hi there. Having a nice day?"

He swallowed hard. Abruptly she realized that the man was afraid of her. She bit back a laugh and tried not to relish the sudden rush of power.

"So, um, where's Jack?" Mo craned his neck, trying to see around her.

"Not here." She walked toward him slowly. "Why are you so nervous?"

"I don't know," he said weakly.

"Come on, Mo. You have nothing to worry about. You and I have never even had a serious argument. Oh, a few disputes now and then when we were all working at the house, but that's about it." She drew closer.

He shrank back in his chair. "I've heard stories."

"From Jack?" She reached the desk and trailed her hand along the front edge. "Did he tell you that I came up with all kinds of creative ways to kill him?"

Mo nodded.

"Did he tell you he deserved them?" She perched on the edge of the desk.

Mo hesitated, then nodded even more vigorously.

Trish picked up a pencil. "Did he mention that I never actually did anything to him?" She jabbed the pencil into the electric sharpener and Mo jumped. "I just talk a good game, Mo. Oh sure, I like to scream." She pulled out the pencil and studied the point. "But did you know, I've never actually hurt a man? I've never backed over one with my car, never pushed one off a cliff. I've never even slapped a man."

"No?" His voice was unnaturally high.

"Nope." She tapped the top of the pencil. "Ouch."

He winced.

"Not yet." Her gaze pinned him to his seat. "But there's a first time for everything."

"Okay, okay, I'll tell you anything you want to know. Just don't hurt me." Mo groaned. "I knew I'd crack under the pressure. Man, I'm such a wimp." He glared at her. "It's all your fault, you know. If you weren't so tall and blond and Amazonian, with a temper to match—"

"Why, thank you, Mo." She grinned. "That's the nicest thing anybody's said to me in a long time."

He slumped back in his chair. "What do you want?"

"I know all about the phony sabotage. I know

there isn't really a problem. And I know it was all a setup to get us back to the island."

"It wasn't my idea," he muttered.

"I know that, Mo," she said with a comforting smile. "It's not your style. What I want to know is whose idea it was in the first place."

"If I lose my job over this—"

"You won't." She pointed the pencil at him and smiled. "Unlike some people, *I* can keep my mouth shut."

He blew a long, resigned sigh. "It was Jack's dad. He called and said you and Jack needed to get back to Paradise Bay. He had already figured there would be minor problems and he thought up the sabotage angle. He said that if Jack could get you alone, you two could work out your problems." Mo narrowed his eyes. "And he mentioned something about living happily ever after."

Trish chuckled. "He's a die-hard romantic. Okay, Mo." She hopped off the desk. "One more thing . . ."

"What?" Mo turned his wrists up and held out his arms. "Blood?"

"Not yours." She grinned. "I'm kidding. I just want to know when Jack found out about all this."

"He didn't know anything until you two were here yesterday. That's when he figured it out." Mo hesitated, then shrugged. "He told me not to tell you."

"Okay. Thanks." A few weeks ago, even a few

days ago, she would have been furious at Jack and his father for trying to control her life. But Russ was only trying to help. And as for Jack . . . How mad could she get at a man who was willing to do whatever he had to do to keep her in his life? "Let's keep this little chat just between us."

Mo snorted. "No problem. I am done with this. Too hazardous to my health."

"Thanks." She started for the door.

"So, are you going to kill him?" Mo sounded like he was about to lose his best friend.

Trish turned toward him. "Worse." She grinned. "I'm going to warm up the doves."

"There aren't any glasses." Trish rummaged through the backpack. "There's Brie, and that great dense bread Maude makes, and mangoes." She glanced up at him and grinned. "I love mangoes."

"Yeah," Jack said slowly, twisting the cork out of the bottle. "Me too." The cork popped free. "So what are we going to do with this without glasses?"

She arched a brow at him. "You've never drunk wine straight from the bottle?"

"Not in years. What about you?"

"Never." She smiled and reached for the wine. She sat cross-legged next to him on the blanket spread on the stone terrace beside the waterfall, the same spot where they'd surveyed the construction site the day before. The atmosphere this evening was dramatically different.

"I'm kind of surprised Maude sent wine instead of coffee."

"Yeah." He'd picked out the bottle himself. "Me too."

She took a swig of the Merlot. "Good year."

"I'm counting on it," he murmured.

"You know, on an island of great views, this has got to be one of the best." Trish gazed straight ahead at the eastern horizon, a slight smile on her lips. "I think I could live here forever."

"It's always been one of my favorite spots." Jack studied her cautiously. This wasn't the same Trish he'd done battle with since the poorly timed arrival of the supply boat. No, this was a throwback to the Trish he'd fallen in love with.

The Trish who had fallen in love with Jack Kendall, not Jack Evans.

He pushed the thought aside. He had enough problems to deal with when it came to this relationship. He didn't need to add past transgressions to the list.

He had no idea what had happened, but it was hard to miss her change in attitude. For one thing, he'd expected her to reject his proposal to spend the night staking out the building site, not because it was a bad plan but because it was *his* plan. Instead, she'd said what a great idea it was and complimented him for thinking of it. She'd even offered to pack one of their backpacks with a blanket and a flashlight and whatever else they might need.

All afternoon her comebacks, as sharp and as quick as always, were edged with good humor instead of dripping with sarcasm. Her eyes sparkled with amusement, and he had the distinct feeling she was laughing, at least to herself, when he wasn't looking. Like she knew something he didn't and thought it was pretty funny. Considering her mood lately, it was a little unnerving.

"Are you staring at me?" she asked without looking at him.

"Yeah."

"Good." That secret smile he'd noticed earlier was back.

"Oh, you like that?" he asked teasingly.

"I like keeping you on your toes."

"Then you must be blissful."

"Ecstatic." She slanted him a quick glance. She was definitely up to something. "What are we supposed to do now?"

"Watch the site and wait." He reached for the bottle.

"How long?"

"As long as it takes." His voice was determined. They could stay here until Hell froze over and they wouldn't see any saboteurs, but of course she didn't know that.

"I don't think we'll see any tourism terrorists

until it's much darker." She turned to meet his gaze. "Do you?"

"Tourism terrorists?"

She laughed. His stomach tightened. He loved her laugh. It seemed like forever since he'd heard it.

"There's not much light left." Trish nodded at the horizon. "I don't think I've ever watched a sunset from the wrong side before."

They sat facing east, overlooking the spot where the inn would stand, the beach and the water. The waterfall splashed behind them, a tall, narrow ribbon of sound, slightly to their right. Behind that, the cliffs and the mountain cut off all sight of the western skies and the sunset.

"Look at that." She propped her elbows on her knees, intertwined her fingers and rested her chin on her hands. "You can actually watch the night move in. The ocean blends right into the sky like they're not separate elements but part of one great whole."

The shadows around them lengthened. They'd lose the light entirely in another few minutes. The growing darkness blurred the outlines of everything more than ten feet away and lent a surreal atmosphere to the setting.

She tilted her head and looked at him. "What do you think, Jack? Can two such different entities really make a whole?"

He stared into her eyes and tried to keep his voice steady. "They do say opposites attract."

"You mean like lovers of adventure and seekers of security?"

He nodded. "Something like that."

"Is it true?" Her voice was low and kind of husky.

"Well," he took a long swig from the bottle, "they'd have to have some irresistible force pulling them together."

"But out there, isn't that blend of water and sky just an illusion?"

"I guess the trick is knowing what's real"—his gaze bored into hers—"and what's not."

"And what is real, Jack?" She took the bottle from him and set it to one side.

"Real?" Why did his voice rise like that? "Maude would probably say reality is relative."

"Maude is pretty perceptive." She unfolded her legs and shifted to face him on her knees. "But my definition of reality might be a little different."

"Oh?"

"Yeah." She reached out, hooked her finger in the vee of his shirt and pulled him closer, until her lips were next to his. "I think this is real." She nibbled at his bottom lip with her teeth.

"You do?" He swallowed hard.

"Uh-huh." She kissed the corner of his mouth. "And this." She ran her tongue along the line of his jaw. "And this. What do you think?"

"Oh, yeah." The words came out in a long, heartfelt sigh. "That's real."

"What did you want to talk about, Jack?" Her tongue traced the lobe of his ear.

"Talk?" Somewhere in that tiny point of his mind not fogged by arousal, a still-lucid voice screamed that this was his chance to clear everything up between them.

"Talk." Her breath whispered against his ear. "That's why we're really here, isn't it?"

"Uh-huh." In another minute he wouldn't remember his name, much less why they were here.

"Talk to me, Jack," she murmured. "Tell me what you want"—her mouth moved back to his and her tongue flicked between his lips—"to say."

He gasped. "Oh, hell." He wrapped his arms around her and they tumbled back onto the blanket. She sprawled on top of him, her mouth covering his, her tongue mating with his own. Heat shot through him and desire spiraled out of control. She ran a trail of urgent kisses down his neck to the opening of his shirt. His hands slipped to the hem of her top and slid up her back, her flesh smooth and hot. Her fingers tunneled through his hair and she pressed her mouth harder against his. He hooked his leg over hers and rolled them both until she faced upward; still, her mouth clung to his as if she wanted to devour him as much as he wanted to devour her.

Her hands grabbed at his shirt and yanked it upwards. He wrenched his mouth from hers, sat up and quickly pulled the shirt over his head and tossed it to one side. She ran her hands over his chest and he shivered.

"You know what I noticed about you the last time?" Her voice was breathless. "No tan lines."

"Oh, yeah." He stretched out beside her and trailed his fingers in a circle over the flat of her stomach, then popped the snap of her shorts and pushed the zipper down. "You know what I noticed about you?" He smiled as his hand slid beneath the khaki fabric. "No panties."

"Oh, I wear them." She arched upward to meet his hand. "I just didn't wear them that night." His fingers moved deeper along her valleys and curves until they dipped into her, hot and wet and wanting. She sucked in a hard breath. "Or tonight."

He lowered his mouth to meet hers and his hand skimmed the long length of her, beneath her shirt. "You're wearing a bra?"

"So shoot me." She pushed him away, sat up and tore at the buttons on her shirt until it fell open. Then she unhooked the front of her bra and drew him back into her arms.

His hands found the soft swell of one breast and his fingers circled her nipple. Her breathing was short and hard. He thought he'd forgotten to breathe at all. She reached for his waist and fumbled with the button of his shorts and then his zipper, and pushed his pants down over his hips. His swollen flesh pressed hard against her. Her fingers wrapped around him, caressing and stroking, and he knew he'd die at any minute. His blood pounded in his veins. His heart thudded in his chest. The night around him throbbed in a chaos of noise and feeling. Trish stilled beneath him.

"What in the hell was that?"

Chapter Nineteen

*While the natives of Paradise Bay are noto-
riously practical, there do exist a handful of
obscure proverbs. Prominent among them is
a saying that those who reveal their hearts beneath the magic of the midnight sky are des-
tined to be one in this life and all the lives to
come.*

*And their love will soar with the stars for-
ever.*

"What?" he said in a tone groggy with desire, like
a sleeper who didn't want to wake up.

"What was that sound?" Trish's voice rose.

"Ignore it. It was me." He nuzzled her neck.
"I'm sure it was me."

"Jack!"

"No really. I make a lot of weird noises when I'm excited."

"You do not. Not like this." She pushed at him. "Shut up and listen."

He sighed and raised his head. "I don't hear anything." He grinned down at her. "I told you it was me."

"It wasn't you." In spite of herself she giggled. "You don't sound like that."

"Like what?"

"Like stuff falling or collapsing. A crash or something."

"Are you sure it wasn't me?" He directed his attention back to her neck. "I probably could make a sound like that if I worked on it. Want me to try?"

"Jack." She didn't mean it to sound like a moan, but it did. "Really . . ." If he'd just stop doing that, she'd be fine. "I think . . ." She was melting all over again. "I mean . . ." Maybe she was mistaken after all.

A dim noise sounded in the distance.

Her heart stopped. "Did you hear that?"

"Yeah." His tone was suddenly serious. "That I heard."

"Shouldn't we do something?"

"I should." He rolled over and got to his feet. The starlight reflected off his broad shoulders and . . . elsewhere, and for a second she wondered if whoever was down there wouldn't mind waiting. He pulled up his shorts. "Where's my shirt?" He glanced around. "When did it get so dark?"

"When we were busy." She hooked her bra closed, buttoned her shirt and scrambled to her feet. "What's going on, Jack?"

"I don't know," he said in a grim voice. "There shouldn't be anybody down there."

"What about security?"

"There is no security." He looked around impatiently. "Now, where is that damn shirt?"

"Oh, yeah, I'd hate for the bad guys to see you improperly attired. What a horrible faux pas that would be," she muttered, zipping up her own shorts. She scanned the area. It wasn't nearly as dark as she'd first thought. The stars overhead were packed so tightly together and the night sky was so clear, there was enough light to make out their backpacks and the bottle of wine. She spotted a wadded up heap of fabric, scooped it up and tossed it at him. "Here."

"Thanks." He caught the shirt and pulled it over his head. "Okay, I'm going to go down there."

"Wait a minute." She grabbed his arm. "I thought this was a joke."

"What do you mean?" he asked cautiously.

"You know what I mean!"

"Shhh!" He put his finger to his lips.

"You know what I mean," she whispered, then shook her head and spoke in a normal voice. "Nobody can hear us up here."

"Just keep it down anyway."

"Fine. Now tell me what's going on. You and I both know there hasn't been any sabotage."

"We do?"

She heaved an exasperated sigh. "Well, I do—and I know you do. Therefore that pretty much means *we* do."

"And you're not mad?" he asked slowly.

"No." She reached up for a quick, firm kiss. "I know you didn't arrange it, you just played along. And it's all right."

"It is?" A surprised smile lifted the corners of his lips.

"It is." She squared her shoulders. "It's also time I stopped being such a pain in the butt and started dealing with all my weird little hang-ups and stopped being so defensive and learned to compromise. And"—she paused to collect her courage—"I think it's time to admit that I do love you."

He cocked his head to one side. "What kind of love?" he quizzed.

"Jack! This isn't the time—"

"What kind of love?" His voice was determined.

She grit her teeth. "Throw-me-on-the-floor-and-screw-my-eyes-out love."

"Maybe later." This time he kissed her, hard and fast and stole her breath in the process. "Now, I'm going down there."

"I don't think so." In spite of the starlight, it was tough to make out the site from this distance. She thought she saw a quick flicker of light, but it might have been a reflection. Her stomach twisted with fear.

"You don't think you're going with me?" he scoffed.

"Are you crazy?" She shook her head. "It could be seriously dangerous down there. Of course I'm not going with you. You're not going."

"Trish, I have to—"

"No, you don't." She crossed her arms. "For all we know, those little accidents might not be accidents after all. Whoever is down there could be a really experienced bad guy. We wait here for a while, we go back to the house, get some help and then we go down there."

"Are you kidding?" He sounded like she was threatening to reveal Superman's secret identity or something equally unthinkable. "We can't do that."

"Why not?"

"Because they'll be gone."

"And that would be bad because . . . ?"

"Trish." His voice was patient, as if he was talking to someone very slow or very young. "I can't let them get away."

"Why not?" she asked again.

"Just because, that's why," he said indignantly.

"I don't believe this." She shook her head. "You *want* to go play hero, don't you? You *want* to chase bad guys, just for the excitement."

"Of course not," he said with absolutely no conviction at all. "That would be stupid."

"You think?" She grabbed his collar with both hands and pulled him close. "Listen to me. I've just found you. I don't want to lose you. I couldn't live if anything happened to you."

"Really?" He grinned.

"You are so egotistical." She released him, turned to find a backpack, then knelt beside it. "All right. We'll need the flashlight, right?"

"We?"

"Yep." She dug through the pack.

He snorted. "You're not going."

"Haven't we had this conversation before? Remember how that one turned out?" She shot him a quick grin. "If you're going, I'm going." She pulled out the high-beam flashlight and tossed it to him. "Look, Jack, I'm scared to death. Remember, I'm the one who hates adventure and excitement."

"Trish," he said gently, "I love you too and I can't stand the idea of you being in danger."

"It's not number one on my list of things to do either, but you don't have many options. Either we go for help together or we do the dumb thing and go down there together because—unless you plan on tying me up—I'm not staying here by myself and I'm not letting you go alone." How could she sound so cool and calm when she was quaking inside? "It's your choice."

"Some choice," he muttered. "Okay, you can come, but you have to do exactly what I say. Agreed?"

"Sure." *Yeah, right.* She stood up. "Let's get it over with."

"I really wish you'd recon—"

"Wait, I forgot something. I found this in the library." She bent down beside the backpack and pulled out an antique pistol. "I brought it as kind of a joke—"

"A joke?"

"Hey, you had your plan for tonight and I had mine. I wanted to make you think I believed this whole scheme. And naturally, if I believed it, having a weapon makes sense. Besides, I thought it would make you nervous."

"Keeping me on my toes again?"

"Absolutely. Here." She handed it to him. "This thing weighs a ton. Anyway, you should be glad I brought it. Now it might—"

"Might what?" he said wryly. "Might make whoever is down there die laughing?"

"You've got a better idea? It's something, anyway. I think the sight of a tall, macho, lunatic hero waving a big old gun around might at least make them think twice."

"Yeah, right, before they shoot us. You take this." He passed her the flashlight and looked at the pistol. "It's not loaded, is it?"

She shrugged. "I don't think so."

"Swell." He hefted the long-barreled gun in his hand. "This thing is probably at least two hundred years old and I have no idea how it works— or if it works."

"I hadn't planned on actually using it," she murmured.

He sighed and took her hand. "Let's go."

They started down the path leading to the road. She flicked on the flashlight.

"Turn that off," he snapped.

"But it's dark," she reasoned.

"They'll see us coming."

"Oh. Whoops." She snapped off the light. "Sorry. This is my first adventure. I'm not up on the rules." She stayed a step behind him, holding his hand in a death grip. The last thing she needed was to tumble down this slope in the dark with tourism terrorists lying in wait. "Jack."

"Shhh."

"Jack," she whispered. "If anything happens—"

"Nothing's going to happen."

"But if it does, I just want you to know I was willing to stand by you when you went to prison."

"What?" He stopped and turned so quickly that she plowed into him.

"Shhh, remember? Bad guys." She pointed down the slop.

"What are you talking about?" he asked in a tense whisper. "Why would I be going to prison?"

"It doesn't matter why. Do you remember when the supply boat came and I thought it was the police?"

"Yeah."

"Well, if I couldn't help you escape, I decided that I would wait for you. I would have come to see you on visiting days."

"Baked me a cake with a file in it?" She could hear the laughter in his voice.

"I don't bake," she said under her breath. "But maybe I would have brought a cake. I know it sounds silly, I just wanted you to know, that's all."

"I don't think it's silly. I think it's nice." He squeezed her hand. "But I don't plan on ever going to prison, and nothing's going to happen to us."

He turned and started down the path. As long as he held her hand she wouldn't fall. The path was steep, although not as bad as the one they'd taken when they climbed the mountain. Of course, it had been daytime when she'd climbed that one. It seemed like hours but was probably less than five minutes before they reached the road.

"Okay," he whispered. "Crouch down and we'll run across the road."

"You can't be serious. How do you run and crouch?"

"I don't know." Annoyance sounded in his voice. "They do it in the movies." He bent over and took a step.

She yanked him back. "What do you mean, in the movies?" Her voice raised in surprise.

"You've never done anything like this before, have you?"

"Be quiet!" He exhaled a long, frustrated breath. "I know it's hard to believe, but no, I've never tried to catch vandals in the middle of the night on a South Pacific island before. Go figure."

"You don't have to be so touchy about it," she muttered. "You certainly gave the impression that you knew what you were doing."

"Shut up and come on." He started off, pulling her behind him.

They crouched low and dashed across the road to a huge crane, one of half a dozen pieces of massive equipment scattered around the site. In the light of day they were immense and impressive; now they were prehistoric monsters waiting for a good meal. He flattened himself against the side of the crane and she followed suit. Her heart pounded wildly. Had she ever been so scared? Had she ever known this kind of fear?

Had she ever had this much fun?

She shoved the ridiculous thought aside. She certainly wasn't having fun. Oh, sure, it was kind of exhilarating, and yeah, that was probably adrenaline pumping through her veins, and maybe, just maybe the thrill zipping up her spine was the tiniest bit enjoyable. But fun?

She giggled nervously.

"Don't crack up on me now, Taylor," he said in a fierce whisper. "Stay here." He bent low and disappeared around the side of the crane.

"Wait!" How could he leave her alone like this? She'd agreed to do whatever he said, but she certainly hadn't meant it. She ducked down and followed the way he'd gone, turned around the crane and stopped. He wasn't there. Anywhere. She froze in panic. What was she supposed to do now?

She took a deep breath and forced herself to calm down. She could handle this. Hadn't she already faced any number of her fears? Hadn't she given up her quest for security in favor of love? Hadn't she realized control might not be as important as compromise? Hadn't she learned to ride that damn motorbike?

Okay. All she had to do now was find Jack and hope she didn't run into any bad guys in the process. She surveyed the site. Even with the starlight, it was an eerie black-and-white scene, and nothing looked like it did in daylight. She remembered that most of the tall, regular shapes were stacks of building materials: plywood, lumber, steel or concrete blocks, but there was a huge empty space between her and any of that. The crane was way too exposed. She had to get to the other side of the clearing. Besides, Jack obviously wasn't over here.

Just like in the movies. She drew a steadying breath, ducked and ran, expecting any second to hear the rat-a-tat of machine-gun fire and see little puffs of dust as the bullets hit the ground around her feet. If they didn't hit her. Maybe this wasn't fun after all.

She reached a stack of cinder blocks and flattened herself against it, struggling to catch her breath. So far so good.

She was still alive. It didn't look like anybody had spotted her. She edged around the corner of the blocks and pulled up short. On one side of her was a stack of plywood, on the other, a huge crate. Abruptly she realized the construction materials that had looked fairly orderly by day looked like a giant, haphazard maze by night. And she was the lab rat. No way was she going in there. Everyone knew what happened to lab rats.

Trish turned and retraced her steps. Oh, this was much better. Now she was exposed. Vulnerable. With no idea which way to go. She had always had a lousy sense of direction. Why hadn't she watched more action movies? Or even one? She racked her brain, but all she could think of were hordes of extras jumping off the sinking *Titanic*. The sinking ship part was appropriate but not especially helpful.

She couldn't just sit here all night, had to do something. Besides, she hadn't heard any strange noises since Jack had disappeared. Maybe whoever had been down here had left? Actually, it made sense: They did what they wanted to do and took off. Why, they could have been long gone by the time she and Jack even made it to the site. The thought bolstered her courage. It seemed to her that she had to choose between cutting back across the open area or the maze. She studied the clearing but couldn't get past the thought of bullets whizzing by her and little clouds of dirt puffing up around her ankles.

She'd rather be a live lab rat than a dead anything. She bolstered her courage and eased around the corner, listening for a second. Nothing. She slipped quietly across the makeshift aisle to the stacked plywood, inched to the corner and peeked around the edge. Nothing.

Okay. She heaved a short sigh of relief. This wasn't that bad. She could deal with it. She hadn't found Jack, but she hadn't found anybody else either. Maybe there was something to be said for adventure after all. Maybe she could even talk Jack into taking her parasailing. Although it sounded like fun, she doubted he'd want to go heli-skiing again. Maybe she could—

A strong hand clapped over her mouth and a powerful arm jerked her backward into a solid body. Something hard rammed into her lower back. Fear, intense and primitive, shot through her. She attempted to scream, but the hand tightened on her mouth. She struggled frantically, trying to kick out with her feet or grab him with her hands, but she was helpless against the man's unyielding grip. She couldn't move, couldn't breathe.

Dear God, I'm going to die and I'll never see Jack again or my mother or Russ or Paradise Bay or the year 2000 or peanut butter cup ice cream

*or cable TV shopping or the children and the dog
we were going to have or Paris in the springtime
or that little black-sequined—*

"I told you to stay put." A harsh, hushed voice
whispered into her ear.

Jack?

She stilled and tried to pull his hand away
from her mouth.

"Are you going to shut up?"

It was definitely Jack. Relief filled her and left
her limp. She collapsed against him. She'd need
a moment to pull herself together so she could
kill him. He'd never see her or Russ or his computer or beer or—

He twirled her to face him. "What are you doing here?"

"Dying of fright thanks to you," she snapped.
"Why did you do that?"

"I didn't want you to scream."

"Next time, try saying, 'Trish, shhh.' My whole
life flashed before my eyes. It was awful. And
why did you have to be so rough, anyway?" She
rubbed the small of her back. "Damn. Was that
the pistol jammed against me?"

"No, I was just glad to see you." In spite of his
low tone, she could hear him chuckle.

"Bite me." She was in no mood for jokes.

"Maybe later." His tone changed abruptly.
"Why didn't you stay where I left you? I thought
we'd agreed you were supposed to do what you
were told?"

"You agreed. I did nothing of the sort."

"You said 'sure.' "

"And I meant it, more or less, but you didn't take me with you. You left me there, alone, in the dark." She poked his chest with her finger. "That wasn't part of the deal."

"I just wanted you to be safe."

"I know that." She smiled in the dark at him. "And that's why I forgive you."

"You forgive . . . ?" He shook his head. "Never mind."

"Did you find anything?"

"No. You?"

"Nothing." She paused for a moment. "Then why are we still whispering?"

"Ambience." His voice changed from a whisper to something approaching normal. "Let's keep it down just in case."

"You think maybe the wind might have knocked something over and that's what we heard?"

"Twice? I don't think so. But I don't think we're going to find anything tonight either." He pulled her into his arms.

"Ouch." She jerked away. "You think you can move your, um, pistol?"

"I don't know." He drew it out of his waistband with a flourish. "It's kind of swashbuckling. I think it's me." With his free arm he yanked her to his side and grinned down at her. She could be mistaken, but she could swear the starlight sparkled in his eyes, like the hero of a silent movie. "What do you think?"

"I definitely think you need to get your swash buckled."

"Want to go home and play pirate and fair maiden?"

"Sure." She grinned back. "Which one do you want to be?"

"Come here, wench." He pulled her closer and kissed her. "Let's get out of here."

"Works for—"

A crash sounded somewhere behind them. Somewhere very close.

"Jack?" Her fear was back, full-force.

"I'd tell you to stay here, but I know you wouldn't." He grabbed her hand. "Just stay right behind me."

"No problem."

They crept silently along the plywood stack. Jack stopped short, drew her to his side and whispered in her ear. "I hear voices on the other side of this wood."

She stifled the urge to run.

"I have an idea. I'll take the flashlight and attract their attention from the front. You circle around and approach them from the back. I'll blind them with the flashlight and you hold the gun on them. Hopefully, they won't realize the pistol is useless."

"Are you crazy? That's the dumbest plan I've ever heard. What if they have real guns and shoot you?"

"If they've been here before, nothing they've done has been serious. At most they're just vandals. Maybe it's just island kids screwing around. I doubt there's any serious danger here." He hesitated. "But if you hear gunshots, go to plan B."

"Plan B?"

"Yeah. Run like hell." He kissed her again. "Now go."

"This is why I hate adventure," she whispered through clenched teeth. "Be careful."

He nodded and turned away. She crept around the stack of wood, wishing she had something other than an antique in her hand. She turned one corner, then halted at the next. He was right: Someone was there. At least two people were talking in very low tones.

She resisted the impulse to peek around the corner for at least ten seconds. Then, very cautiously, she peered around the edge of the wood.

One figure was sitting on the ground, the other kneeling beside him.

"Okay, freeze, right there." Jack's voice boomed and his flashlight illuminated the scene with intense, white light, blinding the vandals. And Trish.

She staggered out from her hiding place holding the pistol in front of her, aiming in the general direction of the bad guys. Or possibly at the light. She couldn't see a thing.

"What in the hell are you two doing here?" Jack said.

"Who's here?" Trish blinked hard.

"Trish, watch what you're doing." Jack's voice rose. "You're aiming the gun straight at me."

"Trish has a gun?" a familiar voice asked. "What idiot let Trish have a gun?"

Trish gasped. "Elliott?"

"So who do you think she'll shoot first?" a wry female voice asked.

"And Maude." Jack sighed. "Put down the gun, Trish."

"Then turn off the damn light so I can see."

He flicked off the flashlight and she stepped closer to the couple on the ground. Her vision adjusted to the subtle glow of starlight and cleared enough to see that it really was Elliott and Maude.

"Help me up, Jack," Elliot said. "I think I twisted something."

Jack grabbed his hand and pulled him to his feet. "What are you two doing here?"

Elliott put his arm around Maude's shoulder and leaned on her. "It was my idea. I thought you could use some help."

"Help?" Trish said cautiously. "What kind of help?"

"You two are going to blow it. Again." Maude sighed. "Look, Trish, Elliott knew Jack was going to bring you here to watch the site tonight. He figured if you heard something, thought maybe there was a real threat, it would make you realize all the problems between you were petty and insignificant and you two would finally be together."

"I didn't know anything about this," Jack said quickly. "All I wanted to do was get you alone so that I could convince you that we belong with each other—"

"And all I wanted was for you to be happy," Elliott said. "I think it would have worked too. I mean, we made enough noise to get you down here and—"

"Although I was doing just fine on my own," Jack mentioned.

"Yeah." Maude smiled. "From what we managed to hear, anyway. In fact, we were just about to leave."

"And I had to go and trip over who knows what." Elliott grimaced. "Sorry."

"Damn, Elliott, I could have shot you," Trish said.

"With that?" Elliott scoffed. "Isn't that the flintlock I looked at in the library today?"

"Yeah," Jack said.

"That thing dates to the early 1700s and probably hasn't been fired in two centuries. Besides, it isn't loaded." Elliott chuckled. "The only damage you could have done with that is if you'd thrown it at me."

"I knew it probably wasn't loaded." Trish passed the pistol to Jack, who tucked it back into his waistband.

"Now that we've cleared all this up . . ." Maude brushed her hair away from her face with her free hand. Trish caught a glimmer of light flashing on her finger. "Let's go—"

"What is that?" Jack grabbed her hand. "It's a ring. No, it's a rock." His gaze jumped to Trish. "Your rock."

"Not anymore," Trish said. "I gave it back. And apparently Elliott gave it to Maude. Congratulations to both of you."

"Thanks." Maude held her hand out and studied the ring glittering in the starlight. "You know, he asked me if I wanted a different one, but since this originally belonged to his mother—"

"Just one of many," Elliott muttered.

"—and it's just so incredibly big, pretentious really."

"I've always kind of liked pretentious." Trish giggled.

"Yeah, me too." Maude grinned.

"Who knew you had so much in common?" Jack turned to Trish. "Why didn't you tell me?"

She shrugged. "I didn't know she liked pretentious."

"Not that. Why didn't you tell me that you gave his ring back?"

"I tried," Trish said thoughtfully. "But you know, you never asked me specifically if I'd given his ring back. I just didn't mention it. It's not like I lied. I mean technically, in the strict definition of the word—"

"This is another part of your master plan to keep me on my toes, isn't it?"

"Isn't everything?"

"Excuse me," Elliott said. "Before we hear something we shouldn't—"

"Like you two playing pirate and fair maiden," Maude said.

"—we're getting out of here. Maude can help me to the road. We hid a couple of scooters up there. I'll ride with her and we'll come back tomorrow and get the other one."

"Are you sure you don't need any help?" Jack asked.

"I've got everything I need." Elliott smiled at Trish. "Good luck."

"You too," Trish added softly.

Elliott leaned on Maude and hobbled off into the night.

"Trish," Jack said. Something in his voice unleashed a flutter of nerves in her stomach and she had to resist the impulse to run again.

"Let's go down to the beach," she said quickly, turned on her heel and maneuvered through the construction maze. She headed for the water. This was it and she wasn't sure she was ready. She stopped and pulled off her shoes, then walked along the water's edge.

"Wait for me." She glanced over her shoulder. Jack was hopping on one foot, trying to take off a shoe. She kept walking. A minute later she heard him approach. He pulled up beside her. "What's wrong?"

"Nothing. Everything." She refused to look at him. "I'm nervous. Scared." Her voice rose. "There aren't any more secrets between us.

There shouldn't be any more of those fears either, but there are."

"Hey." He grabbed her arm and yanked her to a stop. "There's nothing to be afraid of. Besides, I'm willing to compromise as much as you are, and if Elliott really is the type of guy you need, I can be more like him. You know, safety and security and all that."

"Don't even try it." She glared and planted her fists on her hips. "Don't you get it? Haven't you figured it out by now? You're what I need! Except for things like tonight—which I never want to do again, thank you—I want to share adventures with you, and excitement. And passion. And that, Russell Jonathan Evans the Fourth, is all the security I need!"

He stared at her for a minute. "You're just saying that because I have a gun."

"No." She fought back a laugh. "I'm just saying that because you're glad to see me."

"What do you think about telling your mother to put my name on the invitations?"

"I think it's a great idea." She nodded slowly. "Especially since I called her today and told her to go ahead."

"You shouldn't have done that." He shook his head.

Her heart caught. "Why not?"

"I already told her the day we left."

She tried, but couldn't hide her grin.

"I would assume, from the conversations I've had with your mother"—he took her hand—

"that if we were to go someplace like Las Vegas and get married by an Elvis impersonator, she'd kill us and we'd still have to go through with the wedding she's planned, right?"

"Oh, yeah, and besides, there are the doves to consider."

"Doves?"

"You don't know the half of it."

"Trish,"—he paused, as if working up courage—"do you mind that Jack Kendall is really Jonathan Evans?"

"Not now. I might even have fallen in love with you anyway if I'd known."

"It would have been a lot harder, though."

"Oh, yeah." She scoffed. "And this was easy?"

"I wouldn't call it easy, but it was definitely an adventure."

"Well, this is the place for it, all right." She gazed out into the tropical night. The endless black of the ocean met the star-spattered velvet of the sky and it was impossible to see where one ended and the other began. And she knew, deep down inside, that it was the very differences between sea and sky that made them fit together so perfectly when faced with the irresistible force of the night.

"Adventures, huh?" She stepped into his arms, drawn by an irresistible force into a perfect fit. "This was my first, you know."

"But not your last." His lips met hers in a wordless promise of a future filled with everything she'd always wanted and everything she'd been too afraid to hope for. And she knew now what she'd probably known from the moment she'd first met that hulking beast hidden away in a Victorian mansion on a tropical island.

With this man, every day would be an adventure.

And she couldn't wait for the next day to begin.

Epilogue

Sunrise,
New Year's Day, 2000

"More champagne?" Jack held the bottle up for his wife. "Or have you had enough?"

"Come on, Jack." Trish held her glass out to him. "Can you ever have enough champagne?"

"I seem to recall a wedding where the bride had—"

"The bride was very nervous and hadn't eaten that day." Amusement sounded in her voice. "And I believe the groom was—"

"Scared to death." He laughed and refilled her glass, then settled the bottle in the ice chest they'd brought along.

"You know, this is a momentous occasion. We probably shouldn't have ducked out."

"Between my dad playing beneficent monarch and your mother—"

"Always the gracious hostess."

"—I'll bet nobody even knows we're gone."

"Probably not." She sipped her champagne and gazed toward the lightening horizon. He studied her profile for a long moment and, as always, his stomach tightened with desire and love. The odd twists and turns life had taken to bring them together never failed to amaze him.

"Besides," he said, "I didn't want to greet the year 2000 from the patio at the inn. I wanted to see the sunrise from here."

They'd slipped away from the party, changed from tux and formal gown to shorts and shirts embroidered with The Inn on Paradise Bay logo and now waited on the terrace beside the waterfall for the arrival of the first new day of the new year. Work to expand this area and construction on the second restaurant was scheduled to begin in a couple of weeks. This was probably the last time they'd have this spot all to themselves.

"And I didn't want to share this particular dawn with anyone but you," he added softly.

"Me, neither."

He gazed eastward. The sun would be up in just a few minutes. No matter how laid-back he appeared, this was a big deal. Being among the first in the world to greet the first day of the next thousand years was a thrill he wouldn't trade for anything.

"Jack, we need to talk." She set her glass aside and hesitated, as if she was choosing her words carefully. "Now that the inn is up and running, there's not much more for me to do."

"Sure there is. The second restaurant still has to be built. So does the conference center, plus the interior of the main building is only half-finished. There's a ton of work left on the golf course and the pools and—"

"None of that needs me, at least not full-time. At this stage, my input is really minimal." She shrugged and smiled. "My work here is through."

"But Trish—"

She laughed. "Don't give me that look. I'm not dumping you. But I am dumping ESI."

"What?"

"*Dumping* is the wrong word." She thought for a moment. "Look, I've gotten more satisfaction from putting together this project and more fun—"

"I'll say." He smirked at her.

She ignored him. "—than from anything I've ever done. I don't want to go back to corporate PR."

"What do you want to do?" Why did he have the feeling she already knew?

She met his gaze and drew a deep breath. "I want to put together another Inn on Paradise Bay, and another, and—"

Jack shook his head. "I don't think a chain—"

"No, I didn't mean another Inn on Paradise Bay exactly." She gestured in a wide wave at the resort. "This is unique. One of a kind. And it fits in perfectly with its surroundings, as if it wasn't built so much as sprung from the rocks. That's what I want to do. I want to develop resorts and inns and places where people can go for a night or a week or a month and forget their problems and just enjoy life." Enthusiasm sparkled in her eyes. "And not just very expensive, very exclusive projects like this, but resorts for single people and for families—"

"Families?"

"Yeah, families. You know." A soft smile quirked the corners of her mouth. "People with kids, and dogs—they should have places like this."

His heart stopped. "Trish, are you, are we—"

"No. Not yet." She laughed. "I guess you're not ready for that particular adventure."

"Not quite," he said with a strange mix of relief and disappointment.

"Anyway, I've decided to start my own company. Very small. Very focused. One project at a time." Her gaze searched his face. "What do you think?"

"I think ESI has a division—"

"No. I want to do this on my own." She studied him. "So?"

"One of the best things about my life is knowing you're right down the hall during the day. Plus, there's a lot of risk involved in any new

389

business. But if this is what you want—" He heaved a sigh of surrender. "Go for it. You will, no matter what I'd say."

"Yes!" She threw her arms around him. "I knew you'd think this was a great idea and that you'd be wonderfully supportive—"

"That's me." He folded her in his arms and her body molded against his. Was there enough time before sunrise . . . ?

"And you won't mind at all that I'm going to take Elliott and Maude—"

"Wait a minute." He drew back and held her at arm's length. "Elliott is an asset to ESI, and I know Maude enjoyed the restaurant work she did, but Trish, she's a philosopher. A legitimate, card-carrying philosopher."

"She's also a dynamite cook with a gift for planning restaurants—from their menus to their waitstaff. Plus, she's admitted her philosophy career isn't going anywhere. And Elliott is a whiz with finances; that's not my strong point at all."

He narrowed his eyes. "I don't have much of a say in this, do I?"

"Jack," she said patiently, "you're my husband, I'm your wife, we're partners. Equals. I respect your opinion. Even when it's wrong. Even when I'm not going to pay any attention to it."

"No kidding." He pulled her close. "Okay, if they want to go, they're yours."

"Great." She nuzzled his ear. "Oh, yeah, I'm taking Mo, too."

"What?" He jerked back again and glared at her. "I have plans for Mo."

"Come on, Jack." She leaned forward and brushed her lips across his. "I have plans too."

"Trish." He scrambled to his feet. There was no way he could defend himself and his poor, helpless company if she kept doing things like that. "Who else are you stealing on this pillaging raid of yours?"

"No one, really." She stood and brushed off her shorts. "Technically, Ms. Caplan isn't an employee—"

"But she retired two months ago."

"She's bored." Trish shrugged. "Besides, she wants to travel. She's going to scout out sites and write reports for me. Did I ever tell you about the background file I got when I first came to Paradise Bay?"

"I don't think so."

"At first it sounded like an encyclopedia, but each entry got more lyrical and poetic. I started thinking of it as a travel guide, rather than a report." Trish grinned. "Ms. Caplan wrote it."

"She has a secret life, doesn't she?"

Trish laughed. "I think so."

"You know, a less confident man would be upset that you didn't ask me to join your new enterprise."

"Well, thank God for egotism." She shook her head. "Sorry. Russ would kill me. You're the heir apparent, remember? Besides, you'd want to be in charge."

"I seem to recall agreeing once to let you be the lord and master and I'd be the loyal minion."

"Uh-huh. And how long did that last?"

He trapped her gaze with his. "Forever."

She caught her breath. "Have I ever told you that your eyes smolder?"

"That's not the only thing smoldering."

"Come here, Jack." She crooked her finger at him.

He stepped forward. "Yeah?"

"Look." She turned him around to face east. "Sunrise." Trish stepped in front of him, drew his arms around her and leaned back against him.

The black of the night had faded to purple, now chased by pinks and brilliant orange. The first rays of the new year crept slowly into the sky as if waiting for trumpets to herald their arrival. The sea and sky at the horizon, for this moment only, no longer seemed one body but two distinct entities defined by the ever-growing ribbon of light.

"Wow." Trish sighed. "Ms. Caplan certainly did get this right."

"What did she say?"

"Let me think." She paused for a minute. "Okay. Here goes:

" 'There may well be places on earth with a sunrise more spectacular or scenery more lovely. There are indeed places that are more convenient to reach or more developed for comfort. But only here can be found an inherent joy in life for seekers of truth and peace, love and happiness.

" 'For this is indeed where the day and the future begin.' "

"She does have a way with words," he said softly.

"And she's right," Trish said. "I found truth and peace, love and happiness here."

"Me too, but I did better than that." He hugged her tighter. "I found you."

For a moment he wondered whether the reality of Paradise Bay was its physical presence as a tiny spot on a map next to a randomly placed date line, or if its true existence was in the uncharted seas of the heart and the unexplored regions of the soul. And as surely as he'd ever known anything in his life, he knew no matter where he and Trish were, or what they were doing, Paradise Bay would always be a part of them.

For this new day and all the days to come.

I hope you've enjoyed visiting Paradise Bay. While this particular spot doesn't exist, it's loosely based on the island nation of Kiribati. I read a news article about Kiribati two years ago and it captured my imagination.

Kiribati is next to the International Date Line and does indeed claim to be where each new day begins. It's a very tiny country and the article expressed the hopes of its leaders to parlay its position into increasing its tourism—especially for New Year's, 2000. The article also mentioned that, at the time it was written, Kiribati had recently run out of beer.

I doubt if I'll ever get to Kiribati but I am looking forward to the next century. And whether you greet the dawn of the year 2000 under tropical skies in the South Pacific or in your own home, I wish you all a very happy New Year.

Best Wishes,
Victoria

P. S. Write to me at P. O. Box 31544, Omaha, NE 68131

A FAERIE TALE ROMANCE

VICTORIA ALEXANDER

Ophelia Kendrake has barely finished conning the coat off a cardsharp's back when she stumbles into Dead End, Wyoming. Mistaken for the Countess of Bridgewater, Ophelia sees no reason to reveal herself until she has stripped the hamlet of its fortunes and escaped into the sunset. But the free-spirited beauty almost swallows her script when she meets Tyler, the town's virile young mayor. When Tyler Matthews returns from an Ivy League college, he simply wants to settle down and enjoy the simplicity of ranching. But his aunt and uncle are set on making a silk purse out of Dead End, and Tyler is going to be the new mayor. It's a job he takes with little relish—until he catches a glimpse of the village's newest visitor.

_52159-8 $5.50 US/$6.50 CAN

Dorchester Publishing Co., Inc.
P.O. Box 6640
Wayne, PA 19087-8640

Please add $1.75 for shipping and handling for the first book and $.50 for each book thereafter. NY, NYC, and PA residents, please add appropriate sales tax. No cash, stamps, or C.O.D.s. All orders shipped within 6 weeks via postal service book rate. Canadian orders require $2.00 extra postage and must be paid in U.S. dollars through a U.S. banking facility.

Name_____
Address_____
City_____ State_____ Zip_____
I have enclosed $_____ in payment for the checked book(s).
Payment <u>must</u> accompany all orders. ❑ Please send a free catalog.

BELIEVE

Victoria Alexander

Tessa thinks as little of love as she does of the Arthurian legend—it is just a myth. But when an enchanted tome falls into the lovely teacher's hands, she learns that the legend is nothing like she remembers. Galahad the Chaste is everything but—the powerful knight is an expert lover—and not only wizards can weave powerful spells. Still, even in Galahad's muscled embrace, she feels unsure of this man who seemed a myth. But soon the beautiful skeptic is on a quest as real as her heart, and the grail—and Galahad's love—is within reach. All she has to do is believe.

___52267-5 $5.99 US/$6.99 CAN

Christmas means more than just puppy love.

"SHAKESPEARE AND THE THREE KINGS"
Victoria Alexander

Requiring a trainer for his three inherited dogs, Oliver Stanhope meets D. K. Lawrence, and is in for the Christmas surprise—and love—of his life.

"ATHENA'S CHRISTMAS TAIL" Nina Coombs

Mercy wants her marriage to be a match of the heart—and with the help of her very determined dog, Athena, she finds just the right magic of the holiday season.

"AWAY IN A SHELTER" Annie Kimberlin

A dedicated volunteer, Camille Campbell still doesn't want to be stuck in an animal shelter on Christmas Eve—especially with a handsome helper whose touch leaves her starry-eyed.

"MR. WRIGHT'S CHRISTMAS ANGEL"
Miriam Raftery

When Joy's daughter asks Santa for a father, she knows she's in trouble—until a trip to Alaska takes them on a journey into the arms of Nicholas Wright and his amazing dog.

___52235-7 $5.99 US/$6.99 CAN

Dorchester Publishing Co., Inc.
P.O. Box 6640
Wayne, PA 19087-8640

Please add $1.75 for shipping and handling for the first book and $.50 for each book thereafter. NY, NYC, and PA residents, please add appropriate sales tax. No cash, stamps, or C.O.D.s. All orders shipped within 6 weeks via postal service book rate. Canadian orders require $2.00 extra postage and must be paid in U.S. dollars through a U.S. banking facility.

Name_____
Address_____
City_____State_____Zip_____
I have enclosed $_____ in payment for the checked book(s).
Payment <u>must</u> accompany all orders. ❑ Please send a free catalog.

The CAT'S MEOW

Victoria Alexander, Nina Coombs, Coral Smith Saxe & Colleen Shannon

*"To persons of good character,
free feline to stable home"*

The ad seems perfect for what Gisella Lowell, an eccentric Bostonian gypsy, intends. While the newspaper ad offers only the possible adoption of four adorable cats, Gisella's plans are a whisker more complex: four individual tales of magic and romance. As the October nights grow chill and the winds begin to howl, four couples will cuddle before their hearths, protected from the things that go bump in the night. And by Halloween, each will realize that they have been rewarded with the most fulfilling gift of all: a warm, affectionate feline. And, of course, true love.

___52279-9 $5.99 US/$6.99 CAN

Dorchester Publishing Co., Inc.
P.O. Box 6640
Wayne, PA 19087-8640

Please add $1.75 for shipping and handling for the first book and $.50 for each book thereafter. NY, NYC, and PA residents, please add appropriate sales tax. No cash, stamps, or C.O.D.s. All orders shipped within 6 weeks via postal service book rate. Canadian orders require $2.00 extra postage and must be paid in U.S. dollars through a U.S. banking facility.

Name_____
Address_____
City_____State_____Zip_____
I have enclosed $_____ in payment for the checked book(s).
Payment <u>must</u> accompany all orders. ❏ Please send a free catalog.
         CHECK OUT OUR WEBSITE! www.dorchesterpub.com